Other Titles By

Maureen Smith

A HEARTBEAT AWAY

GHOST OF FIRE

WITH EVERY BREATH

Taming the Wolf

Maureen Smith

Parker Publishing, LLC

Taming the Wolf

Dedication

To my husband, Lorrent, who's been heating up my days and nights for eleven years.

Chapter One

Samara Layton needed a drink. Badly.

If not for the fact she was a recovering alcoholic, she would've thrown off the costume she wore and made a beeline for the first wet bar she could find. She already felt practically naked beneath the golden brocade robe draped across her shoulders, concealing the flimsy gown she wore.

One of the stage assistants bustled past her clutching a clipboard, a nondescript girl with dark brown hair shoved haphazardly into a ponytail. "Two minutes!"

Samara nodded, scarcely acknowledging the reminder. Her head throbbed unmercifully with the onset of a migraine that intensified with each blink. She couldn't believe she'd actually agreed to participate in tonight's fashion show. No, that wasn't right. She hadn't *agreed*. She'd been bullied, bullied in a way that would make even the most ruthless mobster cringe.

An assistant hairstylist appeared beside her and paused before lifting a hand to Samara's coiffed black hair. Samara shook her head once, a terse warning to be left alone.

"You know Asha expects me to check everyone's hair before show time," Marianne protested.

"My hair has been spritzed, teased and sprayed more in *one* night than in my entire life," Samara said through gritted teeth. "If my mother values your life *half* as much as she does her own, she would've ordered you to cross my name off the list of models to be messed with."

Heeding the lethal warning in Samara's narrowed dark eyes, Marianne hurried away, muttering under her breath about pampered divas.

Samara's full lips curved wryly at the girl's departing tirade. *Diva.* Anyone who knew Samara Layton would know diva was the *last* word on earth that could describe her. But as for these females around her...well, *they* were a different story.

She shuddered, recalling the scene backstage that had been nothing short of chaotic a few minutes ago. In the main dressing room to the rear of the Kenneth Cole showroom, the models huddled around mirrors, hastily applying absurd layers of makeup. Some were still in their robes while others rushed around naked, searching for their costumes. The hairdresser and makeup artists responsible for doing final touch-ups scurried about like mad scientists, racing after anyone who got away without the proper lipstick color or a loosened coif.

It had been sheer madness.

Behind Samara stood a line of the models that would precede her onto the stage following the opening. The girls' muted conversations filled her ears. The ripple of their nervous laughter reminded Samara of a time when she, too, had greeted each fashion show with unbridled enthusiasm, her stomach was a vicious tangle of nerves and anticipation as she prepared to take the runway. When she had dreamed of following in her mother's footsteps by becoming the toast of haute couture.

A lifetime ago.

"Look alive, girls. It's show time!"

The staccato clap next to her ear jarred Samara from her grim musings. Before she could regain her bearings, she was unceremoniously nudged forward.

It's show time, she mentally repeated the mantra, recognizing the familiar cynicism that clutched painfully in her chest.

Time to razzle-dazzle 'em.

Marcus Wolf shifted restlessly in his front row seat of the crowded showroom. For the umpteenth time that evening, he resisted the urge to check his wristwatch.

He didn't need to see the late hour to know an entire night had been wasted, a night he could have used to catch up on paperwork he'd brought with him to New York. Even if he'd simply returned to his hotel room at the Waldorf-Astoria, freed himself of the Armani monkey suit he wore and plunked down in front of the television for hours of mindless cable programming—*anything* would've been preferable to the torture he would endure once the fashion show started.

Of all the things he'd planned to do while on his business trip to New York, attending the spring fashion premiere of some celebrated fashion designer he knew nothing about was definitely *not* on the list.

His companion leaned toward him, his gravelly voice an amused murmur as he inquired, "Restless already? The show hasn't even started yet."

"I can hardly wait," Marcus muttered under his breath.

This drew an appreciative chuckle from his longtime friend and mentor, Walter Floyd. "You need to broaden your horizons, son. There's more to life than depositions and poring through those legal books you always bury your nose in."

Marcus scowled. "If this is your way of encouraging a better social life for me, Walt," he groused, "you're going to be sorely disappointed. A drink at a local bar would have sufficed."

"We did that the last time you were in town," Walter said, unfazed by Marcus's rancor. "I thought we'd try something a little different. Like I told you before, Asha Dubois is an old friend of mine. I promised her I wouldn't miss this year's premiere, and I had no intention of going back on my word—not even for you, son."

Marcus grunted and fell silent once again. To his right sat a heavily perfumed woman in a sequined evening gown. From her animated conversation with her coiffed companion, Marcus learned *all* of the important members of the press had been invited to the premiere. The editors of *Vogue, Mademoiselle, Essence, Harper's Bazaar,* even some international reporters had consented to grace the event with their presence. Buyers from Neiman-Marcus, Saks Fifth Avenue and Barney's were also supposed to be there.

Apparently, Asha Dubois was even important enough to draw the attendance of her rival fashion designers, although Marcus wouldn't know Manolo Blahnik from Ralph Lauren. At this gathering, *everyone* swept into the fancy showroom with an air of importance, whether they were decked out in glittering evening wear or dressed casually in jeans.

Suppressing a heavy sigh, Marcus flicked his wrist with an impatient gesture and frowned at the Rolex watch peeking from beneath the starched white cuff of his tuxedo shirt.

An air of hushed expectancy fell over the audience as the theater darkened. A plume of smoke drifted from the center of the stage, and then a feral roar erupted from the darkness. A spotlight suddenly illuminated a tiger, huge and magnificent, locked in a metal cage. As the audience gasped, a thunderous roll of drums shattered the air. And then came the percussions, pulsing and almost sensual in their rhythm.

Marcus shifted in his chair once again, settling in for the long haul. A moment later he straightened, his stomach muscles tightening.

At center stage, carried upon the shoulders of two very dark-skinned male models whose muscled chests glistened with oil, was the most exotically beautiful woman Marcus had ever seen.

She sat upon the raised platform, as sublimely regal as Queen Nefertiti being transported by her loyal servants, even right down to the jeweled crown perched atop her head. Halfway down the runway, the models stopped and lowered her gently to the floor. When she glided to her feet, her body was covered in a golden floor-length robe. When the footmen reached to help her, she dismissed them with an elegant sweep of her slender arm. They immediately withdrew, bowing to her in submission. With a look of haughty defiance on her exquisite face, the woman moved to the center of the runway and stopped.

For a moment she was completely still, her head tilted at an angle as if she were listening for something in the distance. Then suddenly she pulled the tiara from her head and shook her hair free, and the silken black tresses spilled over her shoulders and down her back. The footmen started after her as if in protest, and she tossed the crown back at them before continuing down the runway. Before they could reach her, she slid the robe from her shoulders. And there was an audible intake of breath across the theater as the audience beheld what was beneath. The model was glorious in a shimmering pearl-gray goddess gown that clung to every shapely curve of her body. The outfit gave the illusion that she was nude but she really wasn't.

Marcus experienced a sharp punch in his lower abdomen that felt suspiciously like lust.

From overhead, rays of an ancient sun god showered down on the goddess as she stood in all her glory at the end of the runway. The percussions swelled to a crescendo, making heartbeats quicken throughout the theater—Marcus's not excluded. The woman pivoted and started back up the runway, gliding in a turn as she showcased the gown, her sleek brown body gleaming like a heavenly creature's beneath the sheer folds. Then suddenly she stopped, for the tiger had been released from its cage. It stalked toward her, its movements fluid and powerful. The audience held a collective breath, and Marcus found his muscles instinctively primed for the unpredictable.

But he needn't have worried. At the last minute, the animal halted before the woman and sat on its hind legs.

With a look of triumph, she reached out to stroke the tiger, which stretched its neck contentedly. At the center curtain, the footmen lowered their heads and parted as the goddess wafted

Taming the Wolf

toward the archway with the docile beast trailing on her heels. In a puff of smoke they all disappeared, and the stage went completely black. From the projection booth high at the back of the theater appeared the words reflected on the translucent screen above the stage: *Defy Convention. Nubian Expressions by House of Dubois.*

Marcus did not move as the theater exploded into thunderous applause. He didn't notice as, one by one, a procession of obscenely thin models strutted down the runway, giving the audience a preview of their costumes. He spent the next hour hoping vainly for the return of the goddess. Even as he waited, he reminded himself that he'd never been one to fall for a pretty face, and this particular one was probably nothing more than that.

So it was with extreme self-loathing that he found himself casually asking Walter about the identity of the mystery woman during intermission.

"That's Samara, Asha Dubois's daughter," Walt told him cheerfully. His craggy face glowed with pride. "Last time I saw her she was just starting college. She sure has grown up, though. Just as beautiful as her mother. Yes, indeed."

Samara. Marcus mentally rolled the name around his tongue, thinking how fitting it was for the sexy, exotic beauty.

Walt sent him a sidelong glance. "I'd be happy to introduce you to her after the show."

Marcus lifted his shoulders in a dismissive shrug and said in a neutral voice, "Don't go out of your way on my account."

He deliberately ignored Walt's knowing chuckle.

"Absolutely not," Samara said firmly, seated at a table in a private dressing room as she worked furiously to remove the heavy stage makeup. "It's out of the question."

6

Her mother stood behind her, feet planted slightly apart, hands braced on voluptuous hips that defied her forty-seven years. She was the epitome of stylish elegance in one of her original designs, a pale lavender dress with a scooped neckline, narrow skirt and wide sleeves, worn with a pair of matching sling-back stiletto pumps. She was the only person Samara knew who could be subtle and stunning in one breath.

"You are being positively ridiculous," Asha Dubois charged in the cool, controlled voice that often sent her subordinates scurrying for cover. "It's only natural that the reporters would want to interview you. You were a smashing success this evening, darling. They're still buzzing about your performance out there!"

"Be that as it may," Samara said tightly, unmoved by the compliment, although the significance of being lauded by the fashion world's movers and shakers was not lost on her. "I'm not interested in doing any interviews, which I made perfectly clear to you when I agreed to participate in the show."

"Naturally I assumed you would change your mind after the premiere."

"I guess you assumed wrong."

Asha gripped the back of Samara's chair and leaned down until her reflection joined her daughter's in the mirror. Slowly, reluctantly, Samara lifted dark eyes to Asha's face, praying her mother couldn't hear the traitorous hammering of her own heart.

"You're behaving like a spoiled brat," Asha said, her tone low and scathing. "A spoiled, twenty-eight-year-old brat. You're being unreasonable out of pure spite."

Samara was silent, studying her mother's image and marveling, not for the first time, at Asha's exquisite beauty. The slim nose, the high cheekbones, the classically shaped eyebrows arched over exotic dark eyes. Her straightened black hair was fashionably cut in long, breezy layers that perfectly accentuated the sensual contours of her face. Asha had never been a stranger to male attention, turning heads wherever she went. Her stunning beauty made her the envy of countless women and the fantasy of every man who looked upon her.

And in many ways, it had also been her downfall.

Samara raised a defiant chin. "This is *your* world, Mother, not mine. I kept my end of the bargain tonight. I trust you to do the same."

Asha arched one perfectly sculpted eyebrow. "And if I don't?" she challenged.

"It wouldn't be the first time."

Her mother regarded her in shrewd silence, showing no visible reaction to the stinging indictment. "People always comment on how much we look alike," she drawled in a deceptively soft voice. "What a shame the similarities end there."

Samara maintained her steely gaze, refusing to be intimidated, refusing to succumb to the bitter tears that burned at the back of her throat. She was not the same fragile little girl she'd once been, craving her mother's approval, cowering in Asha's larger-than-life shadow.

She would rather die than become that girl again.

A firm knock sounded at the door. Asha straightened and bit out impatiently, "What is it?"

"The natives are getting restless out here," came the saucy retort from Asha's personal assistant, Pierre Jacques. "Will you and the lovely Ms. Layton be joining us for interviews any time soon? The press hounds are becoming quite bloodthirsty, dearest."

"Tell them I'll be right there," Asha said, meeting her daughter's eyes once again as she added wryly, "I'm afraid Ms. Layton won't be able to join us. I had forgotten how terrified of strangers she is."

Pierre gave a snort of disapproval before moving off to do his employer's bidding.

"Will you at least make an appearance at the cocktail reception this evening?" Asha demanded. "It wouldn't look right if my own daughter didn't show up to help celebrate the successful unveiling of my spring collection."

Samara scraped her hair into a makeshift ponytail and rose from the chair, eager to escape the oppressive tension of the tiny dressing room. She knew, realistically, that there was no escaping the volatility that always simmered between her and Asha.

"Samara? I asked you a question."

Smothering a deep sigh of resignation, Samara answered evenly, "I'm going back to my hotel room to pack, Mother. I came here and did what you asked me to do, and now it's time for me to return home where I'm really needed." She paused halfway to the door, her back facing her mother. "Congratulations on another successful premiere. I'll understand if I don't see you tomorrow before I leave."

Her mother said nothing as Samara strode purposefully from the room.

Marcus started across the plush lobby where celebrities and fashion heavyweights milled aimlessly about, basking in the after-glow of the event. He'd excused himself to take a call on his cell phone, ignoring Walt's reproachful look. Walt was not the first person in Marcus's life to complain about his workaholism, and he wouldn't be the last.

Marcus rounded the corner and walked right into the path of Samara Layton. His arms came up automatically to steady her as she lifted her eyes to murmur an apology.

At about five-seven, she wasn't as tall as Marcus had originally estimated. She'd abandoned the sheer goddess gown in favor of a simple white shirt and electric blue jeans that molded long, shapely legs that were made for wrapping around a man's waist and leading him straight to paradise. If he'd thought she was beautiful before, she was even more breathtaking up close. Her rich brown skin was flawless. Lustrous ebony hair stemming from a widow's peak had

Taming the Wolf

been scooped into a ponytail that paid homage to an exquisite face—high 'cheekbones, a slim nose, a delicate chin that hinted at a stubborn streak and a lush, sensual mouth created for pleasuring a man. Marcus got hard just looking at her mouth. And then there were her eyes. Wide and incredibly dark, thick-lashed and tilting exotically at the corners.

Those mesmerizing gypsy eyes settled on his face, registering surprise and a flicker of recognition. But the look was so fleeting Marcus decided he'd only imagined it.

"I'm sorry," she offered in a soft, throaty voice that made his mouth go dry. "I wasn't watching where I was going."

Marcus forced himself to stop staring, a feat requiring the strength of Goliath. Damn, she was fine. "No problem," he said softly. "Where's the fire?"

For a moment she just gazed up at him, as if he hadn't spoken. The look in her eyes, something soft and smoky, almost brought Marcus to his knees.

And then just like that her expression cleared, and her arms stiffened beneath his hands. "If you'll excuse me…" she said pointedly.

He let his arms drop to his sides and took a step back. "Of course," he murmured. "I didn't mean to hold you up."

"Just the pair I was looking for!" boomed a hearty voice across the crowded lobby.

Marcus and Samara glanced up to see Walter Floyd approaching, causing several curious heads to turn in his direction. Tall and solidly built, with silver hair sprinkled liberally at the temples, Walt remained an impressive sight at the age of sixty-two. As a prominent businessman who'd recently been voted "Entrepreneur of the Year" by *Black Enterprise*, Walt could be a shrewd and formidable competitor—and as warm and generous as a beloved grandfather.

As Marcus watched, Samara's lips curved into a smile of undisguised pleasure, and for one insane moment, he envied his friend for getting such a warm response from her.

"If you're coming over here to give me another earful about the tiger," she said lightly as Walt drew near, "you're wasting your breath. Working with Pandora was the only part of the performance I enjoyed, and as I already assured you, my life was never in any danger."

Marcus cocked an amused eyebrow. "Pandora?"

"That's right." There was a hint of defiant pride in the eyes that swung back to him. "She's a South African Bengal tiger, on loan to us from the Johannesburg Zoo. I was there when she was born, and her breeders allowed me to name her."

Walt chuckled, leaning down to plant a fatherly kiss on Samara's forehead. To Marcus he warned, "Don't get this young lady started unless you want to hear a sermon on the importance of humane, responsible breeding to maintain the genetic diversity of the endangered tiger species. Samara has been befriending wild animals for as long as I've known her, sneaking in strays at every available opportunity. If her mother would have allowed it, Samara would've owned a menagerie of pets ranging from parakeets to raccoons."

Samara laughed, the sound as mesmerizing as her voice. "What an exaggeration!" she protested, looking embarrassed as her glance shuttled away from Marcus. He was more intrigued than ever.

Walt grinned. "Anyway, I didn't come over here to lecture you on the dangers of playing with wild animals—although I *do* plan to give your mother a piece of my mind when I find her. I wanted to introduce the two of you, but I see you've already managed on your own."

"Actually," Marcus said, looking at Samara, "we hadn't gotten around to that yet."

"Well, then, allow me to do the honors." With a gallant flourish, Walt made the introductions, explaining to Samara, "Marcus and I met several years ago when we served as committee chairmen on a community revitalization project in Washington, D.C. Marcus was barely out of Georgetown Law School at the time, if memory serves me correctly, but he was already passionate about community issues and brought quite a lot to the table." Walt grinned broadly as if an idea had suddenly struck him. "You two have a lot in common. Samara is very active in the community herself. She works as an executive director for a community outreach organization based in D.C."

"Is that right?" Marcus didn't know which part of the revelation pleased him more — Samara's shared interest in civic affairs or the fact that she lived in Washington, D.C., where he'd recently relocated to. "So you don't live in New York?" he clarified, just to be sure.

Samara shook her head. "I'm only here as a favor to my mother. I don't model on a full-time basis."

"That's surprising," Marcus said. "You were amazing tonight. Captivating."

She inclined her head in simple acknowledgment of the compliment, but Marcus had the vague impression she was less than pleased.

Walt was observing them with sharp, discerning eyes when someone across the lobby called out a greeting to him. "You two keep chatting," he urged his companions as he started away, only too pleased by the diversion. "Get to know each other. You won't be disappointed."

In amused silence, Marcus and Samara watched the older man retreat. "Good ol' Mr. Floyd," Samara drawled wryly. "The art of subtlety was never lost on him."

Marcus chuckled. "Walt's matchmaking attempts aside, would you like to get a drink somewhere? I'd love to hear more about the work you do."

"I can't drink," Samara blurted, then looked as if she wanted to take back the words.

"All right," Marcus said evenly. "No drinks, then. How about dinner?"

She shook her head. "Look, Mr. Wolf, I'm sure you're a very nice guy and really deserving of Walter's high praises—"

His mouth curved with irony. "Which would rationally explain your refusal to have dinner with me."

She bristled at his mocking tone. "Not that I need a 'rational explanation' to refuse your dinner invitation," she said crisply, "but if you must know, in my experience with doing these fashion shows, there are usually three types of men in attendance. Those with a genuine interest in the fashion industry, or those like Walter Floyd who come to support a friend or family member." She paused. "And then there's *your* type, Mr. Wolf."

Marcus lifted a brow. "And what type would that be?" he inquired, a soft challenge in his voice.

"Men who'd rather spend their time anywhere but at a fashion show, but once there, they decide to make the best of the situation by going home with the first decent-looking female they encounter. If it happens to be one of the models, all the better."

Marcus said nothing.

"Do you deny that Walter probably had to drag you out to tonight's premiere?"

"Kicking and screaming."

Point made, she nodded coolly. She hitched the strap of her leather duffel bag more securely onto her shoulder. "It's been a long week, Mr. Wolf, and I have a five-hour drive back home tomorrow morning. So if you'll excuse me, I'd really like to get back to my hotel room and hit the sack. *Alone*."

Marcus inclined his head in the barest hint of a nod. "As you wish. Good evening, Ms. Layton." He stepped aside to let her pass, then stood watching as she headed from the building without a backward glance.

Turning away, he drew a deep, ragged breath and blinked several times, but it was no use. He couldn't erase the image of her round curvy ass squeezed into electric blue denim from his mind. It was permanently stamped upon his brain, like the rest of her.

Samara's heart pounded as the taxicab she'd climbed into hurtled down the busy street, the bright lights of downtown Manhattan whizzing by. Although she automatically gripped the door handle for support, her runaway heartbeat had nothing to do with the cabbie's haphazard driving.

Now, she could thank Marcus Wolf for that.

Lord have mercy, she silently breathed, closing her eyes and leaning her head back against the seat. *No man has the right to be that fine.*

She'd first noticed him at the conclusion of the fashion show, as she stood at the end of the illuminated runway surrounded by photographers vying for the best camera angles. Beyond the flurry of flashing bulbs, she'd seen Marcus seated in the front row reserved for VIP guests. Her pulse rate had accelerated almost immediately. He was already watching her—a silent, penetrating appraisal through dark, heavy-lidded eyes that gave new meaning to the term "bedroom eyes." Rich mahogany skin stretched tight and smooth over chiseled cheekbones, a square jaw. And a firm, sensually molded mouth that made her fantasize about what they'd feel like against her own lips, on her breasts and between her trembling thighs.

As she'd watched from the runway, Marcus slowly stood, unfolding his powerful body from the seat with the fluid ease of a panther. She'd nearly gasped as she took in the sheer size of him, impossibly broad shoulders with a wide chest that tapered down to a trim waist. Samara had attended countless black-tie affairs before. But not once had she been so turned on by the sight of a man in a tuxedo. Marcus Wolf wore the *hell* out of that Armani tux, putting all the other men to shame. Samara wanted to climb him like an oak tree, all six-foot four-inches of him, and wrap *her* limbs around him.

Their eyes had held for several charged moments before Samara forced her gaze away, heeding the flirtatious coaxing of a photographer who'd wanted her to smile for the camera. She was sure her smile had been as wobbly as her knees.

Marcus Wolf was sexier than sin, and his deep, velvety voice laced with Southern heat had been as potent as the rest of the package. Although Samara knew better, she'd been sorely tempted to accept his dinner invitation. Almost at once, she'd imagined them dining by candlelight at a cozy, romantic restaurant, then returning to her hotel room for a nightcap. Or *his* room, whichever was closer.

"Dance with me," he murmured, taking her half-empty wineglass from her hand and setting it down on the table.

He held out his hand to her, and she went willingly into his arms. She closed her eyes and rested her head on his shoulder as they began to slow dance to a nonexistent ballad in front of the moonlit window. She reveled in the strength of his arms around her, the hardness of his chest and belly rubbing against her breasts, making her nipples pucker almost painfully. His muscled thighs slid along hers as he turned her slowly in a circle, one hand at the small of her back, the other at her waist. The heat of his touch seared her through her clothes, which suddenly felt too confining. When his hip brushed against hers, she felt the hard, delicious bulge of his erection, and it made her instantly wet.

She lifted her face to his, and found his dark, smoldering gaze already fixed on her. Her lips parted, and before she could draw breath to speak, he lowered his head and seized her mouth in a hot, mind-numbing kiss that sent liquid fire blazing through her body. She arched into him, pressing her aching breasts to his chest as her hips rocked against him, seeking relief from her torment. He deepened the kiss, giving her his tongue and feasting on her mouth until she was breathless and clinging to him. Soon they were both panting hard.

Forcing his mouth from hers, he whispered huskily, "I want to be inside you."

Her knees almost buckled. She responded by grabbing his face in her hands and pulling his head down to hers for another hot, open-mouthed kiss, leaving no doubt in his mind that she wanted the same thing.

He gave a low growl that she felt all the way down to her toes. His hands went to her buttocks, cupping both cheeks and lifting her from the floor. She wrapped her legs around his waist as he backed her against the wall, then reached for his belt buckle.

"Miss? That'll be $13.80."

Samara's eyes flew open, and for a moment she stared at the cab driver in dazed confusion. As her surroundings slowly came back into focus, she realized her duffel bag was clutched tightly between her thighs. An embarrassed flush heated her face. She'd been fantasizing about Marcus Wolf, and had been on the verge of having sex with him. Her breasts throbbed, and the crotch of her panties was wet.

The cabbie was watching her with interest. "Ma'am?"

Samara fumbled out a twenty from her jeans pocket and passed it to him. "Keep the change."

He flashed a toothy grin as she quickly climbed out of the cab. "Enjoy the rest of your visit to New York!"

Samara scowled as she hurried toward the entrance to the hotel where she was staying. *I'll enjoy it even more*, she thought darkly, *once I get my hands on a damn vibrator.*

Chapter Two

By seven o'clock Monday morning, Samara was settled in her northeast D.C. office, tending to the myriad tasks that were neglected during her absence.

The Fannie Yorkin Institute for Community Outreach and Development—or FYI as it was commonly called—was a nonprofit organization created to serve the educational and socioeconomic needs of the community. Although FYI had flourished for nearly two decades, a combination of recent extenuating circumstances had severely crippled the organization's finances. Samara had been brought on board following the sudden retirement of the Institute's founder and president, and she was charged with the Herculean mission of rescuing FYI from bankruptcy. It was an undertaking she'd wholeheartedly embraced. Despite FYI's severe financial problems, she knew what good the Institute could do: the educational opportunities it had afforded kids who might not otherwise have stepped foot on a college campus, the financial aid provided to struggling families who simply needed a helping hand to get through tough times, and the counseling given to at-risk teenagers.

In many ways, Samara was as indebted to the Fannie Yorkin Institute as were the countless community members who'd benefited from the organization's generosity over the years. The opportunity to work at FYI had come at a low point in her life, when she'd found herself stuck at a marketing job she hated and uncertain about the future. She'd jumped at the chance to start a new career, and had never looked back.

Samara spent the first part of her morning listening to voicemail messages and returning as many phone calls as possible. She'd been working tirelessly to reestablish connections with many of their former investors and corporate sponsors, relationships that had suffered as a result of instability within FYI. Although she'd made great strides in her second year as executive director—facilitating partnerships with other groups and businesses that shared common objectives, creating new community-based programs as well as breathing life into existing ones—the reality was that her efforts would mean nothing without significant financial contributions.

They needed money desperately. And they needed it yesterday.

In the midst of making phone calls, Samara found her thoughts straying to Marcus Wolf. After returning to her hotel room on Saturday night, she'd ordered a bottle of sparkling cider from the menu and filled the Jacuzzi with steaming hot water. While soaking in the marble tub and sipping her chilled drink, she'd allowed her mind to wander back to the fantasy that had been interrupted earlier in the cab. By the time Marcus thrust inside her, she was so caught up in the daydream that she hardly noticed as her wineglass slipped from her fingers and shattered against the floor. The sound was drowned out by her rapturous moans as she masturbated to the rhythm of Marcus's imaginary strokes.

Samara groaned softly at the memory, even as her body throbbed in response. Not for the first time since Saturday night, she called herself all kinds of a damn fool for not accepting Marcus's dinner invitation. At the very least, she would have gotten a good fuck out of it.

"I take it things didn't go too well in New York?" said an amused voice from the doorway.

Samara glanced up and managed a wan smile for the attractive woman who leaned on the doorjamb. "Good morning," Samara greeted her warmly. "Didn't hear you get in."

"Obviously." Melissa Matthews crossed the short distance and put a steaming mug of coffee on Samara's desk, shoving aside a pile of paperwork to make room. "I know you haven't even stopped to breathe, let alone allow yourself some caffeine. And I'm willing to bet you've probably been here since the crack of dawn."

Samara shot the woman a grateful look as she reached for the coffee. "Not quite. Mmm, this is heavenly," she murmured after an appreciative sip of the creamy brew. "Thanks, Melissa."

Melissa waved off her gratitude with a manicured hand, settling her petite frame into the chair opposite Samara's desk. "Did that scowl on your face have anything to do with your week-long excursion to New York?" she asked without preamble.

"What scowl?"

Melissa ignored her, all too familiar with Samara's tendency to answer a question with a question. Particularly questions she wanted to avoid. "How'd the premiere go?"

"It was a smashing success," Samara said dryly. "But, of course, I never expected otherwise. My mother is a very talented designer who knows what people want and, perhaps more importantly, knows how to make them want what they normally might not."

Frowning, Melissa shook her head as if to clear it. Her neat auburn dreadlocks bounced with the gesture. "It's too early in the morning for riddles, Samara. Is that a clever way of telling me that you and your mother had another one of your 'civilized' arguments?"

Samara shrugged, feigning nonchalance as she picked up an engraved silver ballpoint pen that had been a gift to her from the Institute's retiring founder. "Things were business as usual between me and my mother."

But Melissa knew better. Her expression softened. "Want to talk about it?"

"Not particularly." Samara took a long sip of coffee, then leaned back in her swivel chair and crossed her legs. She told herself the sudden churning in her stomach had more to do with ingesting coffee on an empty stomach than the inner turmoil that always accompanied discussions of her mother. "Thanks for holding down the fort. How'd things go?"

"Not too bad. If you don't count the fact that the heater decided to break during the coldest week we've had since the start of spring, and we all had to wear fur coats in the office for three days until the repair guys could work us into their busy schedules. Guess they're still holding it against us for paying our bill late three months in a row."

Samara winced, rolling the ballpoint pen between her fingers and wishing their financial woes could be simply solved with the sale of the expensive pen. "I'll call Fred personally to see if we can set up some sort of payment plan."

Melissa snorted. "You do that, because all of my efforts to date have been miserable failures. He likes you better, anyway—as do most red-blooded males."

An image of Marcus's piercing dark eyes and sensuous lips filled Samara's mind. She ruthlessly shoved the image away. Enough was enough.

"What else?" she demanded, her tone more impatient than she'd intended.

Melissa looked momentarily bewildered. "Nothing," she answered carefully, "except that Brianna missed you terribly, and wants a full report of everyone you saw at the premiere. Namely celebrities."

Samara smiled softly, thinking of the shy nineteen-year-old single mother she'd mentored for the past year, helping her work toward obtaining her G.E.D. "I'll be sure to scour my brain trying to recall as many celebrities as possible. For *both* of you."

Melissa grinned sheepishly. "Well, only if you insist. And since we're back on the subject," she leaned forward expectantly in the chair, "did you get the check?"

It was the question Samara had dreaded the most, the question she'd hoped to avoid for as long as possible. But she should have known better.

Apart from her husband of three years, nothing excited Melissa Matthews more than the prospect of receiving money for the Institute. A CPA who could've had her pick of any Fortune 500 company, she'd served faithfully as the organization's accountant for over a decade—and enjoyed every minute of it.

Samara became suddenly absorbed in the inspection of a scratch on the scarred surface of her desk. "About that check…" she hedged.

Melissa's hazel eyes narrowed suspiciously. "What *about* the check?"

Samara frowned. "I don't exactly have it…in my possession."

"Well, where is it?" When Samara hesitated, Melissa lunged to her feet. "Don't tell me your mother didn't give it to you!"

"All right, I won't tell you."

"Samara!"

Samara cringed. "If you're going to yell at me, could you at least close the door so everyone won't hear you?"

Melissa strode to the door and slammed it before rounding on Samara once again, her eyes flashing. "What happened?"

Samara rubbed the ache creeping into her temples. "There's something you have to understand about my mother," she began tiredly. "Her generosity is…conditional."

"And you met those conditions!" Melissa flared, indignant hands thrust onto dainty hips. "You took an entire week off from work—time that could have been spent enjoying a badly needed vacation, I might add. You traveled to New York to be there to rehearse for *her* spring premiere, which *she* specifically requested your participation in. And the only reason on earth that you agreed to do it was because she promised to give FYI a large donation. That was the deal."

"Keeping deals isn't really my mother's style," Samara muttered.

Melissa opened her mouth with another heated retort, decided against it and snapped her lips shut. She sat back down again. "The organization needs a sizeable donation Samara, or we'll have to close shop. As it is, we're just barely maintaining our operating expenses in an effort to keep most of our programs going. Soon that won't be possible."

"I know," Samara said on a heavy sigh. "I'll think of something, Melissa, don't worry."

"That is easier said than done. Between the fluctuating economy and increased competition for charitable donations, it's harder than ever for small nonprofits like ours to get proper funding. And as you well know, the District's limited resources are allocated to public sector organizations that fall under the Office of Community Outreach." Melissa slumped back against the chair, her expression bleak. "I don't know what else we can do, Samara. We've held fundraisers, sponsored everything from bake sales to book fairs, and cold-called every business in our database. The contributions we're receiving simply aren't enough anymore."

Before Samara could open her mouth, Melissa stabbed a warning finger at her. "And you can't keep outsourcing your services in exchange for donations. Not only are you burning yourself out that way, but that's *not* what you got your MBA for."

"I don't mind," Samara countered. "I enjoy using my marketing background as often as possible. God knows my mother thinks I'm totally wasting the degree," she added cynically.

"Is that what you two argued about in New York?"

"If only it were that simple." Samara stared unseeingly into her coffee cup. When she spoke again, her voice was subdued. "My mother assumed that once the premiere was over, I would change my mind about talking to reporters. But with her, it's never as simple as just doing interviews. With Asha Dubois, the more you give, the more she demands—until she completely usurps your will. Then you find yourself bending to her every whim, acting out a reality not of your own choosing."

Melissa was silent, watching her with a mixture of sympathy and concern. "Don't worry about the check," she said gently. "We'll get the funds somehow, and just chalk up this experience to a loss."

"No." Samara shook her head, her jaw set determinedly. "I kept my end of the bargain. It's time for my mother to be held accountable for keeping hers. I'll call her this afternoon during my lunch break."

"Samara—"

"This is too important, Melissa. We both know that."

With a sigh of resignation, Melissa stood and crossed to the door. She paused, her hand on the doorknob. "You know where to find me if you need to vent afterward."

Samara's smile was warm with gratitude. "I know," she said quietly. "And thanks."

"I knew it wouldn't take you long to come to your senses," Asha drawled, making no attempt to hide her smugness. "As notoriously stubborn as you are, even *you* can admit when you're wrong."

On the other end of the phone, Samara fought to rein her temper. "I didn't call to apologize, Mother," she said as calmly as possible. "I stand by my decision not to be interviewed after the premiere. I know very well your army of publicists was laying a trap for me, hoping the reporters would corner me into announcing my intention to join the House of Dubois. As if I've ever expressed any interest in becoming the mother-daughter design duo you so desperately want."

"Your refusal to take an active role in my company makes no sense whatsoever," Asha said heatedly. "Look at the Asian culture where the children *embrace* their parents' businesses as their own. Drycleaners, restaurants, convenience stores—you name it. *Every* member of the family works together to ensure the success of the business. But not *my* daughter. My daughter would rather wither away at some failing nonprofit organization than put her natural talents to use. Even if you never wanted to model, Samara, the *least* you could have done was head our marketing division. You have an MBA from the Wharton School of Business, for goodness sake!"

"Which I utilize every day in my position as the Institute's executive director," Samara wearily reminded her. The debate was so familiar she could recite it in her sleep.

She was also prepared for her mother's vitriolic rebuttal. "Obviously your 'expertise' isn't working, or the organization wouldn't be in such bad shape!"

"Which brings me to the original reason for my call," Samara said tersely, steeling herself against the inevitable pain caused by her mother's words. No matter how many times they argued, the hurt was always there—a raw, festering wound that refused to heal. "We had an agreement."

"I spoke to the board of trustees," Asha said, "and according to them, giving a donation to the Institute would be like tossing my money to the wind. You're too far in debt."

"That's not true. We've been working with our creditors, who assure us that they will continue to work with us if we show marked improvement in our financial status. That's why the donation is so urgently needed."

"Well…" There was a light tapping on the other end, and Samara could imagine her mother reclining in her plush Manhattan office, drumming her manicured nails impatiently upon the surface of her imported Louis XVI desk. "I don't think it's going to be possible, Samara. The board will never approve it."

Samara's heart plunged sickeningly. She closed her eyes, torn between desperation and the remaining shards of her pride that revolted against begging.

You can't give up, an inner voice pleaded. *It's for a good cause!*

"It's your company," Samara said, despising the low tremor in her voice. "You have the authority to override any of the board's objections. You've done it before."

"That was for something I believed in," Asha retorted. "That isn't the case here."

"But you gave me your word. I trusted you to keep it."

"Don't lay one of your guilt trips on me, Samara. I'm sick to death of it! No matter how much I do for you, it's never enough. You always manage to make it seem like I've failed you somehow. All I've ever tried to be is a good mother to you. Whether you like it or not,

House of Dubois and all of its assets will be yours one day. And I sincerely hope you won't turn your back on the corporation the way you've turned your back on me."

Anger swelled inside Samara's chest. She wanted to shriek at the top of her lungs, and probably would have were she not in a public park, visible to business professionals leisurely enjoying their lunches on the warm March afternoon. "That's so typical of you, Mother," she said bitterly. "Turn the tables on me to divert from the fact that *you're* the one breaking yet another promise."

"I'm not giving you one red cent for that place, Samara. Can't you see that it's a sinking ship? You're going to find yourself out of a job when—"

"Goodbye, Mother. Thanks for your time anyway." Samara disconnected and shoved her cell phone inside her purse. Her hands were trembling violently, and she thrust them between her knees to control the shaking.

She'd failed.

Failed in her efforts to change her mother's mind about the donation. Failed to remain emotionally immune from her mother's manipulative ways.

She sat alone on that park bench and mentally replayed the entire conversation, wondering where she'd gone wrong, wondering if there was a shred of validity to her mother's claims.

As a child Samara had worshipped Asha Dubois, and thought her mother could do no wrong. After all, it wasn't Asha's fault that she'd married at eighteen, and a year later found herself pregnant and divorced. Heartbroken, she'd tried to make the best of her situation, taking menial jobs to keep food in their bellies while they bounced between women's shelters and lived off the kindness of strangers. When Asha got her big break in the form of a modeling contract, it was only natural that she'd jumped at the opportunity, her ticket out of poverty and misery. She'd had no choice but to send Samara to live with her grandmother—the same woman from whom

Asha had concealed Samara's existence for years, because she was ashamed to reveal the byproduct of her failed marriage.

Samara recalled the many months that had passed with no word from Asha, as her various modeling assignments took her from one continent to another. If it wasn't for the fact Asha's face was often splashed across the front covers of magazines, Samara might have forgotten what her mother looked like. Then one day, out of the clear blue, Asha had reappeared, asserting her parental right before whisking Samara off to unknown destinations. When she grew weary of motherhood, Samara was promptly returned to her grand-mother—only to be taken away again when the next whim struck Asha. Every time Samara formed attachments at school, her mother would sweep back into her life as if she were the arriving cavalry. The interruptions occurred so frequently that Samara simply stopped trying to make friends at school and kept to herself.

When she thought about it, she supposed she should be grateful for the many adventures she'd had, the colorful sights and sounds of new countries and lilting dialects. She'd always been accompanied by a tutor, and was fluent in four languages by the time she reached high school.

But then there were the men, Asha's string of discarded lovers, whose lewd gazes crawled over Samara's young body.

Until one decided that merely looking wasn't enough.

Shoving aside the painful memories, Samara rose to her feet and started back toward the office building with brisk, determined strides. Somehow she'd get the money to save FYI from bankruptcy. Somehow she'd make everything right.

Where there's a will, her grandmother had been fond of saying, *there's a way.*

Samara definitely had the will.

Now she just had to find the way.

Later that afternoon, Melissa burst excitedly into Samara's office. "Have you seen today's *Washington Post*? Specifically the Metro section?"

Samara chuckled, looking pointedly at the pile of paperwork before her. "Does it *look* like I've had time to read the newspaper?"

"I think I may have found the solution to our financial crisis," Melissa rushed on as if Samara hadn't spoken. She tossed the Metro section onto Samara's desk, the edges crumpled from her overzealous grip. "Take a look at that."

Samara glanced down and froze. Slowly, almost against her will, she picked up the newspaper and stared at the front page. PROMINENT ATTORNEY BRINGS PRACTICE TO THE BELTWAY, the headline proclaimed.

And there, to her utter astonishment, was a photograph of Marcus Wolf.

Trying hard to form her features into an impassive mask, she glanced up at Melissa. "What does this have to do with our financial situation?"

Scowling, Melissa snatched back the newspaper and sat down in the chair. "Please don't tell me you've never heard of Marcus Wolf? He only happens to be the same attorney who won that landmark class action lawsuit against that school district in Georgia a few years ago, the one that was displaying blatant discrimination in its mistreatment of underprivileged children. The judge awarded the plaintiffs millions of dollars. The case was all over the news, and CNN even compared its significance to *Brown vs. Board of Education.*" Melissa made a sound of disgust when she saw Samara's blank look. "Girl, you need to come up for air once in a while."

"I remember that case," Samara countered defensively. "But I still fail to see the connection between us and Marcus Wolf…" Suddenly it dawned on her, and she groaned loudly. "Please tell me you're not suggesting what I think you're suggesting."

"Why not? Marcus Wolf is an extremely wealthy attorney with practices in Atlanta, and now Washington, D.C. According to this article, his estimated net worth is well over fifty million. Girl, you know I don't believe in coincidence. I think it was divine intervention that brought him to our backyard at this particular time. He's an untapped resource we should solicit for contributions."

"Melissa—"

"And look, it says here he's very active in civic organizations. His law firm awards college scholarships to underprivileged students and between litigating civil and tort cases and serving on various boards, he mentors inner-city youth. It says that he considers it his life's mission to impact as many communities as possible through his work." Melissa glanced up from the newspaper triumphantly. "Now if *that* doesn't sound like something straight out of our mission statement, I don't know what does."

Finally noticing Samara's pained expression, Melissa frowned. "What's wrong? Why do you have that look on your face, like someone just played a bad joke on you?"

"I think someone did," Samara muttered under her breath. At Melissa's perplexed look, she threw her head back against her chair with another low groan. "I met Marcus Wolf over the weekend. He was at the premiere."

"Really?" Grinning, Melissa clapped her hands together. "That's even better! He'll remember you when you call his office."

Samara winced. "That's not necessarily a good thing."

Melissa's grin faded. "And why is that?"

"Let's just say we didn't get off to a very good start. He invited me to dinner, and I sort of turned him down."

"Sort of?"

Samara nodded reluctantly. "And I might have implied that he was, um, a womanizer who attended fashion shows just to pick up women."

"Please tell me you're joking." At Samara's shamefaced look, Melissa slapped a hand to her own forehead. "Are you insane? Does he *look* like the kind of man who needs to resort to such tactics? Did you hear the figures I just quoted you? The man is a multimillionaire! Now, I realize this might not mean a great deal to you—future heiress to a fashion empire—but to the average person, being worth fifty million dollars is nothing to sneeze at! Not to mention the fact that Marcus Wolf is finer than mere words can begin to describe. Furthermore—"

Samara held up a hand to stem the tirade. "Point taken."

"I can't believe you insulted that man! Are you bound and determined to alienate the entire male species?"

Samara glared at her. "Don't you have some account ledgers to review or something?"

Melissa departed in a huff, grumbling as she went, "If the Institute goes under, you'll have no one to blame but yourself." Half a moment later, she stuck her head back in the doorway, looking somewhat contrite. "Okay, that wasn't fair. Of course it won't be your fault if we go under. But I'll be very, *very* disappointed in you if you let this golden opportunity slip through our fingers!"

Samara waited until she was sure Melissa was gone, then reached across her desk for the newspaper. Her gaze lingered on the photo of Marcus Wolf standing on the steps of the district courthouse, arms folded across his wide chest, legs braced apart, prepared to take on the world above a caption that referred to him as the "king of torts." As Samara remembered the vivid details of her fantasy, her belly quivered. Why did the man have to be so damn fine?

Dragging her gaze from the photo, she began to read the article. By the time she finished, she could see why Walter Floyd and Melissa were so impressed with Marcus Wolf. He was smart, successful, tenacious, and most of all, he seemed to genuinely care about others, defending those who couldn't defend themselves.

Could Samara have been wrong about him?

She frowned, setting down the newspaper. Just because Marcus had a humanitarian spirit didn't mean he couldn't also be a womanizer. Congress was filled with politicians who performed good deeds, but still cheated on their spouses. Some also accepted bribes under the table.

When it came down to it, what Marcus did in his private life was none of her business.

Unless she could use it to her advantage.

Samara grew still as an idea formed in her mind. According to the article, Marcus was giving a lecture at his alma mater, Georgetown University, that evening. The event was free and opened to the public. Maybe if Samara showed up and…And what? After the way she'd insulted him in New York, she couldn't very well walk right up to him tonight and ask for a large sum of money. She'd be lucky if he spoke to her at all. But that didn't mean she couldn't try. And if he showed even the least bit of interest in her…well, she would definitely use that to her advantage.

Where there's a will, there's a way.

Chapter Three

When Samara arrived at Georgetown University that evening, twenty minutes late thanks to a traffic accident, the auditorium was filled to standing room only. She joined a row of spectators lined up in the back, then quickly turned her attention to the podium, where Marcus Wolf was already speaking.

Her heart gave an involuntary thump at the sight of him. Even from a distance, he looked fine as hell in a double-breasted charcoal-gray suit that accentuated his powerful build. He appeared relaxed and confident as he discussed the importance of civic engagement, exhorting the law students in attendance to make sure they were entering the profession for the *right* reasons — to change the world. The audience was riveted, and Samara could see why. Marcus Wolf was an incredible speaker, one of the most compelling she'd ever heard. And the sound of his deep, masculine voice set off a slow burn between her legs.

It came as no surprise when, at the end of his presentation, Marcus received a rousing standing ovation that lasted at least three minutes. A flurry of questions followed, many from students who wanted to learn more about his journey to becoming one of the country's leading tort attorneys. Others asked questions about some of the more controversial cases he'd successfully litigated in court. And several people wanted to know whether his firm was hiring and what kind of skills and qualifications he looked for in an associate.

One dark-haired young woman stood and asked him why he wasn't married yet, which drew a round of laughter as everyone in the room awaited Marcus's response. Samara even found herself holding her breath.

A slow, lazy grin curved his mouth as he regarded the student. "Are you proposing?" he drawled.

The girl actually blushed and gave him a flirtatious smile. "I am now. And if it helps my chances any, I'm graduating in the top three percent of my class next month."

Marcus nodded approvingly. "Talk to me afterward," he told her with a wink, and the crowd reacted with more laughter, enjoying the playful exchange.

Not surprisingly, the pretty brunette was the first in line to speak to him when the event was over. And she wasn't alone.

Standing in the back of the auditorium, Samara resigned herself to an unbearably long wait as throngs of people lined up to ask Marcus more questions and to get his autograph. Half an hour passed before the room finally began to empty.

Seeing her chance, Samara drew a deep breath to calm her jittery nerves and approached Marcus just as he finished conversing with an older black gentleman.

When Marcus's gaze landed on hers, her mouth went dry. Up close, he was even finer than she remembered, with his dark, mesmerizing eyes and smooth mahogany skin. His firm, sensuous lips glistened with moisture as he sipped his water. Samara actually found herself envying the bottle of Evian.

If Marcus was surprised to see her, he didn't show it. "Ms. Layton," he murmured in polite greeting.

"I really enjoyed your lecture," Samara told him, smiling warmly. "It was very inspiring."

He inclined his head. "Glad you got something out of it."

"Definitely. And that was a great write-up about you in the *Post*. When we met on Saturday, you didn't mention that you'd recently relocated to D.C."

His mouth twitched. "I would've gotten around to it eventually."

Her smile turned rueful. "If I'd given you a chance," she translated.

"I didn't say that."

"Only because you're too polite."

Marcus chuckled, and her belly flip-flopped at the low, sexy rumble.

She moistened her lips with the tip of her tongue, and watched as his heavy-lidded gaze followed the gesture. She knew the glossy red color she wore showed off her full lips to advantage. *Thank you, MAC.*

She gave Marcus a knowing look. "You must give presentations all the time. Just how many marriage proposals have you received? Or have you lost count?"

"Nah, this was a first." The way his gaze lingered on her lips made her nipples harden. As if he sensed her body's reaction, his dark eyes drifted lower, to the plunging neckline of the sheer red blouse she wore. Her skin burned as if he'd actually leaned down and brushed his mouth over her breast. She trembled at the thought.

"A first, huh?" she murmured, her voice throaty with arousal. "I find that hard to believe."

His eyes returned slowly to her face. "Believe it," he said huskily. "I always remember my firsts."

Heat pooled between Samara's legs. Their gazes locked. The air between them crackled with sexual tension.

"I must admit, Ms. Layton," Marcus said softly. "I was a little surprised when I looked out into the audience tonight and saw you."

His words sent a thrill of pleasure through her. The fact that he'd picked her out in a roomful of over six hundred people meant more to her than he could ever know.

"Despite the way I behaved in New York," she heard herself telling him, "I haven't been able to stop thinking about you."

If Marcus's eyes weren't so dark, she would have sworn his pupils dilated. His nostrils flared slightly, and beneath the expensive suit jacket he wore, his chest seemed to rise and fall more rapidly. Trapped in the smoldering heat of his gaze, Samara felt her own breathing quicken. She hadn't meant to blurt out the confession, but if Marcus kept devouring her with those sexy bedroom eyes, God only knew what else would come out of her mouth.

Make love to me came to mind.

Out of the corner of her eye, she noticed two sharply dressed men and an attractive black woman hovering nearby, watching her and Marcus.

"I shouldn't hold you up any longer," Samara murmured apologetically. "People are still waiting to speak to you."

He released her from his gaze long enough to meet the stares of the others with indifference. "Those are my senior associates. We're supposed to be meeting for drinks after this."

"Well, in that case, I'd better let you go." She reached out and touched his arm, letting her hand linger for a prolonged moment. "It was good to see you again, Mr. Wolf."

"Likewise," he drawled.

As Samara turned and walked away, she was acutely aware of him watching her, his gaze like a physical touch on her back. She knew the picture she made, with her short black skirt clinging to her curves and her stiletto heels accentuating the shapely expanse of her long legs. She was counting on Marcus appreciating the view— appreciating it enough to want more.

She left the auditorium and started toward the double glass doors leading to the parking lot. A number of people were still milling about, chatting in small clusters or talking animatedly on cell phones.

Before Samara reached the exit, she made a detour, rounding a corner and heading down an empty corridor that led to the restrooms.

"Samara."

She turned to find Marcus striding purposefully toward her, his dark, intoxicating gaze locked on hers. She waited, heart hammering wildly in her chest, anticipation pulsing through her veins.

When he'd stopped before her, she stared up at him. "Marcus—"

Without a word, he cupped her face in his large hands and crushed his mouth to hers, his tongue plunging inside and stroking deep.

Samara eagerly responded, wrapping her arms around his neck and reaching on tiptoe to press herself more firmly against his hard, muscular body. Liquid heat coiled inside her, drawing tighter and tighter until she thought she'd explode. She'd never known there could be so much pleasure in a man's hungry kiss. But it was more than just a kiss. It was an all over body experience, the way Marcus sucked on her tongue and rubbed his chest against her breasts, making them swell and her nipples harden to aching points.

"I want something from you," she breathed into his mouth, while she still had the presence of mind to warn him.

"I'm counting on it," he whispered huskily.

Without breaking the kiss, he backed her up, one step at a time, through the open doorway of a dark, empty classroom. He shoved the door closed behind them, then backed her against the wall. He cupped her buttocks and lifted her off the floor as Samara wrapped her legs around his waist, her skirt riding up her thighs. The bulge of his erection pressed against the lace crotch of her panties, making her hot and wet. Their lips met again, meshing and parting as the kiss grew wilder, more intense.

Samara knew what they were doing was the epitome of insanity, but she didn't care. All that mattered was that she needed him, wanted him like nothing she'd ever wanted before. And the reality of this moment was even better than her fantasies.

Dazedly she watched as Marcus reached inside the plunging neckline of her sheer silk blouse. She shivered as his knuckle grazed her skin, searing her to the bone. She sucked in a sharp breath when he cupped one lace-covered breast in his hand. Holding her gaze, he slipped a thumb inside her bra and rubbed it back and forth against her tight nipple, sending waves of pleasure crashing through her. She rocked fitfully against him, trying to position the bulge in his pants right where she wanted it.

With a soft, husky laugh, Marcus bent his head and drew her nipple into the silken heat of his mouth. A ragged moan escaped from her throat. Her back arched as his tongue caressed the sensitive peak, licking and sucking. She felt the pull of his mouth everywhere—in the pit of her stomach, in her trembling thighs, between them. He kissed his way to her other breast and treated it to the same delicious torment. All the while, his hips grind against hers in a slow, subtle rhythm that nearly made her come.

She caught his head between her hands and brought his mouth back to hers, kissing him greedily, showing him just how much she wanted him. As their tongues mated feverishly, he cupped her breasts in his hands, thumbing her wet nipples, rasping them. She writhed against him, mindless with need. She didn't know how much more she could take without begging him to make love to her right where they were.

His hands slid down her back, then grasped her bare buttocks beneath her hiked-up skirt. Samara's heart pounded hard as his fingers edged toward her moist, aching center. Breathing became secondary to the heightened anticipation of his touch. She closed her eyes, then gasped as one finger slid beneath her panties and found her throbbing clitoris.

Her eyes flew open, and she gazed up at him as he began to stroke the slick nub, slow and tantalizing, until a shaking moan rose up in her throat.

Marcus watched her, devouring her with his gaze, his face hard and dark with passion. "You're so wet," he said, the words so low and guttural they were practically a growl. His fingers glided over the folds of her sex, spreading her slick wetness over swollen, sensitive flesh. Her eyes rolled back in her head.

"You like that?" he whispered huskily.

"*Yes*," she moaned breathlessly, rocking against his hand. "That feels *so* good."

It was an understatement if she'd ever heard one, but she could barely speak, let alone think of better adjectives. Besides, she doubted there was a word to describe the sensual pleasure she was experiencing, the exquisite sensations overtaking her body.

All thoughts ceased as Marcus slipped one thick finger deep inside her. She cried out hoarsely and clung to him. She felt the iron steel in his shoulders, the way his muscles bunched and flexed beneath his suit jacket.

He lowered his head and slid his tongue into her mouth, tasting her as his finger moved slow and deep. It was sensory overload, the sweetest torture she'd ever endured. Powerless against the sensual onslaught, Samara arched against his hand, meeting each deep, penetrating thrust with moans that he swallowed in his mouth. Just when she thought she couldn't take anymore, he pushed a second finger inside her.

She cried out, her hips pumping wildly against him as the sensations intensified, burned. His fingers moved deeper and faster inside her. His thumb stroked her clitoris until her body began to convulse uncontrollably.

"Marcus...*Oh yes!*" She rode his fingers as she climaxed, her thighs taut and shaking, waves of ecstasy bursting through her. The spasms ceased after several moments, releasing her from the grip of the most powerful orgasm she'd ever had in her life.

Weak and spent, she dropped her head against Marcus's solid chest and closed her eyes, trying to catch her breath. She could feel the rapid beat of his heart, and she felt a twinge of guilt that he'd done all the hard work and received so little in return.

She lifted her head to survey his shadowed face in the moonlit darkness of the room. His eyes were glittering onyx as he gazed back at her, his lids at half-mast. Damn, he was sexy.

"I've kept you from your friends," was all she could say.

Marcus chuckled, the sound low and rough and innately masculine. "You don't hear me complaining."

A smile tugged at the corners of her mouth. "That's because you're too polite."

He chuckled again. "Get to know me a little better and you'll see that I'm anything but polite."

Samara laughed, thinking just how *much* better she'd like to get to know him. In every wicked way imaginable.

Reluctantly, she unwrapped her legs from his waist, and he eased her down and stepped back. While he adjusted his silk tie, she straightened her blouse and tugged her skirt back into place. Her inner thighs were slick with moisture. She'd come all over Marcus's hand, but instead of feeling self-conscious or ashamed, she felt only deliciously satisfied. And rather amazed. If Marcus Wolf could rock her world with just one finger, she could only imagine the kind of damage his rock-hard dick would do. Her nipples puckered at the mere thought.

She retrieved her purse from the floor and reached inside for a business card. As she passed it to Marcus, their fingers brushed, and her skin tingled with awakened nerve endings. Their gazes met and held.

"Call me sometime," Samara murmured. Without waiting for his response, she turned and slipped quietly out of the room.

Marcus was still nursing a hard-on by the time he joined his colleagues at the downtown sports bar where they'd agreed to meet for drinks.

As he sat down at the table, Donovan Ware, his former college roommate and current employee, sent a triumphant look at the blond-haired man seated across from him. "Ha, I was right! Pay up, Blair!"

Scowling, Timothy Blair dug inside his wallet, retrieved a twenty-dollar bill and tossed it grudgingly across the table. "You got lucky this time, Ware," he grumbled.

Donovan laughed, cheerfully pocketing the money.

Marcus watched the exchange with a raised brow. "Did I miss something?"

Timothy threw him a disgruntled look. "You weren't supposed to show up. I bet your buddy here you'd blow us off for that hot number you were talking to before we left."

Marcus chuckled, shaking his head. "Good to know the money I pay you guys is being put to good use. I'll have a scotch," he told the young redhead who appeared at their table to take his order.

Her wide green eyes were latched onto his face. "Excuse me for asking, but aren't you Marcus Wolf?"

Marcus smiled lazily. "Last I checked."

She beamed. "Oh my God! I saw the article in today's paper. I'm a *huge* fan of yours, Mr. Wolf. My name's Meagan."

"Pleasure to meet you, Meagan."

Excitedly, she tore off a sheet of paper from her notepad. "Could I have your autograph?"

"Of course." Marcus signed the paper and handed it back to the waitress, who clutched it to her chest as if it were a winning lottery ticket.

"Thank you *so* much," she gushed. "I'll be right back with your drink."

As she moved off, Donovan grinned and shook his smooth bald head at Marcus. "You're gonna have to start beating them off with a stick, man."

"Or you could just hand them over to me," Timothy suggested. "Starting with that hottie back at the university. *Man*, she was beautiful."

Donovan snorted. "You wouldn't know what to do with a woman like that, Blair."

"And *you* would?"

Taming the Wolf

"Damn straight!"

Marcus tuned out their bickering as his mind wandered back to the erotic encounter with Samara Layton. He still couldn't believe it had happened. Since meeting her in New York on Saturday, he hadn't been able to get her off his mind. When he first saw her tonight, standing in the back of the auditorium, he'd thought his mind was playing tricks on him. It was only after she'd stepped to him, and he found himself gazing down into those dark gypsy eyes, that he realized she wasn't a figment of his imagination. When she smiled at him, his heart leaped. When she actually reached out and touched him, blood rushed straight to his groin. Her sultry confession—*I haven't been able to stop thinking about you*—had pretty much sealed the deal. What man in his right mind *wouldn't* have followed her after hearing something like that?

And while her plump breasts were filling his hands, and her long curvy legs were wrapped around his waist, he hadn't stopped to question his good fortune. He didn't care that just two nights ago, Samara Layton had wanted nothing to do with him. All that mattered was being inside her honey-wet heat, and damn she'd felt incredible. So incredible that his dick throbbed at the memory of it.

He reached for the glass of scotch the waitress had brought and tossed down half the contents in one gulp.

"Don't feel bad about losing the bet, Blair," Donovan was consoling his colleague. "For a while there, *I* didn't think Marcus would find his way here either. Not with the way he went after—" He stopped, looking slyly at Marcus. "You *did* catch her name, didn't you?"

"Hell, yeah."

When Marcus offered no more, Donovan and Timothy stared at him. "Well?" they demanded in unison.

Marcus swallowed more scotch. "Her name's Samara."

"Beautiful name," Timothy said.

"Beautiful woman." Donovan grinned at Marcus. "So what happened when you caught up to her?"

40

"None of your damn business."

"Aw, come on, man," Donovan laughingly protested. "You're holding out on *me*? How long have we known each other?"

"Too long." Seventeen years, to be exact. They'd met as freshmen at Morehouse College, and quickly became friends when they discovered how much they had in common. They both had grown up in Atlanta and were raised by single fathers. As political science majors, they'd both dreamed of attending law school and becoming high-powered attorneys. After graduation, Donovan's law school plans had been delayed when his father got sick. While Marcus left home to attend Georgetown University, Donovan had stayed behind to care for his ailing father until he passed away two years later. After that, he'd enrolled in law school at Emory University, preferring to remain close to home. But he and Marcus never lost contact with each other. When Marcus returned to Atlanta to launch his own law firm, Donovan was nothing but supportive. When Marcus decided to expand the practice, after three years of flying solo, Donovan was the first staff attorney he'd hired.

"Where's Helen?" Marcus asked, belatedly realizing that the fourth member of their party was missing, although her Louis Vuitton purse occupied the chair across from him.

"She stepped outside to take a call from a client," Donovan answered. "Her phone rang just as she was about to join the bet on whether or not you'd make it here. Wanna know what *she* thought?"

"Not really." It was one thing to discuss his exploits with the fellas, but to have another woman speculating about his sex life just didn't seem right. Especially a woman who worked for him.

"I envy you, Wolf," Timothy said, reaching into the glass bowl on their table and scooping out a handful of peanuts. "Even before you opened your mouth to speak tonight, you were getting *do me* looks from practically every woman in the room. You could've gone home with any one of those females who lined up to talk to you afterward." He shook his head, munching thoughtfully. "You're a lucky man, boss."

Chuckling, Marcus signaled the waitress for another round of drinks. It was only then that he remembered Samara telling him she wanted something from him. He wondered if she were just talking dirty... Or had she meant something else?

Whatever it was, he intended to find out what she wanted. And if his so-called luck held up, he and Samara Layton would be lovers before the end of the week.

Chapter Four

I'm so sorry we won't be doing business together this year," lamented Vickie Paige, special events coordinator of Capitol Fun Rentals. "We always look forward to helping FYI with Founder's Day. It's an annual tradition."

"I know," Samara said on the other end of the phone. "I was really hoping we could hold the event this year, but the funds just aren't there."

"I understand. Shoot, I wish I could just let you guys use everything for free."

Samara smiled. "I know you would if you could, Vickie, and I appreciate that. But even if I let you do that, there's no way you could get away with not charging for a carousel, a moonwalk, a dunking machine, a couple of helium tanks, several tents—not to mention the cotton candy, hot dog, nacho, popcorn and snow cone machines."

Vickie chuckled. "That *is* a lot to account for. But what if you scaled back on a few things? Would that make it more feasible?"

Samara sighed heavily. "I thought about that, even crunched some numbers. But, no, it still wouldn't work. And Founder's Day isn't just about the carnival. We also hold the annual scholarship drawing that a lot of teens and parents look forward to. I can't bear the thought of telling them that no scholarships will be awarded this year. Call me a coward," she added ruefully.

"You're not a coward," Vickie said quietly. "You're doing everything you can to save the Institute, and that takes a lot of courage. I admire you, Samara, and I know I'm not alone."

"Thank you, Vickie. That really means a lot to me." Swallowing past the lump in her throat, Samara glanced down at the checklist on her blotter. She still had several more calls to make before the end of the day. "I have to run, Vickie, but I'll be in touch if anything changes."

"All right. You hang in there, Samara. Everything's gonna work out just fine, you'll see."

Samara thanked the woman again and hung up the phone, wishing she shared Vickie Paige's optimism about FYI's future. But it was hard to remain optimistic with a stack of overdue notices perched on a corner of her desk, and spreadsheet after spreadsheet shouting that they were in the red. To add insult to injury, Melissa had introduced the dreaded *D* word over coffee that morning— downsizing. If the Institute's financial situation didn't improve soon, Samara would have to start laying off employees.

With a long, weary sigh, she swiveled away from her desk to gaze out the window, which overlooked a well-manicured park across the street. The sky was pewter-gray and cloudy with the threat of rain; the gloomy weather matched her mood.

She didn't even *want* to think about downsizing any of her nine employees. And where would she start? Every staff member was invaluable to the organization, from the loyal receptionist who'd been with the Institute since its inception, to the grant writer who'd secured much of their funding over the years. And Melissa. God, she couldn't even imagine terminating Melissa. It was inconceivable.

Don't get discouraged, an inner voice consoled her. *You still have your back-up plan.*

At the thought of Marcus Wolf, Samara's belly quivered. Two days later, she still couldn't believe what she'd done with him—a virtual stranger. She'd gone to the university intending to flirt with him, to use her feminine wiles to renew his interest in her. It wasn't until she actually saw him again that she realized she wouldn't be satisfied with merely having a cup of coffee with him afterward and pleading her case.

No, she'd wanted more.

She'd wanted him.

And there was no way she would have left without tasting his sweet, juicy lips and feeling his hard, muscled body pressed against hers. The pleasure she'd experienced in his arms was unlike anything she'd ever imagined. And if she had to do it all over again, she wouldn't have thought twice about making love to him right there in that classroom. Now that she'd had a taste of Marcus Wolf, she only craved more.

Groaning in frustration, Samara leaned her head back against the chair and closed her eyes. *This is ridiculous*, she thought. *FYI is in dire financial straits and all you can think about is getting laid.*

Her phone rang, startling her. She swiveled around and reached across the desk to pick it up. "Yes?"

"Samara, you have a visitor in the lobby," the receptionist told her, a note of unmistakable excitement in her voice.

"Who is it, Diane?" Samara asked curiously.

"His name's Marcus Wolf."

Samara's heart slammed against her rib cage. After two days of waiting for Marcus to call, she'd been on the verge of picking up the phone herself and making the next move. "Thanks, Diane," she said somewhat breathlessly. "Tell him I'll be right down."

She hung up the phone and quickly straightened the papers on her desk, then grabbed the stack of overdue invoices and hid them in the bottom drawer. She pulled a tube of red lipstick from her purse and applied a fresh coat, ran a comb through her relaxed mane and popped an Altoid into her mouth. Pausing to take a deep breath, she strode from the office and headed downstairs to the lobby.

Marcus stood at the large oak reception desk, tall, dark and incredibly handsome in another two-thousand-dollar Italian suit, this one in navy blue. His hands were thrust casually into his pants pockets as he conversed with Diane Rawlings, the receptionist. When he flashed that killer grin, the fifty-seven-year-old woman giggled and blushed to the gray roots of her scalp. Samara couldn't believe it. Diane, who was both feared and respected for her no-nonsense personality, had actually *giggled* and *blushed*.

Was any woman on the planet immune to Marcus Wolf?

He glanced up at Samara's approach, and her heart skidded to a halt as their eyes met and held. Images of their erotic encounter instantly filled her mind, making her temperature rise.

"Mr. Wolf," she greeted him, hand outstretched. "A pleasure to see you again."

Marcus clasped her palm in the solid warmth of his own, sending tingles up and down her spine. "The pleasure's all mine, Ms. Layton," he drawled in that deep, mesmerizing voice that made her want to cross her legs. *Tightly*.

"Would you like to join me in my office?" she murmured.

Something hot and wicked flashed in his dark eyes, and Samara realized he was reacting to the wording she'd used. *Join me in my office. Join me.*

Her mouth went dry at the accompanying mental picture.

"Lead the way," he said softly.

"Diane, please hold my calls."

"Of course, Samara."

As Samara turned and led Marcus up the stairs, she could feel his bold gaze all over her backside, burning through her creamy silk blouse and pencil-slim brown skirt, as if he had X-ray vision. Never before had she been so aroused by a man undressing her with his eyes.

By the time they reached her office on the second floor, she was almost dizzy with desire. As she closed the door behind them, Marcus caught her arm, turning her around to face him. She felt a thrill of excitement as he pulled her roughly into his arms.

Sinking his hands into her hair, he lowered his head and took her mouth in a deep, provocative kiss that drugged her senses and made her breasts ache. She pressed against him, opening her mouth to receive the hot, silky penetration of his tongue. He tasted of chocolate and peppermint, warm and delicious. She deepened the kiss, sucking greedily on his tongue while her hands slid up and down the muscled hardness of his back. She wanted nothing more than to be naked with him, to feel his powerful body mounted above hers as he thrust in and out of her. Though she knew this wasn't the time or place. She couldn't help but moan as he cupped her buttocks, lifting her hips more fully against his so she could feel the bulge of his erection. Almost mindlessly, she ground herself into him, and this time he uttered a low, guttural moan of pleasure.

Dragging his mouth from hers, he whispered huskily against her throat, "Damn, I can't get enough of you."

She tipped her head back, making it easier for him to kiss her there. "Then what took you so long to find me?"

She felt him smile against the sensitized hollow of her neck. "I wanted to test the limits of my endurance. As you can see, I didn't make it very far."

She chuckled softly. "You don't hear me complaining."

"No," Marcus agreed, lifting his head to search her face with a sudden keenness she found unsettling, "I *don't* hear you complaining."

With a sinking feeling in the pit of her stomach, Samara pulled out of his arms and walked over to her desk and sat down. Marcus followed more slowly, his dark gaze never leaving her face as he ignored the visitor's chair and rounded the desk, perching his hip on the edge of it so she had to tilt her head up to look at him.

"I'm curious about something," he said thoughtfully. "Maybe you can help me."

Samara leaned back in the chair and smoothly crossed her legs. The moment of truth had arrived. "What is it?"

"When we met in New York," Marcus said slowly, "you couldn't get away from me fast enough. And then on Monday night you showed up where I was speaking and practically propositioned me on the spot."

"I didn't proposition—" He arched a dubious brow, cutting short her protest. She grinned sheepishly. "All right, maybe I did proposition you."

Marcus chuckled. "Not that I'm complaining, but you can see how a brother might be a little confused by your behavior. What changed your mind about me?"

She shrugged. "Maybe I was playing hard to get in New York."

"Were you?"

Samara met his gaze unflinchingly. "If you're asking whether I'm really attracted to you, and if I meant it when I told you that since we met, I haven't stopped thinking about you, the answer is yes on both counts. If you doubt my sincerity, I can think of a hundred different ways I can prove my attraction to you."

His hooded eyes drifted to her lips. "A hundred, huh?"

"At least."

"I just might take you up on that offer, Ms. Layton," he said silkily.

Her nipples hardened. She licked her lips, murmuring softly, "I hope you will, Mr. Wolf." And, oh, how she meant it.

"That said," she continued after a moment, "in the spirit of full disclosure, I did have another reason for showing up at the university that night."

"Ahh, yes. Of course." Straightening from the desk, Marcus tucked his hands into his pockets and wandered over to the window. "The Fannie Yorkin Institute."

"Yes." Samara drew a deep breath. "As you probably know, we've experienced some financial setbacks over the last few years, and now we're facing the possibility of bankruptcy."

"That's too bad," Marcus said quietly. "You've done a lot of positive work in the community."

"Yes, we have. But if we don't receive some funding very soon, we'll be forced to close shop." She paused. "I went to Georgetown to talk to you about donating to the organization. But after the way

I treated you in New York, I knew there was no way I could come right out and ask for your help."

He glanced over his shoulder at her. "So you decided to seduce me instead."

Samara hesitated, searching his face for any signs of anger or hostility. But his expression was unreadable. She said meekly, "Let's just say I thought it best to soften you up a little before I petitioned you for money." When he turned back to the window without a word, she hastened to add, "If you'd prefer, I can call and schedule an appointment with your secretary. And then I could come to your office and give a presentation for you and your senior associates—"

Marcus shook his head. "They've gone back to Atlanta to tie up some loose ends at headquarters and won't return until the end of next week, when we officially open for business. I'm still trying to get the office organized, so it's not really ideal for visitors yet." He turned slowly, his dark gaze roaming across her face with an intensity that made her breath quicken. "Have dinner with me tonight."

"Dinner?" she echoed.

"Yes, dinner." Wry humor lifted the corners of his mouth. "I know we've already tried that once before, but this time we'll call it a business meeting. You can bring as many materials as you need and give your presentation. You'll have my undivided attention."

Samara smiled, hope blooming in her chest for the first time in weeks. "All right, Marcus. That sounds like a plan."

He glanced at his Rolex watch. "I have a meeting with the city council this afternoon. I can pick you up afterward, say around six-thirty?"

"That's fine. I still have a lot of paperwork to catch up on, so you can pick me up here." No *way* was she inviting Marcus Wolf to her house. They'd never make it out the front door.

She rose from her chair and escorted him downstairs to the lobby. Melissa was behind the reception desk manning the phone for Diane, who'd left early to attend a function at her grandson's elementary school.

Melissa's hazel eyes widened in shock when she saw Marcus. Samara quickly performed the introductions, praying her friend wouldn't say anything to embarrass her.

"It's so nice to meet you, Mr. Wolf," Melissa said, eagerly shaking his hand. "I've followed your career since you worked for the ACLU here in D.C. I really wanted to attend your presentation the other night, but I'd already made plans with my husband. But I heard from my friend, a law professor at the university, that you were absolutely wonderful. Do you know Louise Fletcher?"

"As a matter of fact, I do," Marcus answered easily. "We met a few years ago through the D.C. bar association. She and her colleagues were generous enough to take me out to dinner before the lecture."

Melissa beamed. "Well, she speaks very highly of you. What brings you here this afternoon?"

He glanced lazily in Samara's direction. "Ms. Layton and I had a few things to clear up."

"Really?" Undisguised curiosity filled Melissa's eyes as she looked from Marcus to Samara.

"We'd better not hold you up any longer," Samara told Marcus, discreetly ushering him toward the front entrance. "You wouldn't want to keep those city council members waiting. I've heard they're an ornery lot."

Marcus seemed vaguely amused as he paused at the door to look down at her. "I'll see you at six-thirty," he said softly.

She smiled at him, aware of Melissa's speculative gaze. "I'll be ready."

When he'd gone, Melissa leaned across the counter and exclaimed, "You have a *date* with Marcus Wolf?"

"Shhh, not so loud! And it's not a date. It's a business meeting."

"How did this happen? The last time we spoke, you thought he was a womanizer."

"He probably is," Samara blithely retorted. "But if he can help bail us out of debt, I don't care what he is. Now if you'll excuse me, I have some work to finish up before my *meeting* with Mr. Wolf."

Melissa grinned from ear to ear. "Atta, girl. I'll want a full report in the morning."

Samara chuckled dryly. "I wouldn't expect otherwise."

Chapter Five

Three hours later, Samara climbed into the luxurious interior of Marcus's silver Bentley Continental GT. The leather seats were so soft and sumptuous she felt like a knife sinking through melted butter.

"Nice," she murmured appreciatively as Marcus slid behind the wheel. She ran her fingers over the gleaming wood surface of the console. "*Very* nice."

Marcus sent her an amused sidelong glance. "You like?"

"Oh, most definitely." With a luxuriant sigh, Samara closed her eyes and sank more deeply into the enveloping comfort of the passenger seat. As she did, she felt the tensions of the day slowly ebb from her body. "Mmm, I could fall asleep right now."

Marcus chuckled softly. "I'll try not to take it personally."

She opened one eye to look at him. "If anything, you should take it as a compliment."

"How's that?"

"If I feel relaxed enough around you to fall asleep that says something good about you. You're trustworthy, easy to be with."

Marcus shook his head. "Sounds boring to me."

Samara smiled lazily. "Believe me, Marcus. That's one word that could *never* be used to describe you."

His grin flashed white in the dim interior of the car. "I wasn't fishing for compliments, but I'll take it."

Samara laughed, then turned to gaze out the window as they maneuvered through the snarl of downtown traffic, following Pennsylvania Avenue as it wound past government office buildings and historic landmarks. A gray mist clung to the cool March air, but so far the forecasted showers hadn't arrived.

"Where are you staying, Marcus?"

"Foggy Bottom. Wanted to be as close as possible to the court-house." He glanced over at her. "What about you? Where do you live?"

"All the way over in southeast D.C." She made a face. "Everyone keeps telling me that I need to move closer to the office, but I can't bring myself to put my house up for sale. It was my grandmother's— I practically grew up there. I can't imagine living anywhere else."

Marcus nodded sympathetically. "I understand how you feel. It was hard for me to convince my father to sell our old house. He had strong ties to the community, but the neighborhood was going to hell. Once my brother and I moved away from home, we didn't feel comfortable leaving the old man there alone—retired cop or not."

Samara chuckled. "A retired cop, huh? He must have put up quite a struggle about leaving his turf. Where is he now?"

"We bought him a house in Stone Mountain, right outside of Atlanta. The way he complains, you would think he'd been exiled to some desert wasteland."

Samara shook her head in exaggerated disbelief. "Ingrate," she pronounced in judgment.

Marcus laughed, and damn if it wasn't the sexiest sound she'd ever heard. She crossed her legs and willed her pulse rate to slow down.

Soon they arrived at an upscale Georgetown restaurant renowned for its award-winning cuisine and stunning views of the Potomac River. Marcus helped Samara from the Bentley, relin-quished the car to the valet, then guided her inside with a warm hand at the small of her back. The maître d' greeted him by name and ushered them to a candlelit table in a private corner of the elegant restaurant. A fire glowed softly in a stone fireplace nearby, and tall French doors opened to a terrace that boasted the best water-front views in the city. In warmer weather, customers lined up to enjoy the outdoor seating. It was perfectly romantic, the kind of restaurant Samara had envisioned in her fantasy about Marcus. And even as she reminded herself that this was *not* a date, she couldn't help but wonder what else the night had in store for them.

As soon as they were seated, a white-jacketed waiter materialized to take their drink orders. "We have an excellent wine list," he proclaimed, then proceeded to recite his recommendations.

"I'll just have a club soda," Samara told him.

Marcus ordered a glass of Burgundy wine and appetizers. As the waiter bustled away, Marcus gazed at Samara across the linen-covered table. Candlelight flickered across his face, softening the hard angles and planes and accentuating the lush, sensual contours of his lips. He was too fine for words. It would take some serious willpower to keep her mind on business. At the moment, all she could think about was climbing across the table, straddling Marcus and riding him like a champion thoroughbred.

"I'm going to ask you a personal question," he said, "but please feel free to tell me to mind my own damn business."

A rueful smile touched her lips. She already knew what he was going to ask, so she saved him the trouble. "I'd love to tell you that I don't drink alcohol for religious reasons, but I think you've already figured out that I'm not a good little church girl. The truth is, Marcus, I'm a recovering alcoholic. I celebrated three years of sobriety this past January."

His expression softened. "Congratulations," he said quietly.

"Thank you. Of all the things I've accomplished in my life, sobriety is probably the hardest thing I've ever had to work for, which is why it's an accomplishment I'm especially proud of."

"You should be. It takes an extraordinary person to overcome an addiction like that, Samara. You have my utmost respect and admiration."

Samara could have leaned across the table and kissed him. Later, when they were alone, she would. And she wasn't so sure she'd stop at just kissing him.

The waiter returned with their drinks and appetizers, then took their meal orders.

As they began eating their crab bisque, Marcus said, "I met Richard Yorkin at a local fund-raiser a few years ago. I remember how passionate he was about the Institute. I was kind of surprised to learn he'd retired."

Samara swallowed her soup, mentally deliberating how much information to divulge about the founder's real reasons for retiring. She finally decided honesty was the best policy, especially if Marcus—as a potential donor—was to understand that the Yorkin Institute hadn't simply fallen on hard times due to negligence or misappropriation of funds.

"Long before Richard decided to retire, which was a very difficult decision for him, he suffered a personal tragedy in his life. He lost his wife of thirty years to breast cancer."

"I'm sorry to hear that," Marcus murmured.

"Naturally it devastated him. They had no children, so he pretty much had to grieve alone." And with the support of the local chapter of Alcoholics Anonymous where he and Samara had met; they both found themselves barreling down a path of self-destruction.

"The Institute suffered financially during this period," she continued, "and by the time Richard rebounded from his grief, it was too late. Against the wishes of his financial advisors, he still wanted to keep the Institute open for business. He and his wife Fannie—whom the Institute is named after—had established FYI together, and he knew she would want the work to continue with or without her. But the cost of her chemotherapy and related medical expenses over the years had taken a toll on their personal finances. Richard poured what little remained of their savings back into the Institute, then hired me to replace him as executive director when he decided to retire. He was confident my marketing background could help breathe new life into the place."

Marcus nodded. "Does he remain active in the Institute?"

"Not really. Last year he moved to Cape Cod, where he and Fannie honeymooned. He said he feels closer to her there." Samara stroked her spoon absently through the creamy bisque. "He calls every once in a while to check up on everyone. But I think he's more concerned with our general morale than the financial status of the organization. That's just the kind of person he is—caring and generous to a fault."

Marcus took a sip of his wine, watching her over the rim. "You said you have a marketing background. What were you doing before coming to the Yorkin Institute?"

"I worked as a marketing manager at a top advertising firm after earning my MBA."

"Impressive."

She gave a dismissive shrug. "It had its perks, I guess. The signing bonus, six-figure salary, corner office with a view…"

"But it wasn't what you wanted," Marcus surmised.

Samara glanced up from her bowl, met his penetrating gaze and felt incredibly transparent. "No," she said quietly. "It wasn't what I wanted. There's a huge difference between using my degree to improve the bottom line of some faceless corporation versus using those same marketing skills to come up with programs that members of the community can benefit from." She paused, studying him. "Just as I'm sure you can appreciate the difference between practicing corporate law behind a desk versus defending real, everyday people whose basic civil rights have been violated."

"I can't argue with that," Marcus agreed.

"That's probably a first."

"What?"

"You. A lawyer not arguing."

Marcus laughed. "You got lawyer jokes, huh?"

Samara smiled across the table at him, enjoying their cama-raderie. "Sorry. I couldn't resist."

As their meals arrived, she asked, "So what about you, Mr. King of Torts? Have you always felt a calling to save the world?"

His mouth curved ruefully. "I don't know about all that. But I guess my father had other ideas. He named me after Marcus Garvey."

Samara grinned. "Quite a legacy to fulfill."

"I know. No pressure, right?"

As they dug into their meals, Marcus told Samara how he'd learned about Nelson Mandela and the African National Congress while he was a political science major at Morehouse, and how he'd returned home brimming with stories about Mandela's imprisonment and his subsequent efforts to end apartheid in South Africa.

"That was all I talked about that summer, until my brother got sick and tired of hearing my fight-the-power lectures and told me to write Nelson Mandela a damn letter."

Samara laughed. "And did you?" she asked, equally riveted by his tale and the deep, intoxicating timbre of his voice. His voice was so damn sexy, her legs would stay *permanently* crossed.

Marcus chuckled. "I had no choice. My brother threatened me with bodily harm if I didn't. To my absolute surprise, I not only received a letter of response from Nelson Mandela, but an invitation to join him in South Africa the following summer. I felt like I'd won the lottery, Samara. Not only had I been given a rare opportunity to meet one of my heroes, but I also used the experience to learn a new language and conduct research on the inner workings of the African National Congress."

"Wait a minute," Samara said, pausing with her fork halfway to her mouth. "Did you write an article that was published in the *Georgetown Law Journal*?"

Marcus nodded. "During my second year there."

"Get out of here! I came across that article during college while doing some research for a sociology paper. Excellent resource, by the way. Very thought-provoking and well researched."

Marcus inclined his head with unaffected modesty. "I'm glad you enjoyed it. What was your paper about?"

They continued talking as they finished their meals. Plates were discreetly cleared from the table, rich desserts enjoyed, coffee poured and refilled—and still they lingered, completely engrossed in each other. They were oblivious to the emptying restaurant and the surreptitious looks they received from the wait staff. Samara couldn't take her eyes off Marcus, and apparently the feeling was mutual. His dark, focused gaze heated the blood in her veins and set off a sweet, pulsing throb between her legs. She wanted his mouth down there, wanted to feel his tongue stroking the slick folds of her sex before plunging deep inside. The thought of it turned her on so hard and so fast, she got wet.

As if he'd read her dirty mind, Marcus smiled, a wickedly sexy smile that made her stomach clench. As she stared at him, his tongue snaked out and slowly glided over the juicy, sensuous curve of his bottom lip. Samara watched as if in a trance, her nipples hardening, her clitoris throbbing.

With a supreme effort, she dragged her gaze away and glanced down at her watch. "Goodness," she choked out. "I didn't realize how late it was. And I haven't even given you my presentation!"

"No time like the present," Marcus drawled, looking relaxed and content as he leaned back in his chair. Samara wanted to crawl under the table, kneel between his legs, unzip his pants and give him the blowjob of his life. She could almost taste the salty-sweet flavor of his cum when he exploded in her mouth.

Shaking off the vividly erotic image, Samara reached into the leather attaché case she'd brought and withdrew several glossy brochures. Spreading them across the table, she briefly explained the various programs offered by the Institute.

"We've collaborated with many organizations on different projects. For instance, we work with area hospitals and the healthcare industry to encourage safe-sex practices among teens, and we sponsor wellness programs geared for mothers and newborns as well as the entire family. We've also partnered with several employment agencies that provide us with current job vacancies for our onsite employment counseling center.

"The program I'm currently interested in spearheading is called Youth for the Arts and Literacy. We already know of several students from local schools and universities who are interested in participating. One of my ideas is to have the students involved in a dance troupe that performs throughout the community, and I'd also like to make visiting artists available to conduct workshops and other programs for anyone interested in attending. The Institute would collaborate with neighborhood associations and build ties with local community development corporations, which would also result in needed revenue going back into the Institute—something our financial advisors would greatly appreciate," she added dryly.

Throughout her presentation and as he sifted through the brochures, Marcus' expression had remained impassive. Samara wondered nervously if opposing counsel ever found themselves unnerved by his demeanor as they delivered their closing arguments.

But when she'd finished speaking, Marcus gave a slow, approving nod. "I can see why Richard Yorkin entrusted you with the position of executive director when he retired. You really have a vision for the organization, Samara. And there's no doubt in my mind that closure of the Institute would be a huge loss to the community."

"I'm glad you feel that way," Samara said, silently releasing the pent-up breath she hadn't realized she was holding. "Although FYI has done some tremendous work in the past, I'm one-hundred percent confident that with increased funding, we can accomplish even greater things in the future."

"I agree." Marcus reached inside his breast pocket and withdrew his checkbook. As the waiter removed the last of their dishes and glided away promising to return with the bill, Marcus filled out a check and passed it to Samara across the table.

She thought her eyes were deceiving her when she saw the seven-figure amount. Even as her heart performed somersaults, she lifted incredulous eyes to Marcus's face. "I...I can't accept this much."

He looked faintly amused. "You're not," he said pointedly. "The Yorkin Institute is."

Samara drew a deep breath, the check trembling in her hand. "When I told you about Richard losing his wife to cancer, it wasn't to play on your sympathies or anything. I simply wanted you to know how much FYI meant to him, that he didn't jeopardize its future by squandering funds."

"The thought never crossed my mind. As I told you before, I met the man myself. His passion for community service made an impression on me. A very distinct impression." Marcus leaned forward in his chair, his dark gaze intent on hers. "*Your* passion made an impression on me."

She swallowed with difficulty. "Please don't think I'm ungrateful, Marcus. Nothing could be further from the truth. It's just that—"

Again, he interrupted her protests. "If I were some anonymous benefactor," he challenged, "would you have a problem accepting the money?"

"Well...probably not. But that's not the case here."

"The Institute needs the donation, Samara. It would be ridiculous for you not to accept it just because we've gotten a little acquainted."

"Wait a minute." Almost frantically, she dug into her attaché case and extracted a calculator. She began configuring numbers. "I can do some pro bono consulting work for your law firm—marketing proposals, market research, budget reports, press releases, anything you need. At my old firm, I charged our clients an hourly fee based on my degree and experience. Let's just say—"

"Samara." Marcus reached across the table, gently laying his hand over hers to retrieve the calculator. "I'm not trying to turn you into an indentured servant, baby girl. This isn't a loan. I want you to take the money and put it to good use. Can you do that for me?"

She pulled her bottom lip between her teeth, tingling from the warmth of his hand and the tender endearment he'd used. She knew her behavior was irrational, absurd even. After all, she *had* arranged the meeting with him in the hopes of receiving a large donation, and the reality was that they desperately needed the money. If Melissa were here, she would strangle Samara for attempting to sabotage the Institute's chance at financial rescue—a chance that might never come again.

"All right," she finally conceded. She placed the check carefully inside her purse, intending to guard it with her very life until it could be safely deposited. Lifting her head, she gazed earnestly at Marcus. "I want you to know how much I appreciate your tremendous generosity, as will everyone else who benefits from it."

"You're very welcome," he said.

"But I want you to promise me that you'll allow me to provide my services to your firm. Absolutely *anything* you can think of, I mean it."

"That really won't be—"

"At least keep it under consideration. Will you promise me that?"

Marcus chuckled, torn between amusement and exasperation. "All right, I promise."

She gave him a grateful smile. "Thank you." She began gathering her brochures, returning them to the attaché case as Marcus handled the bill.

"Marcus?"

"Hmm?"

Her expression was sheepish. "Could I have my calculator back?"

"Nah," he said lazily. "I think I'll keep it as collateral."

Marcus couldn't remember the last time he'd so thoroughly enjoyed a woman's company. Even after the bill was settled and their table had been cleared, he and Samara lingered at the restaurant for another hour, talking about anything and everything. Just as their mutual friend Walter Floyd had predicted, they had a lot in common and shared many of the same interests. Marcus couldn't get enough of her, with her throaty laughter, smoky eyes, sexy mouth and luscious body.

He didn't want the night to end.

And judging by the looks Samara was giving him on the ride back to the Yorkin Institute, she didn't either.

All too soon they reached their destination, where Samara's burgundy Toyota Avalon sat alone in the parking lot. Marcus pulled up alongside the car and killed the ignition.

Their eyes met and held in the shadowy darkness.

"Marcus…"

"Samara…"

When they spoke at the same time, he chuckled quietly. "Ladies first."

"I had a wonderful time tonight," Samara said softly.

"Me, too."

"I'm sure those waiters were beginning to wonder if we'd have to be forcibly removed from the restaurant."

"Yeah. I think I saw a couple of cops circling the building at one point. I didn't know if they were there to get us, or the leftover pastries."

Samara laughed, making his pulse leap. Damn, she had a sexy laugh.

Moments later they were still chuckling quietly, calmly, the joke just an excuse for their eyes to linger over each other.

"Will you be available to take a photo sometime this week?" Samara asked. "Nothing elaborate, just a simple photo of us shaking hands somewhere. Our community relations director will want to include an article about your generous donation in the next issue of our monthly newsletter. So, will you be available this week?"

"Actually, Samara, I hadn't really planned on publicizing the donation. Where it came from isn't really important, is it?"

She frowned. "Well…no. But I really like to give credit where credit is due. Besides, we always include articles in the newsletter about substantial donations we receive. Our contributors appreciate the recognition."

"I don't need recognition," Marcus said gently. "When I give, it's for something I really believe in. As long as you put that money to good use, that's all I care about." When her frown persisted, he sighed, realizing that he'd unintentionally offended her. "Tell you what. Let me think about it some more. If I change my mind, I'll give you a call. How does that sound?"

She gave him one of those smiles that took his breath away, the kind of smile that would make a man do anything. "All right, Marcus. I'll respect your wishes, whatever you decide." She glanced at the clock mounted on the dashboard and shook her head. "I can't believe how late it is. I don't think I've ever spent four hours at a restaurant."

"Was it that long? See, I hardly even noticed."

"Neither did I. Time flies when you're having fun." Their gazes locked for a moment, then Samara reached for the door handle. "Good night, Marcus."

"Wait. I'll walk you to your car."

She laughed, because he had parked right beside the Avalon. But she played along and stayed put as he climbed out and walked around to open the door for her. As she accepted his hand and stepped from the vehicle, he admired her long, curvy legs accentuated by a pair of strappy stiletto heels. Remembering those long legs wrapped around his waist made him spring an erection faster than he could complete the next thought.

As Samara emerged from the car, he gave her hand a little tug, enough to throw her off balance. And then he caught her in his arms as she fell against him, her eyes wide with surprise.

"Hey, you did that on—"

Marcus cupped her face between his hands, turned it up and captured her mouth with his. Instead of protesting, she slid her

63

hands up his chest and around his neck, kissing him back so hungrily his head swam. He traced the silken contours of her lips with his tongue, coaxing them to part, and when they did, he drove into the sweet warmth of her mouth like a starving man. He tried not to devour her, to take his time and savor her, but he'd already learned that when it came to kissing Samara, patience was a virtue he didn't possess.

Forcing himself to slow down, he dragged his lips from hers and brushed a kiss along her cheekbone. Samara turned her head, blindly seeking his mouth, but he pulled back from her. He rubbed his thumb over her lush bottom lip, trying to resist the silent allure in her dark, sultry eyes. When she opened her mouth and gently suckled his thumb, raw need tore through him. With a ragged groan, he pinned her against the side of the car and wedged his knee between her legs, lifting her slightly off the ground. She moaned and threw her head back against the roof of the car. Like a heat-seeking missile, he homed in on her arched throat, suckling her so hard he knew he'd leave a mark.

Their heads slanted this way and that as they kissed more urgently, their tongues mating frantically as their groping bodies tried to merge into one. They were so absorbed in each other that it took several minutes before they realized it had started raining.

Slowly they opened their eyes and drew apart. In unison they stared up at the falling rain, then at each other.

"It finally came," Samara murmured breathlessly. He must have given her a strange look, because she clarified, "It's been cloudy all day. It finally rained."

"Yeah." Marcus wanted her so badly he ached, but he also needed the decision to come from her. The last thing he wanted was for her to feel obligated to sleep with him just because he'd donated money to the Institute.

"I guess we'd better head for cover before we get soaked," she joked as the rain began to fall harder.

The only kind of soaking Marcus cared about was getting soaked between the sheets with Samara, whose nipples were now protruding from her pale silk blouse.

His mouth watered like the skies above them. "Have a good night, Samara," he said thickly.

"You, too, Marcus."

He waited until she'd climbed inside her car before walking back to his own. Removing his wet suit jacket, he tossed it carelessly across the leather seat and slid behind the wheel of his climate-controlled vehicle. Too bad the engineers who'd built his Bentley hadn't come up with the technology to cool a man's raging libido, he thought darkly.

Turning his head, he watched through the passenger window as Samara leaned her head back and smoothed her wet hair off her face. Looking at her, he felt like a horny teenager who'd stumbled upon a peephole leading into the girls' locker room.

Samara started her car and backed out of the space, pausing to smile and wave at him. Marcus nodded back at her, then sat and watched as she drove out of the parking lot.

It was only when he glanced down at the floor that he saw she'd forgotten her attaché case. He threw the car into drive and started after her, then stopped.

His mouth curved in a slow, satisfied smile.

All the signs were there. He and Samara Layton were meant to be together. And the sooner, the better.

Because if he didn't have her soon, he was going to lose his damn mind.

Chapter Six

S amara had barely entered the building the next morning when she was approached by Melissa. She grabbed Samara's arm and hustled her up the stairs to her own office, closing the door behind them.

Removing a stack of spreadsheets from the visitor's chair opposite her desk, she gestured Samara into the seat before planting herself directly in front of her. "Well?" she demanded, her eyes sparkling with anticipation. "How'd it go last night?"

"Good morning to you, too, Melissa," Samara said dryly.

"I've been waiting for you over half an hour! You're in later than usual this morning."

Samara checked her watch and arched a skeptical brow. "It's only seven-thirty. I always come in around this time."

"Yesterday you were here at seven," Melissa pointed out. Her bronze-painted lips spread in a wicked grin. "Did you and Mr. Wolf have a late night, by any chance?"

"For your information, I was home before midnight." *Just barely.*

"Come on, girl. Give up the goods. How'd the meeting go?"

"It went very well. We had an opportunity to discuss many topics, including the matter for which we were meeting in the first place. Marcus was very impressed with the programs we currently have and the programs we *could* offer, if we had proper funding. In fact, he was so impressed that he agreed to help us out of our financial bind."

Melissa grew very still. "How much 'help' are we talking about?"

"Well…" Samara prolonged the announcement, relishing every moment of it. "Let's just say it was more than I expected. Far more, in fact."

"Spill it, woman!"

Samara reached inside her purse and withdrew the deposit slip, waving it triumphantly under Melissa's nose. "Try this on for size."

Melissa snatched the bank receipt out of her hand and stared at it, her eyes widening almost to the point of hysteria. "Oh my God! That's well over—"

"I know! I was just as shocked as you are."

"Do you know what this means?"

Samara laughed. "Do *I* know what it means? Girl, I could hardly sleep a wink last night, I was so excited. We're back in business, Melissa!"

With a squeal, Melissa grabbed her out of the chair and hugged her, then they jumped up and down like giddy teenagers at a sleep-over—something Samara had never gotten to enjoy when she was growing up.

"Thank God for Marcus Wolf!" Melissa exclaimed when they'd finally settled down. "Didn't I tell you that it was divine intervention that brought him back to Washington, D.C.?"

Samara grinned. "Yes, Melissa. You did."

"And just think. If you two hadn't met at the fashion show in New York, you never would've reached out to him for a donation." She paused, her lips pursed thoughtfully. "In an ironic way, I guess we can thank your mother for making this possible."

Samara didn't want to thank Asha Dubois for a single thing, but she could see Melissa's point. She also realized that if her mother hadn't reneged on their deal, she wouldn't have had a reason to seek out Marcus and get to know him better. And that would have been a damn shame.

"This calls for a celebration," Melissa declared. "Let's treat the staff to lunch this afternoon. They've worked tirelessly under these trying circumstances. I think they've earned a free meal, don't you?"

Samara gave her friend a surprised look. Melissa Matthews was notoriously frugal, and had been long before the Institute fell into financial trouble. As their accountant, it was her duty to cut corners wherever possible, and she took the responsibility seriously—almost to an extreme.

"Why, Melissa, that's awfully generous of you," Samara teased.

Melissa snorted. "Don't get too happy. I'm only ordering pizza. Speaking of food, where did you and Marcus…" she trailed off. Her eyes suddenly fastened on Samara's neck. "Oh my God. Is that what I think it is? Is that a *hickey*?"

Samara's hand shot to her throat. The silk scarf she'd worn that morning to conceal the incriminating mark had slipped off while she and Melissa were jumping up and down.

Oh, great. Now I've got some 'splainin to do.

Melissa was gaping at her, open mouth and all. "What exactly happened between you two last night?"

An embarrassed flush heated Samara's face. "Do we have to discuss this right now? I haven't even had my first cup of coffee yet, and I've got a ton of phone calls to make and letters to draft."

"Details," Melissa commanded, pushing her back down in the chair. "I want details."

Samara chuckled, shaking her head in resignation. "First off, I should have told you yesterday that I went to see Marcus when he spoke at Georgetown on Monday night."

"You were there?"

"Yes. And your law professor friend was right. Marcus *was* wonderful. He had everyone hanging onto his every word—including me. You know, after you and I talked on Monday, I got to thinking about what you'd said about him being an untapped resource and all that. So I went to the university to speak to him about giving FYI a donation. But after the way I'd dissed him in New York, I knew I'd have to be somewhat, uh, creative in my approach."

Melissa grinned slowly. "How creative?"

"Creative enough to hold his attention. I flirted with him, we chatted a little. One thing led to another and…"

"*And?*"

"We wound up in an empty classroom making out."

"Stop playing! You didn't!"

"I did." Samara grinned unabashedly. "Enjoyed every second of it, too."

Melissa laughed. "I'll bet. That man looks like he would be *quite* enjoyable. Lord, he is scrumptious! Was he mad when he found out you wanted money from him?"

Samara frowned, feeling a pang of guilt. "Maybe a little, but it didn't last very long. He was pretty mature and forgiving about the whole thing."

"Obviously. He wrote you a nice fat check. That must have been one helluva kiss you gave him—and vice versa," she added, with a pointed look at the hickey on Samara's throat. Her eyes twinkled with mischief as Samara bent to retrieve her scarf from the floor. "Are you going to see him again?"

"I hope so," Samara answered without hesitation. At Melissa's knowing look, she smiled shyly. "We had a really great time last night. We talked for hours, and we had so much in common it was scary. And you know what else? It was the first time I'd ever been with a man who didn't ask me what it was like to be Asha Dubois's daughter, a man who wasn't remotely interested in hearing about my mother's sexual exploits. It was such a refreshing change, Melissa. I felt like we really connected. It was the best non-date I've ever had."

"Sounds like it was," Melissa said with a soft, intuitive smile. "Sounds to me like the Marcus Wolf Fan Club just gained a devoted new member."

Samara laughed, rising from the chair and walking to the door. "The man rescued us from bankruptcy. I'm not only a *member* of his fan club—I'm the new president!"

That afternoon, Marcus had just hung up the phone with a prospective client when the intercom on his desk buzzed. "Mr.

Wolf, you have a call," the receptionist informed him. "It's your father."

Smiling, Marcus picked up the phone. "How are you doing, Dad?"

"Same as I was two days ago," came Sterling Wolf's gruff reply. "Restless from rattling around in this big ol' house you and your brother insist on keeping me trapped in."

"You're not trapped," Marcus said patiently. He was used to his father's complaints. "You have a more active social life than most men your age. You belong to the senior basketball league; you have your weekly poker group—"

"What you've just described sounds awfully similar to the activities of an inmate at one of those retirement homes."

Marcus laughed. "Hey, don't forget your upcoming fishing trip with the fellas."

"Well…that's different," his father conceded, an unmistakable note of pleasure creeping into his voice. After years of resenting the forced move to Stone Mountain, Sterling Wolf had been pleased to find a group of retired police officers with whom he could commiserate over the current state of law enforcement.

"Taking your meds okay?" Marcus asked.

"Yeah, so don't you start with me."

Marcus grinned at his father's irascible tone. "Do what the doctor tells you and I won't have to."

After thirty years on the force, the toll of sleepless nights, stress and poor eating habits had resulted in Sterling Wolf developing high blood pressure and suffering a mild heart attack. His physician had not only ordered him to retire, but had recommended a complete change of scenery. After ranting and raving for weeks, Sterling eventually consented to selling the family home and relocating to the less congested, more peaceful confines of Stone Mountain. In less than a year, his health had dramatically improved, confirming the wisdom of the move—although Sterling would sooner walk through fire than admit it.

"When do you think you'll be heading back this way?" he asked.

"Actually, I might fly down this weekend. My senior associates in Atlanta have been hinting that there may be trouble in the waters regarding one of our pending class-action lawsuits."

"What kind of trouble?"

"Some disagreement between the parties, minor discrepancies in their deposition statements."

"So they want you to come put out the fires." Sterling grunted his mild disapproval. "Son, you've come a long way from leasing an office space the size of a broom closet and doing pro bono work in exchange for client referrals. You are the founder and CEO of a thriving legal practice—the Atlanta division rakes in millions, and I don't doubt the new branch will do the same. You left the Atlanta firm in the hands of four very capable attorneys. At this point, the *last* thing you should be doing is flying back and forth between offices to do a little handholding. If anything, you should be taking more of a behind-the-scenes role and enjoying the fruits of your labor, the way most people in your position would do. I read about them all the time in the *Wall Street Journal*, these enterprising young fellas who start their own businesses. Once they've achieved success, they take more of a backseat role in the company and spend most of their time golfing and sailing on their luxury yachts."

"Dad," Marcus said dryly, "you know I never opened the practice just to become a figurehead. I like litigating, and I enjoy interacting with my clients and working on their behalf."

"But at the expense of a personal life?"

Marcus rubbed his temple wearily. "We're not going to have this discussion today, Dad." There was enough of an edge in his voice to warn his father off.

Sterling, to his credit, took the hint. "Did your brother tell you he's seeing someone? She comes into his restaurant pretty regularly with her clients. I think she's an investment broker or something. Anyway, she seems like a nice enough young lady, though she's probably not the type *I* would've chosen for Michael. A bit highfalutin', if you ask me."

"I'm sure Mike won't ask you," Marcus drawled, wry humor curving his mouth.

"Why? Because my marriage failed, therefore I can't be a credible authority on such matters?"

"You know that's not what I meant, Dad."

"I know, I know." Sterling Wolf pushed out a deep, heavy sigh. "Your mother called today. She said she'd been trying to reach you for weeks and wanted to get your new number. I told her you'd only been in D.C. for a few weeks settling in."

Marcus stiffened. When he didn't immediately respond, his father quietly continued, "I gave her your number, son. I hope you don't mind."

Marcus clenched his jaw. "That's fine," he said shortly.

"She might be going with Grant to Baltimore in a few weeks for some sort of medical conference at Johns Hopkins. She was hoping to see you then."

Anger threaded through Marcus's body, but he controlled it with practice. "If I'm not too busy."

"Make time, son," Sterling gently implored. "She's your mother."

So many things hovered bitterly on the tip of Marcus's tongue. He held them carefully in check. "I've gotta run, Dad. Got some case briefs to finish reading before a meeting this afternoon."

"Sure, I understand." Sterling Wolf knew better than anyone how Marcus felt about his mother. Since the divorce, Sterling had been trying unsuccessfully to repair the breach between mother and son. "I'll talk to you when I get back from my trip?"

"Of course. Have a good time, Dad. Catch a big one for me."

"Will do. Love you, son."

"Love you, too."

Marcus hung up the phone, then closed his eyes in an unsuccessful attempt to shut out the memories that had haunted him for the last twenty-five years.

Try as he might, he'd never been able to erase the memory of coming home early from school one afternoon and catching his mother in the arms of another man. It had taken all of her tearful pleas to keep an enraged Marcus from pulverizing her lover, a surgeon at the hospital where she worked. The coward beat a hasty retreat while Celeste Wolf wrestled her ten-year-old son to the floor, restraining him with a strength borne of sheer desperation.

But it hadn't mattered at that point anyway. Just as the rage had quickly consumed Marcus, he soon lay spent in his mother's arms, filled with a crushing despair, knowing that their lives would never be the same again.

"Baby, please," Celeste had sobbed. "Please try to understand. I didn't know you would be home early! I never would have let you see me with Grant that way if I had known!"

Marcus untangled himself and got slowly to his feet. He couldn't even look at her. His sweet, beautiful mother doing unspeakable things with another man in his father's house.

His throat felt raw when he finally spoke. "Does Dad know?"

She hesitated, pulling her satin robe protectively around her. "I was going to tell him, Marcus. I swear."

"Why?"

"Because he deserves to know—"

"No!" he roared, and she jumped. "I meant why'd you do it? Why, Ma?"

Tears rolled down Celeste Wolf's face, smearing her mascara. "Marcus, there are so many things about your father and me that you don't understand. We've been having problems—"

"So you brought another man in here?"

"Baby, please listen to me. I'm your mother—"

The icy, unforgiving look on Marcus's face had stopped her cold. He stood over her with clenched fists, half man and half wounded boy. When he spoke, his voice was flat and cold. *"I don't have a mother anymore."*

She gasped. "Marcus, baby, please!" Desperate, she hurled herself at his legs, but he turned sharply on his heel and walked out, slamming the front door so hard that the family portraits on the wall rattled and fell.

Even now Marcus's gut tightened in anger.

Sterling Wolf had been shattered by his wife's infidelity. Following the divorce, Marcus and his brother had watched help-lessly as their father lapsed into depression, throwing himself into work like never before. He was never negligent as a parent. He'd attended their basketball games whenever possible, and stayed on them about getting good grades and making something of them-selves. And he'd taken them camping and fishing every summer.

But Sterling was never the same after his wife's betrayal.

Although her absence from their lives gave him an opportunity to grow closer to his sons, he firmly believed that the bond between mother and child should never be broken. So he'd made excuses for Celeste whenever she forgot her sons' birthdays or missed important events in their lives, like Michael's championship basketball game in which he'd been named MVP. Or Marcus's graduation from law school, which coincided with her vacation with her new husband.

Even if Marcus could have forgiven his mother those transgres-sions, he would never forgive her for betraying his father. For causing irreparable damage to their family.

For rendering Marcus incapable of ever trusting another woman's love.

Oh, he wasn't a misogynist or anything crazy like that. Sterling had raised his sons to be gentlemen, to treat females with the utmost respect. Marcus loved women of all shapes and sizes, and had enjoyed his fair share of lovers. He especially appreciated those who understood when it was time to move on, who weren't determined to suck more out of him than he was willing to give. Marcus had no intention of settling down with anyone. Not any time soon, and possibly never. Considering how his own father's marriage had ended, Marcus figured it wasn't worth the risk. He didn't need the aggravation of a broken heart or shattered dreams. And he was just superstitious enough to believe in history repeating itself.

The reality was that his success attracted all types of women, many of whom were after his bank account and not much else. God knows he'd encountered more than enough of them in his life. Even Samara, who could have her pick of any man she wanted, had an ulterior motive when she'd approached Marcus on Monday night. He wasn't mad at her or anything, but he couldn't let himself forget that. Because as soon as he let his guard down, he'd be hers for the taking. Just as she'd subdued that wild tiger during the fashion show, she would tame Marcus.

No way in hell would he ever let himself be tamed by any woman.

Not even a fine ass woman like Samara Layton.

Samara had made up her mind.

Tonight, on a night when the moon shone bright and full in the sky, she was going to catch a wolf.

Marcus Wolf, to be exact.

She figured she'd waited an appropriate length of time — twenty-four hours — to prove she wasn't offering sex as payment for the generous donation he'd given FYI. And even if twenty-four hours *wasn't* enough time, she didn't care. For once in her life, she was going after what she wanted, and to hell with the consequences.

She'd set the plan in motion by calling his office that afternoon. His receptionist had put her through almost immediately.

"Hey, beautiful," Marcus greeted her, the husky timbre of his voice pouring heat into her ear. "I was just thinking about you."

Samara's nipples got hard. She licked her lips. "Were you?"

"Yeah. You left your attaché case in my car. I figured you'd probably want it back at some point."

She chuckled softly. "Actually, that's why I'm calling. I was going to stop by your office today to pick it up, but I wanted to find out when you'd be there."

"I have a meeting in half an hour. But I should be back around five-thirty, and then I'll probably be here for the rest of the night buried in paperwork."

Or buried in me. Samara smiled wickedly at the thought. "That works for me. I have a ton of things to do before I leave here anyway. If I drop by around seven, would that be too late?"

"Not at all," Marcus murmured. "I'll be here."

After Samara hung up the phone, she finished what she'd been working on until five o'clock. Then she grabbed her belongings and left, surprising her employees, who were used to their boss pulling late nights at the office.

She'd spent a productive day making phone calls and drafting letters to neighborhood associations and corporations that had expressed an interest in participating in the Youth for the Arts and Literacy project. Now that FYI had the necessary funds to officially launch the venture, there was a lot of work to do.

But not tonight, thought Samara, climbing into her Avalon. She'd spent the last two years pouring blood, sweat and tears into preserving the Institute's legacy of community service, doing whatever was necessary to keep the organization afloat. Dinner with Marcus last night had been about business.

Tonight was strictly for pleasure.

When she arrived home, she filled her tub with scented bath crystals from Victoria's Secret and took a hot bath. When she'd finished, she rubbed mango body butter all over herself, slipped into the sexiest lingerie she owned, then stepped into a pair of six-inch stiletto heels she'd once bought on a whim and never really intended to wear. The shoes were downright lethal to walk in, but years of runway training—courtesy of her mother—had given

Samara the confidence and skill to walk in just about anything. And her legs looked positively *fierce* in the stiletto heels, if she didn't say so herself.

Slicking her lips with red and finger-combing her hair, Samara donned her black Burberry trench coat, cinched the belt around her waist, then left the house humming Beyoncé's "Naughty Girl."

Marcus's law firm was strategically located on the northeast end of Massachusetts Avenue—close enough to the city's political presence and Capitol Hillers, but easily accessible to the historic H Street urban corridor with its disenfranchised residents. His practice specialized in civil litigation on behalf of plaintiffs in personal injury, wrongful death, medical malpractice, environmental and products liability, defamation and a number of other tort cases.

The firm occupied the entire tenth floor of a large glass office building. Samara boarded the elevator. As she watched each passing floor number light up, anticipation grew within her until it was a throbbing ache between her thighs. She was horny as hell, but Marcus Wolf was the only man on earth who could satisfy her hunger.

Just seeing his name prominently displayed on the double glass doors made her body tingle all over. THE LAW OFFICES OF MARCUS WOLF & ASSOCIATES.

Watch out, counselor. Court is now in session.

Samara pushed open the door and entered the large reception area. Although it was after hours, a solitary lamp glowed from a table in the far corner of the room. Behind the U-shaped reception desk, boxes containing manila folders and office supplies waited to be unpacked and filed. Lush landscapes and seascapes captured on canvas hung on the gallery-white walls, which looked freshly painted.

Stepping further into the office, Samara called out, "Marcus?"

After another moment of silence, he answered, "Come on back, Samara."

Taking a deep breath, she started down the corridor. As she walked, her heels sank into a thick pile of Berber that absorbed her footfalls.

Marcus's office was located at the end of the hallway, confirmed by the brass nameplate on the door that read MARCUS WOLF, J.D., ESQ., FOUNDER AND CEO.

The man himself was seated behind an enormous mahogany desk in a large office suite featuring mahogany-paneled walls and floor-to-ceiling windows that offered an impressive view of the downtown skyline, now shadowed in nightfall. More cardboard boxes were piled on the floor and on a round worktable in the middle of the room.

Marcus was on the phone with a client. When he glanced up and saw Samara standing in the doorway, he went very still. Her nipples grew erect as his dark eyes slowly raked over her, taking in her long bare legs and sexy stiletto heels. She could tell, by the way his lids grew hooded, that he liked what he saw.

She couldn't wait to show him more.

"Thanks again for calling, Mr. Toussaint," Marcus said into the phone. "I look forward to meeting you tomorrow."

Samara stepped into the office as he hung up the phone and slowly rose to his feet, never taking his eyes off hers. He'd shed his suit jacket and tie, and the sleeves of his gray pinstriped shirt were rolled to his elbows. He looked breathtakingly masculine, and sexy as all get out.

"You should know that the doors were unlocked," she told him, toying with her belt strap. "If I'd been some deranged defendant who'd lost to you in court, you'd be in trouble right now, Mr. Wolf."

His mouth twitched. "Is that right?" he murmured, rounding the desk to walk toward her. With each step that brought him closer, her heart drummed wildly in anticipation. When he'd reached her, he gazed down at her. "And what about you, Ms. Layton? Am I in any danger with you?"

Samara licked her lips into a sultry smile. *"You* tell me." Without another word, she untied her trench coat and let it fall open to reveal her half-naked body.

Marcus's eyes widened, and he swore softly under his breath. His gaze devoured her like she was the last morsel of food on a starving man's plate.

"You like?" she whispered seductively.

He nodded wordlessly, his heavy-lidded eyes following her hands as she moved them slowly across her flat, softly muscled belly and up toward her ribcage. When she reached the underside of her breasts, she paused, then slowly, tantalizingly, squeezed herself.

Marcus closed his eyes and groaned as if he were in pain. *"Samara…"*

She loved the way he said her name, especially now, when he was so turned on she could feel the heat radiating from his body. It aroused her to know she could wield this power over him, this gorgeous, powerful man who could have any woman he wanted.

"Open your eyes, Marcus," she softly commanded.

His thick, ebony lashes lifted to reveal eyes that glittered with desire. She felt a shiver of anticipation for what was to come.

Holding his gaze, she slid the trench coat from her shoulders with deliberate slowness and let it fall to the floor around her. He made a rough, inarticulate sound, then reached out and grabbed her, hauling her into his arms and kissing her so hungrily her head spun. With a soft moan, she wrapped her arms around his neck and feasted on his lips and tongue until they were both groaning with need.

Breaking the kiss, Samara reached up and began to unbutton his shirt. He watched her, his lids at half-mast, his breathing shallow and ragged. When she'd finished her task, he shrugged out of his shirt and impatiently tossed it aside, then reached for her again.

But Samara had other ideas. Evading his grasp, she turned and crossed to the door with a provocative sway of her hips, feeling his burning gaze on her scantily clad body. Because she was a workaholic, she didn't get to the gym as often as she would've liked, but she knew she looked good in the skimpy lingerie she wore, with her round breasts, shapely ass and long, curvy legs.

She closed and locked the door, just in case the cleaning crew hadn't finished their nightly rounds yet. She didn't want anything or anyone to interrupt the business she and Marcus were about to conduct.

As she turned and started back across the room, he watched her like a ravenous wolf about to pounce on its prey. With his chest bared, he was a magnificent sight to behold, with beautiful mahogany skin and muscles that rippled over broad shoulders and an impressively sculpted abdomen. Just looking at him made Samara want to go for a long, hard ride astride him. Her breath quickened at the thought.

Reaching him, she kissed his soft lips, then skated her open mouth along the rugged curve of his jaw. He cupped her bottom as she rained hot kisses down the smooth hardness of his chest. When she drew a dark nipple into her mouth, he shuddered. She laved and suckled the flat bud with her tongue until it hardened in response.

"Samara," Marcus said, low and hoarse. "I—"

She pressed a finger against his lips, silencing him. Smoldering dark eyes followed her as she knelt in front of him and slowly unzipped his pants. She felt him tense as she reached inside his boxers, and then he groaned as her hand closed around his throbbing erection, freeing him. Just as she'd suspected, the man was *hung*, mouthwateringly so.

She felt a rush of heat between her thighs when she raised her gaze to his, and watched him watching her as she grasped the base of his long, thick penis and flicked her tongue over the head, snakelike. He sucked in a sharp breath.

"A hundred ways," she murmured seductively, reminding him of the conversation they'd had in her office yesterday. "I can show you a hundred different ways how much I want you."

She took him in her mouth, and he swore savagely and gripped the back of her head. She sucked him hard and greedily, using her lips and tongue, squeezing his swollen testicles in her hand until she tasted the salt of pre-cum juice. She swallowed and suckled him harder, faster, unbearably aroused by the ragged moans that erupted from his throat. Just when she thought he might explode in her mouth, he sank his hand into her hair and pulled her head back. The intensity of his smoldering gaze sent liquid fire blazing through her.

He lifted her in his arms, swept the contents of the desk to the floor, then set her down on it. He unhooked the front clasp of her bra and slid the straps off her shoulders, then cupped her breasts in his large hands. He pushed them together, taking both erect nipples into his mouth and suckling them. She gasped and arched her back, flames of ecstasy whipping through her body. She had never hungered for another man the way she did for Marcus.

"Ease up," he whispered in her ear. She raised her hips, and he grasped her panties and dragged them slowly off her legs and over her stiletto heels. She watched, her breath trapped in her throat as he rubbed the scrap of red silk over his face, inhaling her scent. When his tongue flicked out to taste the crotch, she nearly climaxed; it was so blatantly erotic. He smiled, slow and sexy, before tucking her panties into his pants pocket, claiming possession.

"A souvenir," he murmured. And then he just stood there, drinking his fill of her before whispering huskily, "You are so damn beautiful."

Samara felt a shiver of warmth puddle in her groin. She closed her eyes and let out a shuddering breath as he drew her right leg over his shoulder and began kissing his way slowly down her inner thigh, igniting a trail of fire along her nerve endings. Anticipation coiled inside her, tighter and tighter, until she thought she would die. At the first touch of his mouth on her, she threw back her head, a sharp cry escaping her throat. She moaned and gripped the edge of the desk for support as he licked her clitoris and the slippery folds of her sex, then plunged his tongue deep inside her.

Samara didn't last even a minute. Marcus captured her wild cry in his mouth as she came apart in his arms, writhing against him as wetness ran down her bottom.

But that was just the appetizer. The main course had yet to be served.

Marcus reached inside his pants pocket, removed a condom from his wallet and quickly sheathed himself. Samara spread her thighs wide and he stepped between them, their gazes locked as she wrapped her legs around his waist. In one deep, mind-numbing thrust he filled her, groaning thickly as their bodies found a rhythm. When his hands slid down her back to grasp her bottom, she arched forward. His fingers kneaded her buttocks, lifting her off the desk and holding her tightly against him. He pounded in and out of her, thrusting so hard she felt his testicles slamming heavily against her.

"*Oh God, oh God…*" she whimpered over and over again, her nails digging into his back as she clung desperately to him. She'd never known that her body could burn with this kind of savage, unbridled lust.

Laying her down on the desk, Marcus lifted her legs higher around his torso, giving him a deeper angle of penetration. He felt huge inside her, huge and magnificently hard. Her heart pounded violently against her ribs. She stared at his face above hers—dark, handsome and powerfully sensual. She didn't know what tomorrow would bring, but tonight he was hers, hers for the taking and pleasuring.

As an exquisite pressure built inside her, her thighs began to shake uncontrollably. "I'm coming," she cried breathlessly. "Ohhh, Marcus…*Marcus!*"

Her hips arched off the desk as a blinding orgasm tore through her, rhythmically convulsing her body. The spasms were so intense she thought she would faint. A moment later, Marcus moaned and bucked against her as he came. Her flesh quivered from the impact of his powerful thrusts as he rode her through his release.

Moments later he collapsed on top of her, his chest heaving as he gasped for breath, his heart hammering against her own. Samara wrapped her arms around his back and burrowed her face in his neck, inhaling his delicious scent, mingled with the musk of their lovemaking.

They remained like that for several minutes, his throbbing penis buried inside her, her legs locked around his waist. At length he lifted his head and gazed down into her flushed face.

"Are you okay?" he asked huskily.

Her lips curved in a sultry smile. "I've never been better. That was quite a closing argument, counselor."

A wolfish gleam filled his eyes. "Who said anything about closing?"

Samara couldn't recall how many times they made love that night. From the desk they moved to a leather sofa in the corner of the room, panting and rolling around and falling to the floor without missing a beat. She came so many times she lost count.

Finally, when she was so exhausted she could barely move, she collapsed in a boneless heap against him on the floor. Marcus gathered her in his arms, holding her so close that the sweat from their bodies sealed them together like two spoons dipped in syrup.

Yawning deeply, she mumbled, "I should probably head home at some point."

"Not yet," Marcus whispered against the nape of her neck. "Sleep first."

Samara nodded drowsily, too weak to protest even if she'd wanted to. Which, for the record, she didn't.

Chapter Seven

I'm so glad you finally agreed to have lunch with me," said Paul Borden, smiling easily at Samara across the linen-covered table in B. Smith's the next afternoon. The popular Union Station restaurant bustled with some of the city's political movers and shakers, business professionals and midday shoppers.

Samara looked across the table at her lunch companion, an attractive light-skinned man with warm brown eyes that crinkled at the corners whenever he smiled, which he'd been doing a lot ever since Samara showed up at the restaurant—alone. She didn't have the heart to tell him that she hadn't actually agreed to have lunch with him, because Melissa had failed to mention his name when she'd invited Samara to join her and her husband, Gary, for lunch. If Samara had had inkling that Paul Borden would be present, she wouldn't have accepted Melissa's invitation. Paul, who worked with Melissa's husband at a downtown software firm, had been asking Samara out since they first met two years ago. Unwilling to encourage his interest, she'd always politely turned down his advances.

The fact that both Melissa and Gary had backed out of lunch at the last minute, citing previous appointments they'd conveniently forgotten, set Samara's back teeth on edge. She couldn't believe she'd been set up, by two of her closest friends, at that. Heads were going to roll when she returned to the office.

But since she was there, she might as well enjoy her lunch. The Swamp Thing, a mixed seafood dish over Southern-style greens, was her favorite entrée on the menu. Not that it mattered anyway, since she was hungry enough to eat just about anything. After having sex with Marcus all night long, she'd worked up quite an appetite.

They'd been so caught up in what they were doing last night they hadn't given dinner a passing thought, feasting on each other instead.

"Doesn't it feel good to get out of the office once in a while, to enjoy lunch somewhere other than your desk?" Paul remarked.

"I don't mind eating at my desk," Samara countered mildly. "I get a lot of work done with everyone out of the office at the same time."

"Maybe," Paul said with a dismissive shrug of his shoulders, "but what fun is that? Besides, you have cause to celebrate. Melissa tells me that the Institute recently received a large donation which will keep the doors open for business—and keep you guys out of the unemployment line."

"Yep, that's right."

Paul's brown eyes twinkled. "So are you going to reveal the identity of this mystery benefactor? Melissa's been pretty tight-lipped about it, and Gary won't betray her confidence no matter how hard I try to pry it out of him."

Samara took a sip of water. "Well, the donor has specifically expressed a desire for anonymity," she explained, "so naturally we intend to honor that wish."

Paul shook his head, bemused. "Can't imagine who wouldn't want to receive credit for donating such a large sum of money. Guy must be a saint or wanted by the Mafia."

Samara was about to respond when she happened to glance across the room just in time to see none other than Marcus Wolf enter the restaurant.

Her heart lurched traitorously at the sight of him, then did a nosedive when she noticed his companion. A tall, leggy, impossibly gorgeous dark-skinned woman was latched possessively onto his arm, and Samara couldn't help noting what a striking pair they made. A well-dressed older gentleman followed closely behind, wearing an expression of approval as he smiled at Marcus and the statuesque woman.

Taming the Wolf

As if sensing her appraisal from across the room, Marcus's dark gaze slid in Samara's direction. She felt an actual jolt as their eyes met and held for what seemed an eternity—but was probably only a few seconds—before she forced herself to look away.

But Paul had also noticed Marcus's arrival. "Hey, isn't that the famous tort attorney who just opened another practice here? The one who was featured in the *Post?*"

"Hmm?" Samara feigned only mild interest as she glanced vaguely toward Marcus, careful not to look directly at him. "Yes, I think you're right, Paul. It is him."

"Everyone at the office has been talking about him, saying what great things he's going to do for the community." A note of skepticism crept into Paul's voice. "Time will tell, I guess."

"Mmm," Samara murmured, noncommittal. Suddenly, she had no appetite. All she could think about was Marcus making love to her, bringing her to one mind-blowing orgasm after another.

Who the hell was that woman on his arm?

She was not at all prepared when he and his companions suddenly appeared at her table. "Good afternoon, Samara," Marcus murmured, those dark, piercing eyes fixed on her face.

"Hello, Marcus," she managed, forcing herself to sound normal. As if she hadn't spent the night clawing his back and sobbing his name in the throes of ecstasy. As if she hadn't snuck out of his office at the crack of dawn wearing no panties beneath her trench coat because he'd refused to relinquish her underwear. "Nice to see you again. I'd like you to meet a friend of mine. Paul Borden, this is Marcus Wolf."

The two men exchanged cordial greetings. When Marcus introduced his companions, Samara told herself it was *not* relief she felt upon learning that the beautiful woman at his side was merely a client's daughter.

Antoinette Toussaint's catlike amber gaze narrowed on Samara's face. "You look familiar," she said, her sultry voice the stuff of men's fantasies. "Have we met before?"

86

"I don't think so," Samara answered coolly.

"You're probably thinking about her mother, Asha Dubois," Paul supplied. "She's been on every magazine cover you can imagine, and Samara looks just like her."

Antoinette snapped her manicured fingers. "That's it! I knew I wasn't crazy." Her full lips curved in the semblance of a smile that was more predatory than congenial. "I used to model for your mother. And then I landed an international assignment that took me overseas for a while. I just returned from Milan, as a matter of fact."

"Sounds wonderful," Samara murmured.

"Oh, it was. Of course, the men over there aren't *nearly* as handsome as ours here in the States," she purred, sliding an intimate look at Marcus. Samara didn't know how to interpret the lazy smile he gave her in return.

Antoinette turned back to Samara, her head tilted to one side as she regarded her thoughtfully. "Why don't you model professionally, Samara?"

"That's more my mother's cup of tea."

"I see. And you're not quite tall enough anyway. What are you—five-five?"

"Five-seven," Samara corrected lightly.

"I hate to interrupt this little tête-à-tête," Antoinette's father interjected with a laugh, "but our table is ready, princess, and considering what Marcus's billable hours are, I'm eager to get this meeting under way."

"You took the words right out of my mouth, William," Marcus drawled humorously. He tipped his head politely to Paul, then Samara. "Enjoy your lunch."

"Same to you," Samara murmured, relieved as the threesome moved off. As she silently exhaled, she couldn't help but wonder if she'd only imagined the flash of anger she'd glimpsed in Marcus's eyes before he walked away.

"That Antoinette Toussaint was mighty territorial," Paul observed, faintly amused as he looked at Samara. "From the way she was acting, you would think the two of you were fighting over Marcus Wolf."

Samara forced a lopsided smile. "Crazy, isn't it?" She glanced quickly at her watch. "We'd better ask for the check. We've been here over an hour, and from what Gary tells Melissa, your boss can be real anal about you guys taking long lunches."

From across the crowded restaurant, Marcus watched as Samara and Paul Borden rose from their table and prepared to leave. As Samara slid the strap of her purse over her shoulder, she happened to glance in Marcus's direction. Awareness punched him in the gut when their eyes connected.

Without a single word passing between them, Marcus understood that she wanted him to follow her.

He'd already intended to do just that.

He waited until she and Borden left before politely excusing himself from his companions and casually strolling after them. Outside the restaurant was an indoor bazaar in which vendors sold exotic imports from around the world. Marcus hung back, waiting with mounting impatience for Samara and her friend to part ways. Borden seemed reluctant to leave her, lingering at her side as she paused to admire some African woodwork and sculptures. After glancing at his watch a few times, he must have finally realized she planned to take a while to browse through the marketplace. His fear of getting in trouble for taking an extended lunch break eventually won out over his desire to prolong his time with her.

Marcus was surprised by the anger that filled him as Borden leaned down and planted a chaste kiss on Samara's cheek. As Marcus glared after the man's departing back, he realized that he was jealous. For the first time in his life, he felt territorial over a woman. When he thought about Samara with Paul Borden, or *any* other man, something dark and startlingly primitive came over him.

What the hell was wrong with him?

He walked up behind Samara, bending low to murmur in her ear, "Have a good lunch?"

She turned and looked at him, her expression carefully neutral. "I did, as a matter of fact." She paused. "Just as I'm sure you'll enjoy your lunch with the lovely Ms. Toussaint."

Marcus frowned. "Her father is a new client."

"I know. Which is why you probably shouldn't keep him waiting. You know, billable hours and all that." She picked up a beautifully beaded necklace and took a moment to admire it while the smiling vendor looked on hopefully. After a discreet glance at the price tag, Samara set down the necklace and moved on to the next item.

"Samara."

She glanced over her shoulder at him. When he said nothing, she arched an expectant brow at him. "What's up?"

"Go away with me this weekend." The minute the words left his mouth, Marcus wondered where they'd come from. He hadn't planned on asking her something like that…or had he?

Samara looked as surprised as he felt. "Did you just say what I think you did?"

"Depends on what you think you heard. I asked you to spend the weekend with me. Is that what you heard?"

"Yes." She stared up at him, the trinket she held all but forgotten. Chuckling softly, Marcus took it from her hand and set it down, then drew her gently away from the table.

"I'm going to Atlanta for the weekend to take care of some business at the other office. I want you to come with me." Realizing how unromantic his invitation sounded, he added, "I'll only be at the office for a couple of hours. We'll be together the rest of the time."

When she blushed, he knew she was remembering their long night of passion. It was all *he'd* thought about since she left his office early that morning, looking tousled and sexy as hell in those fetish-inducing heels. Knowing she was practically naked beneath her trench coat had made him so hard he almost hadn't let her go. The idea of having her all to himself for two whole days had his body thrumming with anticipation.

The only problem was, she still hadn't given him an answer. "Samara?"

She bit her bottom lip indecisively. "I don't know, Marcus. It's such short notice, and I was planning to spend the weekend catching up on some paperwork."

He picked up her hand and used the pad of his thumb to trace an idle pattern in the center of her palm, watching as her sooty lashes fluttered and her lush lips parted on a soundless breath.

"Please?" he implored, low and husky. "Come."

The dark eyes that lifted to his were hazy with desire. "Has any woman ever said no to you, Marcus Wolf?"

His mouth curved in a slow, teasing grin. "You did, the first time we met. I'm doing everything in my power to convince you it was a terrible lapse in judgment."

She laughed, gazing at their joined hands. After another moment, she looked up at him. "I already know it was," she said softly.

Just like that, Marcus wanted her again, hard and deep, right against the nearest wall. If he didn't have a client waiting for him inside the restaurant, he definitely would have tried to coax her into accompanying him back to his apartment. He couldn't get enough of her, even after their all-night lovemaking marathon. If anything, last night had only made him hunger for more.

"All right, Marcus. I'll go to Atlanta with you." She chuckled quietly. "I can hardly refuse the man who single-handedly bailed my employer out of financial ruin."

Marcus grinned, not above using her gratitude to his advantage, if that's what it took to get her on the plane with him. "I'll pick you up tomorrow morning at eight. And pack something dressy. I'm going to take you to my brother's restaurant."

"Your brother owns a restaurant?"

He nodded. "It's called Wolf's Soul. Saturday night marks the fourth year since it opened. I'd like you to commemorate the special occasion with me."

She smiled. "I'm looking forward to it."

So was Marcus. She had no idea just how much.

Samara couldn't believe what an incredible week she was having.

First, the Institute had received the necessary funds to stay in business. And she'd had the privilege of informing nine employees that they wouldn't have to start looking for another job.

And then she'd experienced the most incredible sex of her life, having more orgasms in *one* night than she'd had in five years.

Now she had a romantic weekend getaway to look forward to.

Life didn't get any better than this, and she had Marcus Wolf to thank on all counts.

"Does that smile mean it's safe to show my face?"

Samara glanced up from sifting through a pile of quarterly reports to find Melissa hovering uncertainly in the doorway of her office.

Samara scowled at her. "Just so you know, I didn't appreciate being tricked into having lunch with Paul."

"I know," Melissa groaned, looking guilty as she stepped into the office. "For the record, I felt really horrible about doing that to you. But it wasn't my idea."

Samara's eyes narrowed dangerously. "Whose idea was it?"

Melissa swallowed hard. "Um, Gary's."

"I hope you're ready to become a widow," Samara grumbled, "because when I get my hands on your husband, I'm going to kill him. Actually, I should kill both of you, because *you* should have known better than to set me up like that. Why in the world did you agree to such a thing, Melissa?"

"Paul covered for Gary on a big project a few weeks ago while he was out sick with the flu. Gary wanted to do something nice for him in return, and he knows how much Paul likes you."

"Which is *exactly* why I've never gone out with Paul," Samara said, exasperated. "I don't want to lead him on, and I think what you guys did today was incredibly unfair to him—to *both* of us. Not to mention the fact that Marcus was there with a client, and I felt really awkward when he came over to say hello. I mean, we're not officially dating or anything, but that might change in the near future. Being caught on a 'date' with another man is *not* the best way to start a relationship."

Melissa sighed heavily. "I know. I'm truly sorry, Samara. And so is Gary."

"You should be," Samara snapped. "I would never do that to you. To *either* of you."

"I'm really sorry. If it makes any difference, I guess I didn't realize that you and Marcus were getting serious. If I'd known, I never would've agreed to Gary's idea. How can we make it up to you?"

"I don't know," Samara muttered darkly. "Give me a few days to come up with something really diabolical."

Melissa grinned, relieved. "Fair enough. In the meantime, we'd love to have you over for dinner this weekend. We'll make whatever you want, and I promise Paul will be nowhere in sight."

"Sounds tempting, but I can't make it this weekend."

"Why not?"

"If you must know, I'm going out of town." She hesitated. "With Marcus."

Melissa's eyes widened. *"Seriously?"*

"Seriously. We're going to Atlanta, and that's all I know at this point so don't ask me a million questions."

Melissa grinned knowingly. "So you and Marcus Wolf *are* getting serious about each other. You just met on Saturday, and you're already taking trips together?"

Samara smiled sheepishly. "I know it sounds crazy, Melissa. I can't really explain it myself."

"Girl, no explanation necessary. He's Marcus Wolf—enough said."

Long after Melissa left her office, Samara couldn't stop reflecting on their conversation. Melissa was right. Things *were* moving fast between Marcus and Samara, and it was totally out of character for her. The Samara everyone knew—hell, the Samara *she* knew—didn't do the things she'd done with Marcus over the past week.

Granted, Samara was no wide-eyed innocent . She'd been curious about sex ever since she was a little girl, when she'd accidentally walked in on her mother and her latest beau getting it on in the shower. At the age of sixteen, while traveling overseas with Asha, she'd lost her virginity to a smooth-talking Belgian boy who'd introduced her to the heady delights of French kissing—and a number of other things.

Samara had always maintained a healthy attitude about sex. It was meant to be enjoyed. Although in her experience, not enough men seemed to grasp the concept of how to actually *make* it enjoyable.

Thank God Marcus did.

Still, it would be foolish to fall for him. Men like Marcus Wolf didn't commit to monogamous relationships. They played the field, running through women faster than water through a colander, leaving behind a trail of broken hearts. And when these men finally decided to settle down—*if* they ever settled down—they married trophy wives, and kept a string of mistresses on the side. Samara had no interest in becoming someone's trophy wife or brokenhearted ex-lover. She was too smart for that.

Life had taught her the dangers of surrendering her heart to anyone. The first man who'd betrayed her had been her very own father. From all accounts, Nathaniel Layton was a kind, decent man who'd done the right thing by marrying the girl he'd accidentally impregnated. Yet he hadn't even stuck around for Samara's birth. He'd packed his belongings and stole away like a thief in the night, never looking back. Not caring that he left two shattered lives in his wake, that his departure would set a course in motion of heartache and disillusionment.

Samara would not make the same mistake her mother had. She wouldn't leave herself vulnerable to any man, no matter how generous, compelling and sexy he was.

She'd enjoy this little fling with Marcus, and when it was over, she'd walk away with her dignity—and her heart—intact.

Her very survival depended on it.

Chapter Eight

By nine o'clock Saturday morning, Marcus and Samara were aboard his private jet bound for Atlanta.

Samara looked incredibly sexy in an orange tube top and a pair of low-rise blue jeans that fit her like a glove and had Marcus itching to peel it off her body and eat her like a Dove bar. Her healthy black hair was neatly braided and hung in a thick plait between her shoulder blades. Marcus thought she looked as delicious as the soft shade of raisin lip-gloss she wore, the moist sheen making her lips appear even juicier than usual.

A vision of her mouth wrapped around his penis gave him an instant erection. He shifted slightly in the cushioned seat, wondering if he'd be able to keep his hands off her until they reached their destination. It was only a two-hour flight. But he was so horny, even *that* seemed too long to wait.

Oblivious to his predicament, Samara was staring out the window at tufts of white clouds interspersed with patches of pale blue sky. "No matter how many times I traveled as a child," she murmured, "I never got quite used to being on a plane."

Marcus leaned toward her. "But you're all right now?" he said, both question and gentle assurance.

Samara turned to look at him. "I'm fine. But you should probably get the Dramamine from my carry-on, just in case." At his slightly alarmed expression, she laughed and covered his hand with hers, warm satin sliding over his skin and into his bones. "Relax, Marcus. It was a joke."

His mouth curved in a slow grin. "Very funny."

"*I* thought so."

"Just for that, I should keep the little gift I brought for you."

She looked at him in surprise. "You brought me a gift?"

He nodded. "Close your eyes." As she did, he reached under his seat and withdrew a rectangular box containing the beaded African necklace she'd been admiring yesterday. "Don't peek," he reminded her, then smiled as she squeezed her eyelids tightly shut. He reached around her, clasping the necklace around her throat.

"There," he murmured. "Now you can look."

She opened her eyes, then squealed in shock when she saw the necklace around her throat. "Oh, Marcus! It's beautiful! I was admiring it yesterday at the bazaar. How did you—"

He chuckled softly. "I was there, remember?"

She smiled, gently fingering the exotic beads circling her slender throat. The necklace looked even better nestled against her beautiful brown skin. "You shouldn't have bought this. It was ridiculously expensive, and God knows you've already given me enough money."

"I gave the Institute money," Marcus corrected her. "And don't tell me how to spend my money, woman."

The look she gave him was so tender, his throat went dry. *Man, she's low maintenance,* he silently marveled. He'd heard of women who didn't bat an eyelash at receiving $20,000 diamond earrings.

"Thank you, Marcus," Samara said softly. "This was incredibly sweet of you. I'll never forget it."

"You're welcome," he said huskily. "You look like a Nubian goddess. That's what I thought of you when you first appeared onstage at the fashion show."

She chuckled grimly. "I don't even want to know what you thought of me *after* you met me."

He grinned. "I wouldn't tell you anyway," he said with a mischievous wink. "Too X-rated."

She laughed, her cheeks flushing as she settled back against her seat.

Marcus stretched out his long legs in the spacious cabin. "So you traveled a lot as a child. With your mother?"

Samara nodded. "She often took me with her on photo shoots. We went everywhere. From Versailles to Tokyo to Sydney, you name it."

"That must have been exciting."

She shrugged, gazing out the window. "It had its moments. After a while though, I simply craved the stability of my grandmother's house. I got homesick a lot."

"That's understandable." Marcus studied her rigid posture, reading the nonverbal language. It was a topic she didn't discuss often and probably with good reason. Although he knew very little about the fashion industry, he could only imagine how overwhelming the lifestyle must be — especially to a kid forced to keep up with the frenetic pace.

"Did you ever want to follow your mother into the fashion business?"

"Once. A long, long time ago." She turned to look at him, surprising him with the frankness of her next words. "You've probably already figured out that my mother and I aren't close, not even remotely. She thinks I should take more of an active role in her company; I disagree. When I say this to people, they think I'm insane. After all, what *sane* individual would turn down the opportunity to call their own shots at a multimillion-dollar empire? What *sane* individual wouldn't leap at the chance to live in the spotlight, to enjoy a jet-setting lifestyle?"

Marcus met her heated gaze calmly. "I don't think you're insane."

Her eyes grew soft, her smile warm with gratitude. The combination hit him squarely in the chest. "That's why you're different, Marcus."

"So are you, baby girl. And that's what makes you special. Don't ever let anyone tell you different."

Damn, why had he said that? The more she looked at him like that, with those mesmerizing dark eyes and bewitching smile, the more he felt himself falling under her spell.

Clearing his throat, he continued, "Walter Floyd tells me your mother used to work for him. That's how he met you."

Samara nodded. "My mother was working as a maid for a family in Philadelphia when Walt hired her to manage his store part-time. She'd been married and divorced at a very young age. She did what she could to keep a roof over our heads, but she had her pride too. When her employer made a sexual advance one day, my mother told him off—and we got thrown out of their house. For about two weeks, we'd sneak into Walt's shop after closing time and sleep in the storeroom. And then one day he arrived earlier than usual and caught us fast asleep on the floor. He and his wife were kind enough to take us in for a while, until my mother finally worked up the courage to return home to D.C. to accept help from her mother."

Her low chuckle was mirthless. "You can imagine how shocked my grandmother was to discover that the daughter she'd sent off to college had not only gotten married and divorced, but was now herself a mother."

"Your mother kept your existence a secret?" Marcus asked, unable to mask his surprise. "How'd she pull that off?"

"By telling her mother that she really liked Philadelphia and planned to remain there after college. By inventing stories of study abroad internships whenever my grandmother wanted to visit her at school. Their relationship had been strained to begin with because they could never see eye to eye on anything. Once my mother left home for college, it was that much easier for them to grow further apart." Samara gazed out the window, absently fingering her necklace. "I guess my mother and I are repeating the same vicious cycle."

Marcus fell silent, wanting to offer her some measure of comfort but not knowing how. While her story saddened him, it also strengthened his conviction that a relationship between them could never work. Samara had suffered enough hardship in her life. She didn't need the added burden of being involved with a man who could never love her as completely as she deserved, who would bring his own set of emotional baggage to the table.

They were both damaged goods. Nothing could ever come of their attraction to each other, no matter how intense it was.

But that's okay, Marcus told himself. He and Samara were two mature, consenting adults enjoying a mutually satisfying relationship. As long as they kept their expectations simple, there was no reason they couldn't continue seeing, and satisfying each other, for a long time.

A *very* long time, he amended, watching Samara's round, curvy bottom as she excused herself to use the restroom. He felt a straining at his zipper and realized that at the rate he was going, it would take twice as long as usual to get this particular woman out of his system.

When Samara returned from using the restroom, Marcus was setting out breakfast on the small cherry table across the aisle from their seats.

She paused to admire the sight of him in a black T-shirt and faded jeans that clung to the corded muscles of his thighs and hugged an ass you could bounce quarters off. It was the first time she'd ever seen him out of a suit—except, of course, when he'd been gloriously naked and lying on top of her.

He turned at that moment and caught her drooling over his butt. The answering hunger in his dark eyes made heat pool between her legs.

To hell with breakfast, she thought. The only thing she had an appetite for was the man standing before her.

She couldn't remember who moved first. The next thing she knew, she and Marcus were kissing and frantically undressing each other. Clothes went flying across the cabin. Hard, urgent fingers bit into her flesh as Marcus knelt, gripping the waistband of her jeans and panties and dragging them off her body. With a ragged groan, he buried his face in her abdomen, his warm breath fanning the flames licking through her like wildfire.

When he stood, lifting her into his arms, she locked her legs around his waist and closed her eyes. She heard a condom package tear, then cried out as he impaled her with one deep, powerful stroke.

They tumbled backward, Samara landing on top of him as they fell into one of the seats. She straddled him, bracing her hands on his big, muscled shoulders as he grasped her buttocks. He thrust rhythmically inside her, hot and huge, whispering erotic promises that singed her cheeks and left her quivering.

Up and down she slid on him, riding him, their bodies making wet slapping sounds as sweat gathered on their skin. Their coupling was rough, elemental, purely carnal. With each desperate thrust, the burning ache between her legs intensified, driving her toward a shattering climax.

She leaned down, letting strands of her loosened hair brush his nipples, then moaning as he reached up and flicked his wet tongue over *her* distended nipples. She threw back her head and arched backward as he feasted on her breasts, setting her whole body on fire. It was too much. She never wanted their lovemaking to end.

Marcus reached up, cradling the back of her head and bringing their mouths together for a hot, mind-numbing kiss that left her panting for more.

"Look at us." His voice was a rough, husky command. "Then look at me. I want to see your face when you come."

She shivered at his words, then let her eyes wander downward to where their bodies joined. She watched in breathless fascination as his thick, dark penis slid in and out of her. Aroused by what she saw, she began to move faster and faster, gliding up and slamming down the rigid length of his shaft until her inner muscles began to clench spasmodically around him. Their gazes locked. She called his name hoarsely as they exploded in unison, soaring higher than any airplane could take them.

Wolf's Soul was located in the hub of downtown Atlanta, just a few blocks from the famed Fox Theater. Marcus and Samara had barely entered the restaurant that evening before people started greeting them. Stylishly dressed men approached to exchange vigorous handshakes with Marcus while beautiful women slid coy smiles at him. Marcus moved easily through the crowd as he greeted old friends from Morehouse, clients of the Atlanta firm and former business associates, keeping one hand at the small of Samara's back the entire time.

Framed portraits of various celebrities and prominent athletes who had visited the restaurant graced the walls. With the high ceilings and recessed lights turned strategically low, the restaurant gave patrons the illusion of being in the heart of a deep, plush cavern. Music drifted from a baby grand piano tucked into a shadowy corner, the tinkling notes of a jazz number blending with the muted din of voices. The bar at the rear of the restaurant was long and backed by a mirror that reflected its full length, and doubled the light from above. Tier upon tier of liquor bottles with contents of amber, gold and red liquids sparkled from behind proud old labels.

"There you are!" called a deep, resonant voice from across the room.

The minute Samara saw the owner of the voice, she knew he was Michael Wolf. Tall and broad-shouldered with smooth dark skin, he had the same chiseled cheekbones, square jaw, strong nose and firm chin as his brother. Even their haircuts were the same, cropped close to the scalp and faded along the sides.

He buried Marcus in a quick bear hug before drawing back to give him an affectionate chuck on the chin. "Glad you could make it, Little Man," he teased, although he was at least four inches shorter than his younger brother.

Marcus chuckled. "You knew I would. It's your fourth anniversary." He turned to Samara behind him, gently bringing her around to his side. Michael's dark eyes widened a fraction before roaming across Samara's face with undisguised male appreciation.

"Nice to meet you, Michael," Samara said, shaking his hand once Marcus performed the introductions.

"The pleasure's all mine," Michael Wolf said smoothly. He dipped his head to place a gallant kiss upon her hand, leaving no doubt in Samara's mind that he, like his brother, had broken plenty of hearts.

She swept an appreciative look around the restaurant. "This is a very nice place you have, Michael."

"Thank you very much, Samara. It's my pride and joy."

Marcus feigned a wounded look. "I thought *I* was your pride and joy."

"Nah," Michael said with a conspiratorial wink at Samara, "You've been replaced. Come on, I saved your table near the stage. The band will be starting in a few."

Marcus and Samara followed him to a round black lacquered table positioned before a small, unobtrusive stage. A blues quartet rehearsed quietly onstage, striking intermittent chords.

"The chef is preparing your meals right now," Michael informed them, pulling out Samara's chair with a flourish. "I want you both to try our newest house specialty. Crab and mushroom stuffed salmon with Creole couscous, sautéed spinach and sauce aurora."

"Sounds good," Marcus and Samara said in unison.

With a pleased grin, Michael moved off to greet other guests.

"You were right about him," Samara remarked, watching him go from table to table, answering questions and putting his customers at ease. "He's a natural."

"The best," Marcus said, and there was no mistaking the deep pride in his voice.

Over lunch that afternoon, he'd told Samara how his older brother, the self-appointed family cook, had always dreamed of owning a restaurant. Four years ago when his job at an engineering firm was downsized, he'd decided to follow his dreams, pouring all of his savings into a restaurant venture. His gamble had paid off. Four years later, Wolf's Soul still received rave reviews and boasted a clientele that included celebrities and high-ranking politicians.

In no time at all, Marcus and Samara's meals were served and enjoyed with great relish, as Michael promised. While they ate, the live band entertained the customers with the fluid rhythm of one selection after another, from toe-tapping ragtime tunes to soulful jazz renditions.

Samara was secretly grateful for the distraction the music provided. With Marcus seated so close to her at the small table, she had enough difficulty performing the simple act of breathing—let alone attempting conversation. Not that conversation had ranked high on their list of priorities that day.

After arriving in Atlanta that morning, they'd checked into their luxurious hotel suite, placed their bags in separate rooms, then wound up on the floor in the living room, making love as fervently as if it were their first time. They came up for air several hours later to enjoy a leisurely lunch on the balcony before taking a romantic stroll through the lush, secluded gardens tucked away behind their hotel room. When Marcus took her against a tree, Samara knew she'd never look at another Japanese maple the same way again.

Blushing at the memory, she glanced up from her plate to find Marcus watching her. The glittering heat in his eyes sent a tingle of pure sexual awareness dancing up her spine.

"Stop that," she whispered accusingly.

"What?"

"You know very well what. Stop looking at me like that, like you're already thinking of another location for us to christen."

His mouth curved in a slow pirate's grin. "Now that you mention it, there *is* a tiny room in the back—"

"*Marcus,*" she groaned helplessly.

He chuckled low in his throat, the sound curling her toes. "All right, I'll back off for a while. Don't want you thinking the only reason I invited you down here was to turn you into my sex slave."

She laughed. "The thought *had* crossed my mind." As if becoming Marcus Wolf's sex slave would be such a terrible fate.

"Seriously though, Samara. I want you to have fun this weekend, relax and unwind. You work too hard."

"Said the pot to the kettle."

"Actually," Marcus said huskily, "I've never been more relaxed in my life."

She held his focused gaze, her heart racing. "I was just thinking the same thing."

The band took a break after completing the first set, and Michael Wolf stepped onto the stage and grabbed the microphone. "Evening, ladies and gentlemen. Is everyone having a good time tonight?"

His query was met with buoyant applause and cheers. Michael grinned. "We've come to that portion of the evening where we like to hear from our guests. We don't call it karaoke exactly. It's more of an opportunity for some of you budding songbirds out there to show us what you've got. Hey, you never know—Tina Turner was discovered this way."

There was a smattering of laughter as Michael's dark eyes began a deliberate scan of the audience. "Let's see, who can get us started this evening…"

Samara was taking a sip of her club soda when his searching gaze landed on her. Dread filled her chest as his lips curved in a slow, triumphant grin. She began to shake her head from side to side, but it was too late.

"Ladies and gentlemen," Michael announced, "I present to you a personal guest of mine this evening—the very lovely and talented Samara Layton!"

Marcus leaned toward her with a faintly amused expression. "You don't have to go up there if you don't want to."

"I *don't* want to," Samara muttered under her breath. "And how does he know I'm talented? I can barely carry a note!"

"Samara?" Michael prompted from the stage, still grinning.

Samara wanted to sink through the floor as every smiling face in the restaurant turned in her direction. Soon the audience jumped on the bandwagon, whistling and calling encouragements to her.

Samara was no stranger to the spotlight. Thanks to her mother, she'd grown up participating in various beauty pageants and fashion shows. Just a week ago, she'd strutted down a New York runway before a crowd filled with celebrities and fashion industry bigwigs— a crowd far bigger and more intimidating than this one.

Live a little, Samara.

Marcus had made eye contact with his brother, signaling him to find another sacrificial lamb.

But Samara stood, albeit on wobbly legs, and walked toward the stage. Michael took her hand and gently helped her up. "Just relax and have fun. What do you want to sing?"

" 'At Last' by Etta James," Samara answered, because it was the only song she felt remotely confident enough to sing beyond her shower stall. It had been one of her grandmother's favorites.

Michael whispered her selection to the pianist and climbed off the stage to join Marcus at the table. A hushed silence descended upon the room, broken by scattered whistles of male admiration as the spotlight illuminated Samara. She stood before the microphone and took a deep, steadying breath as the familiar opening strains of the song began.

"At last…my love has come along…" Her voice was soft, surprisingly fluid even to her own ears. She smiled shyly, gratified as the audience responded with immediate approval. *"My lonely days are over…and life is like a song…"*

Seated at the table, Marcus grew completely still as he watched Samara, transfixed. He couldn't take his eyes off her in that tiny slip of a red dress, and he knew he wasn't the only brother in the house with that problem. She was fine as hell, possessing the kind of looks that made grown men act a fool. Even his brother hadn't been totally immune.

But what ensnared Marcus went beyond Samara's exotic beauty, or the whiskey-soaked voice that poured over his flesh and into his soul. It was the whole package. The combination of intelligence and wit, sensitivity and fieriness, innocence and eroticism. She was everything he'd ever wanted in a woman—something he hadn't realized until that very moment.

Watching Marcus out of the corner of his eye, Michael leaned over to whisper, "You're falling in love with her. You know that, don't you?"

Marcus swallowed the sudden tightness in his throat, then dropped his gaze, wanting to strangle his brother. "You don't know what you're talking about," he growled under his breath. "I just met her."

"So did I," Michael countered mildly, "and I can tell you right now that she feels the same way about you."

Marcus lifted his eyes to Samara once again, and found her already watching him as she crooned the words to Etta James's classic hit.

Michael didn't know what the hell he was talking about, he thought darkly. Marcus was no more in love with Samara than she was with him. Just because she possessed all the qualities he'd want in a wife—*if* he'd wanted a wife—didn't mean a damn thing.

Before he knew it, the song had ended. Amid boisterous applause and calls for an encore, Samara executed a brief curtsy and headed off the stage.

Marcus stood at her approach. "A woman of many talents," he murmured in her ear.

Samara gave him an embarrassed smile before reclaiming her seat and taking a long sip of her club soda.

Marcus barely paid attention as his brother sang Samara's praises, and solicited more volunteers whose talent levels ranged from comical to downright good, as the band returned to the stage to resume playing. All he could think about was what Michael had said.

Marcus was *not* in love with Samara.

But damn his brother for planting such a crazy idea in his mind.

Chapter Nine

A re you absolutely sure you don't want to hang out at the hotel until I get back from my meeting?" Marcus asked Samara the next day as they left downtown Atlanta in his other vehicle, a black Lincoln Navigator he stored at the parking garage of his law firm so he wouldn't have to rent a car whenever he came to town.

"I'm positive, Marcus," Samara told him for the umpteenth time.

"You could have gone downstairs to the spa, or done a little shopping and sightseeing—"

She laughed. "I didn't need to visit the spa. The massages we received this morning gave me all the pampering I'll need for a long time, thank you very much. And I don't have to go sightseeing, since I've been to Atlanta several times before. Besides, I'm looking forward to meeting your father."

Sterling Wolf had called Marcus's cell phone that morning to let him know his fishing trip had been cut short when a member of his group came down with food poisoning. Upon learning that his son was in town, and accompanied by a woman, Sterling had insisted that Marcus bring Samara over to the house to meet him before they flew back to D.C. that evening. He hadn't taken no for an answer.

"I should only be gone for a couple of hours," Marcus assured Samara.

She nodded, smothering a wide yawn. "Take as long as you need. If your father doesn't mind, I just might grab a nap while I'm over there. You have worn a sista out, Marcus Wolf."

He chuckled softly, glancing at her. His eyes were indiscernible behind the dark mirrored sunglasses he wore. "Think we overdid it by going dancing last night?"

Her mouth curved in a lazy grin. "I think we overdid it before we arrived in Atlanta yesterday morning." She paused, then added demurely, "I've never made love on an airplane before. That was quite an experience."

"Mmmm," Marcus agreed, low and husky. "And just think. We have the trip home tonight to look forward to."

Smiling at the thought, Samara leaned her head back on the headrest and closed her eyes against the early afternoon sunlight slanting through the windshield. She felt boneless, deliciously drowsy. She couldn't remember the last time she'd felt so relaxed, so free of worry or tension. Although she'd teased Marcus about wearing her out, the truth was that she was enjoying every single moment with him, whether they were making love or working it out on the dance floor—which, of course, had only led to more love-making.

She was having the time of her life. A part of her didn't want the weekend to end.

A very *big* part of her.

Marcus reached over, gently kneading the nape of her neck until a soft moan of pleasure escaped her lips. Oh, he was good at this. *Too good.*

Without opening her eyes, she murmured, "Do you do this very often? Whisk women away for romantic weekend getaways?"

His fingers stilled for a moment, and she could feel him looking at her behind the mirrored lenses of his sunglasses. For a minute she thought he wouldn't answer her, but then he said quietly, "Would it bother you if I said yes?"

"Of course not," she said, forcing a nonchalant tone. "I was just curious, that's all. You really know how to show a woman a good time."

109

When he made no reply, Samara mentally kicked herself. Why had she gone and said something like that? Not only had she ruined the mellow mood between them, but now Marcus would think she was the jealous, possessive type, and nothing could be further from the truth. What he did with other women was none of her business. If he invited another woman—say, Antoinette Toussaint—to spend the following weekend with him in Jamaica, Samara wouldn't care.

That's what she told herself anyway.

With downtown Atlanta behind them, Marcus exited onto a country road that took a winding curve and gave way to an explosion of blooming magnolias. A sprawling red brick house rolled into view, and Marcus steered the Navigator down the long cobblestone driveway, past acres of manicured green lawn and a small lake at the center of the property.

"Oh, Marcus," Samara murmured, breaking the awkward silence that had fallen between them. "This place is breathtaking."

Marcus smiled. "Tell my father that. Maybe he'll believe it coming from a beautiful woman."

He parked in the driveway behind a silver Buick Park Avenue, then climbed out of the SUV and came around to open the door for her. As they started up the walk, she admired the large house, which boasted bi-level decks, an upper balcony facing the lake and plenty of steep French windows.

They were met at the front door by a tall, dark-skinned man who could only be Marcus's father. After one look at Sterling Wolf, Samara could see where the Wolf brothers had gotten their good looks. In his early sixties, Sterling was ruggedly handsome in a hunter-green chambray shirt and corduroy trousers worn over dusty leather boots. His salt-and-pepper hair was neatly trimmed, and his eyes were dark and sharply intelligent. In a flash of insight, Samara imagined the tough, hard-nosed homicide detective he'd been. He must have investigated his cases with the tenacity of a pit bull, breaking rules and stepping on bureaucratic toes left and right.

Those keen eyes zeroed in on Marcus's hand at Samara's back before a low, gritty chuckle rumbled up from his chest. "Well, this is certainly a nice surprise."

"Hey, Dad," Marcus greeted him. "This is Samara Layton. Samara, I'd like you to meet my father, Sterling Wolf."

Samara smiled at the older man. "It's nice to meet you, Mr. Wolf."

Sterling Wolf's large, callused hand swallowed hers in a firm handshake. "Nice to meet *you*, Ms. Layton," he said, his Southern drawl even more pronounced than Marcus's Opening the door wider, he ushered them inside.

Vaulted ceilings and a winding staircase to the upper level punctuated the sheer elegance of the house. To their immediate right was a high arched entranceway to the spacious living room. Aubusson rugs were spread across golden pinewood floors that shined with brilliance from the afternoon sunlight.

"Y'all are just in time for lunch," Sterling said. "Michael's just finishing up in the kitchen. When he heard about the fishing trip being cut short, he took pity on his old man and came right over to fix me lunch since Frizell is off this week." Seeing Marcus glance at his watch, he said warningly, "I won't hear a word about you not joining us for lunch, son. You're the boss of those folks. They'll understand if you show up a little late to a meeting *they* requested. And on a Sunday, at that."

Marcus chuckled dryly. "I've got some time. Who got food poisoning? You didn't say on the phone."

Sterling grunted. "It was Charlie. He was sick as a dog all over the place. We decided to cut our losses and head back home on the first flight outta there." He shrugged broad shoulders. "Fish weren't biting much anyway."

Michael emerged from the kitchen, wiping his hands on a dishtowel and smiling at Samara. "So my eyes weren't deceiving me last night. You *are* as beautiful as I thought you were."

She smiled. "And you're still as charming as I remember. Do you need help with anything in the kitchen?"

"Nope. Everything's ready."

"Good, 'cause I'm starving," Sterling announced. "You know I can't eat that mess they serve on planes. Rubber coated with food coloring, that's all it is."

"I thought we could eat out on the deck," Michael suggested. "The weather's great."

"Sounds good to me." Sterling winked at Samara. "Why don't we go on ahead, let the boys bring out the food while we get better acquainted?"

His charm was infectious. Samara grinned at him. "Lead the way."

She followed him to a pair of French doors leading onto an enormous veranda facing the rear of the house. At one end of the deck was a gazebo painted white with a red brick roof to match the exterior of the main house. A one-level guesthouse graced the opposite end of the deck. Winding flagstone walkways served as connecting paths between the gazebo and guesthouse, and centered on a small pool that shimmered sapphire blue in the dappled sunlight. A series of lush garden beds framed the terraced walkways, adding brilliant splashes of color to the landscape. The surrounding canopy of trees formed a leafy backdrop and provided an enchanting sense of seclusion.

The overall effect was nothing short of breathtaking.

"You like it out here?" Sterling asked, observing her rapt expression with a pleased smile.

"It's absolutely beautiful," Samara said. "You must spend a lot of time out here."

"It's hard not to." He swept an appreciative look around the scenic environment. "The boys and I didn't have anything like this back in the old neighborhood. I guess we were long overdue. Marcus will have to give you a tour of the garden. It was featured in one of those magazines last year—*Better Homes and Gardens*, I think it was." He cleared his throat, adding gruffly, "Not that I pay attention to that kinda stuff, mind you."

Samara suppressed a knowing grin. "I'd love a tour of the garden. Especially now that I know how famous it is."

Sterling's smile deepened as he offered his arm. "Shall we?"

Samara slipped her arm companionably through his as they walked to the gazebo. Four wrought-iron chairs were arranged around a matching white table draped with linen.

"Thank you kindly, sir," Samara said as Sterling pushed in her chair.

He took a seat beside her. "Is this your first trip to Georgia?"

She shook her head. "First time in Stone Mountain though. It's lovely out here. So peaceful."

"It's a far cry from where we came from, that's for sure."

She arched an inquisitive brow. "And you don't think that's a good thing?"

"To hear my sons tell it, it's the best thing that ever happened to me. And maybe they're right. But you know how it is with human nature. When we get accustomed to one way of life, we often find it hard to adjust to something new, something different." He grinned ruefully. "I suppose it's true you can't teach an old dog new tricks, eh?"

"I suppose," Samara agreed, making an exaggerated show of looking around the yard and under the table. "But I don't see any old dogs around here."

Sterling laughed, a deep, pleasant rumble. "I think we're going to get along just fine, Samara Layton. Just fine."

Marcus and Michael emerged from the house to serve lunch. Over the next hour, conversation flowed freely as the foursome discussed everything from politics to sports. As Samara bantered easily with the Wolf men, she couldn't help envying the closeness they shared. She'd always wanted a sibling, perhaps even more than she'd craved a good relationship with her mother. Marcus had the best of both worlds.

Taming the Wolf

But throughout the meal, she never felt like an outsider. If anything, Sterling and Michael embraced her as if she were a member of the family. And on several occasions, she'd glanced up and caught Marcus watching her, studying her. The heat he sent through his dark eyes surrounded her, leaving her with a liquid rush in unspeakable parts of her body.

When he left for his meeting, she walked him outside to the Navigator. She was telling him how much she'd enjoyed lunch when, without warning, he pulled her into his arms and kissed her senseless.

When he finally released her, his dark eyes smoldered with an intensity that shook her to the core. She could only stare at him, stunned and breathless, as he climbed into the truck and drove away.

She watched until the Navigator was out of sight before turning and slowly heading back toward the house, wondering what was up with Marcus.

On her way to the kitchen to help Michael finish clearing the dishes, she passed Sterling and a group of his friends seated around a table in the den. After lunch, he'd called and invited them over for their weekly poker game, previously postponed in lieu of the fishing trip.

Their raucous male laughter reverberated around the room as they regaled one another with ribald jokes and anecdotes of wayward grandchildren.

"Well, you know I would trade places with you *any* day," Sterling was saying. "I'm gonna have one foot in the grave by the time my sons decide to give me any grandchildren."

"Sterl, I hate to break it to you," came the sage reply, "but you've already got one foot in the grave!"

Samara couldn't help but grin as more laughter and guffaws rumbled around the room.

Sterling wasn't amused. "Ha ha, that's real clever, George. How long did it take you to come up with that one? Now if we don't get this game started soon, I'm gonna start tossing you fellas out of my house—starting with you, Mr. Wise Guy."

"Where's Charlie's replacement?" another voice piped up.

"What do you mean?" Sterling asked. "Isn't Charlie coming? He seemed like he was feeling better on the plane."

"Nah, didn't George tell you? Charlie's still sick. George spoke to him before he left the house. He said his wife was putting him to bed."

Out of the ensuing mutters, Sterling demanded, "And when were you going to share this information with the rest of us, George?"

"Sorry," came George's sheepish response. "Must've slipped my mind."

"Yeah, like your brain," Sterling retorted.

More scattered chortles. "Why don't you ask one of your boys to fill in for Charlie?" George asked. "They're both still here, aren't they?"

Sterling grunted in disbelief. "*My* boys? Have you lost your mind? Marcus and Michael would wipe the floor with you fellas. I taught 'em everything I know about poker."

"Which ain't much," George snickered.

Ignoring the barb, Sterling continued, "Nah, we need to find someone else. I don't feel much like losing today, not after we had to cut the fishing trip short."

Samara, belatedly realizing she'd been standing in one spot as she enjoyed their bickering, now tried to tiptoe past the room without detection.

"Is that you out there, Samara?" Sterling called to her. "Come on in here. Let me introduce you to everyone."

Silently cursing her own nosiness, Samara turned and retraced her steps to the den. Seven pairs of eyes lifted at her appearance.

Sterling beamed proudly as he made the introductions. Samara struggled not to cringe when he presented her as Marcus's "special lady friend."

She nodded at each man in turn. "Nice to meet you, gentlemen."

"Say, can you play poker, Samara?" the one nicknamed Bubba asked.

Samara opened her mouth to respond when a derisive snicker from George forestalled her. "Everyone knows poker is a man's game," he scoffed.

"Is that right?" Samara said, unable to resist the challenge. Injecting saccharine into her voice, she drawled, "Well, I suppose that's probably true. I haven't met too many female champion poker players."

"And you never will," George declared emphatically.

"So how about it, Samara?" Sterling prompted. "Can you play well enough to be our eighth man? I'll even spot you the money so you don't have to spend your own. We don't play for high stakes here. All of us are either living on a fixed income and/or the generosity of our children."

"Well..." With an exaggerated display of reluctance, Samara said, "I suppose I could give it a try. But I don't want you gentlemen going easy on me simply because I'm a woman."

George's dark eyes gleamed with anticipation as she sat in the chair opposite him. He looked like the proverbial cat that had cornered the mouse. "Don't you worry, Ms. Layton. We'll beat—I mean, *treat*—you fair and square."

Samara smiled sweetly at him. She saw no point in telling George that as a bartender in college, her favorite pastime had been playing poker with her coworkers during downtime. Maybe after the game she would let him know about the trophy proudly displayed in her curio cabinet at home, a trophy crowning her the champion in a national poker tournament.

When Marcus returned from his meeting later that afternoon, the last thing he expected was to find Samara playing poker with his father and his buddies.

Every Friday night, Sterling Wolf's den was converted into the poker domain, complete with an octagonal-shaped table that served as the room's centerpiece. Other than the players themselves, no one entered the poker domain on Friday nights—not even his father's indomitable housekeeper. It became a testosterone-filled cave ripe with the stench of cigar smoke, male sweat and rowdy laughter.

So it seemed impossible that Marcus would find Samara seated at the table with the seven retired cops, as out of place as a ballerina at a rodeo.

His first instinct was to march into the room and snatch her from the table—a reaction not even *he* understood.

He was stopped by his brother, who'd hung around after Marcus left to work on a presentation he was giving at a restaurateur's convention next week.

Leaning in the doorway of the den, Michael reached out, detaining Marcus with a hand on his shoulder. Shaking his head wordlessly, Michael pointed across the room, clearly amused by what he'd been watching.

A roar of incredulous male groans erupted from the poker table. "Another royal flush!" George Wilkins cried in disgust. "I don't believe this!"

Neither did Marcus. He watched, in amazement, as a grinning Samara leaned forward to haul in her earnings from the pot. "You fellas are making me quite a rich woman this afternoon," she drawled, making a show of counting her money before pocketing it.

Sterling laughed uproariously. "Gentlemen, I think we might've been better off if we'd asked one of my boys to join us!"

"Too late now," grumbled Bernard "Bubba" Ward. "Anyway, she's got an unfair advantage over the rest of us."

"And what's that, Bubba?" Sterling inquired.

"Look at her! She's as pretty as the dickens. I can hardly concentrate on my cards."

The complaint was followed by another round of laughter and guffaws. Sterling removed his porkpie hat from his head—the lucky hat from his detective days at the Atlanta PD—and settled it atop Samara's head. The brim slanted crookedly across her eyebrows, partially obscuring her face but doing nothing to hide the megawatt grin.

"Does that help, Bubba?" Sterling demanded.

A red flush crept across Bubba's pale face. "Well, maybe just a little."

The others ribbed him good-naturedly.

"Let's face it, fellas," Melvin Tooks announced. "We've been outmatched by a superior opponent."

"That's right," Sterling chimed in. "It just hasn't been our week. But you know what the best part is? There's only *one* of us here who has to eat crow for underestimating Ms. Layton."

Seven pairs of eyes swung to George Wilkins, who seemed to shrink down into his chair. "So I was wrong about her," he muttered sheepishly. "I've been wrong before."

Sterling grinned in satisfaction. "Samara, is there anything you'd like to say to our good friend George before we call it quits?"

Samara's grin widened. "It's been a real pleasure doing business with you, Mr. Wilkins. Now if you kind gentlemen will excuse me," she said, rising from the table, "I think I'll head on out and decide what to do with all this loot. And, no, Mr. Wilkins, going on a shopping spree is *not* one of my options, so don't you even go there."

He grinned and ducked his head as the others laughed. Samara rounded the table and planted a conciliatory kiss on his ruddy cheek, and Marcus would have sworn the man blushed if he weren't so dark-skinned.

"Where's *my* kiss?" Bubba protested. "And can you go to the movies with us tonight?"

Samara sighed dramatically. "Thanks for the invite, Mr. Ward, but I'm afraid I'll have to take a rain check. You fellas enjoy your-selves—and let me know if y'all need to borrow any money for tickets."

She left a trail of raucous laughter in her wake as she started from room.

Grinning, Michael leaned over to Marcus. "*Where* did you find her? She's incredible."

Marcus didn't answer, too busy staring at Samara as she paused to speak to his father, managing to look both adorable and sexy in Sterling's porkpie hat. When she glanced up and saw Marcus standing there, her smile widened with pleasure. It nearly knocked him off his feet.

He must have looked as dumbstruck as he felt, because Michael chuckled and shook his head in disbelief. "Well, I'll be damned. I never thought I'd live to see the day."

Marcus swallowed hard. "What day?"

"You've finally met your match, Little Man. You've finally been tamed."

Marcus said absolutely nothing, afraid his brother's words were too close to the truth.

Chapter Ten

S amara, Brianna Lynch is here to see you."

"Thanks, Diane. Please send her up." Samara put the finishing touches on a report she'd been working on, saved the file and exited the program. She swiveled away from the computer just as Brianna Lynch appeared in her doorway.

"Hi, Samara. I came as soon as I got your message."

Samara smiled at her. "Thanks for coming, Brianna. Please close the door and have a seat."

Brianna complied, sitting down almost gingerly in the chair opposite Samara's desk. She still wore her waitress uniform from the downtown restaurant where she worked, a simple white blouse over a pleated black skirt. In her haste, she'd forgotten to remove the little green apron bearing the restaurant's name and insignia. Raindrops glistened on flawless cheeks the color of café au lait. Thick shoulder-length braids marched back neatly from her face, still gently rounded from the weight she'd gained during pregnancy.

Brianna and her four-month-old daughter, Lola, had been abandoned when Brianna's boyfriend panicked and decided he couldn't handle the responsibility of fatherhood. A pregnant, devastated Brianna had come to the Yorkin Institute in search of help and a nonjudgmental shoulder to lean on. She and Samara had bonded almost immediately.

"Is it raining hard out there?" Samara asked.

"It's not too bad." Brianna set aside her umbrella and wiped moisture from her face.

"I know you're on your lunch break," Samara said, "so I'll make this quick. The reason I called is because we have a job opening here I thought you might be interested in. The coordinator of our employment counseling center has accepted a position with another company. She's graduating from college in May and wants to begin working in her chosen field, so it's a wonderful opportunity for her. But it leaves us with a vacancy that needs to be filled rather quickly. Our human resources manager, who supervises the counseling center, is stretched pretty thin as it is."

Brianna's thick-lashed brown eyes grew wide with disbelief. "You want *me* to work in the employment counseling center?"

Samara nodded, smiling. "I think you'd be perfect, Brianna. You're smart, organized and conscientious. I've seen you in action at the restaurant, and you have excellent customer service skills, which are an important part of the coordinator position—being able to assist job seekers when they come to the center. Many don't have regular access to computers, so they're not familiar with how to navigate their way around our database. They need someone to provide technical assistance and, sometimes, a sympathetic listening ear." She paused. "You've been in their shoes, Brianna. You understand just where they're coming from."

"B-But I don't have a college degree," Brianna said faintly.

"Neither did Crystal when she first started here. She worked part-time and attended classes at night. Before she resigned, we were going to bump her up to full-time now that we have the available funds, because we really need someone in the center on a full-time basis. Joanne, our human resources manager, will train you on the database and teach you the filing system. Once you finish your GED classes and start college next year, we can arrange some type of flextime schedule. And don't tell me you're not going to college," Samara warned before Brianna could open her mouth, "because you *are*, even if I have to enroll you myself and pick your classes for you—although I'd much rather leave that part to you."

Taming the Wolf

Brianna smiled tremulously. Her eyes glittered with excitement. "I-I don't know what to say, Samara."

"Say you'll accept the job."

"Yes! Yes, I'll accept the job. Thank you so much, Samara. I don't know how to repay you."

"You don't have to repay me. Just prove me right and do a good job like I know you're capable of, and that will be repayment enough." Samara's tone softened. "This isn't charity, Brianna. I'm giving you this opportunity because I truly believe in you and want to see you succeed in life. The starting salary is entry-level, but I'm sure it's a bit more than what you're earning now at the restaurant. As a full-time employee, you'll also receive benefits—tuition assistance, 401(k), health care. No more coming out of the pocket to take Lola to the doctor."

"How soon can I start?" Brianna asked eagerly.

"Crystal has agreed to stay on through next week and help train the new coordinator. So the sooner you can quit your job at the restaurant, the better."

"Consider it done." Grinning, Brianna glanced at her watch. "I'd better get back before my lunch break ends. It's really busy this time of day."

Samara nodded as Brianna rose from the chair. The girl's expression was earnest. "I can't thank you enough for all you've done for me, Samara. I promise not to let you down with this job, or anything else for that matter."

"I know," Samara said with a soft smile. "Oh, Brianna, before you leave..." She opened the bottom desk drawer and grabbed her purse. She withdrew a sealed envelope containing the money from her poker winnings and handed it to Brianna with a wink. "Just a little something I picked up over the weekend."

Puzzled, Brianna tore open the envelope and peeked inside. Her eyes bulged at the sight that greeted her. "Oh my God! There's over four hundred dollars in here!" She raised incredulous eyes to Samara's face. "I-I can't accept all this money, Samara."

"Sure you can," Samara countered briskly. "Consider it a signing bonus. Or, if you want, think of it as tips you deserved but never received from cheap customers."

Tears misted the girl's eyes even as she grinned. What waitress couldn't relate to being stiffed by cheap customers? Samara certainly remembered those days.

"What should I do with the money?" Brianna asked, her voice thick with emotion.

"Whatever you want. Buy a nice Easter dress for Lola and yourself, then use the rest to open a savings account. Just a suggestion."

"Thank you, Samara. Thank you so much." Overcome with gratitude, Brianna hurried around the desk and threw her arms tightly around Samara's neck. Samara laughed and hugged her back, feeling a bit misty-eyed herself. In many ways, Brianna Lynch had become the little sister she never had, but had always wanted.

"You're going to be just fine," Samara whispered into Brianna's hair. After another moment, she drew back and tweaked the girl's nose affectionately. "Now get out of here before you're late. I don't want those folks firing you before you have a chance to quit."

Brianna grinned as she bent to retrieve her umbrella from the floor. "We're supposed to get back our test results in class tonight. I'll call and let you know my grade."

"You do that. And kiss Lola for me."

"I will. Thanks again, Samara." Brianna left the office giving a shy wave.

Samara dialed Joanne Newsome's extension to inform the relieved human resources manager about their new hire and to request the necessary forms to begin the paperwork.

After she hung up the phone, she consulted her watch and saw that it was two-thirty. She'd worked straight through lunch, making phone calls and finalizing details for the summer launch of the Youth for the Arts and Literacy project. That morning she'd attended a meeting with Jasmine Woodbury, a dance instructor at the Duke Ellington School of Performing Arts. The teacher was excited about the YAL project and already knew of several well-known artists who'd be willing to conduct community workshops. Before the school year ended, Jasmine would hold auditions for the dance troupe, and once the student participants were selected, they could begin practicing for summer performances.

That week, Samara had meetings with two of their former corporate sponsors interested in renewing partnerships with the Institute. FYI's debts would soon be settled, their creditors appeased. Things were finally looking up for FYI.

So why does it feel as if something's still missing?

Samara chewed her bottom lip, staring blindly at her computer screen. For the umpteenth time in two days, her thoughts strayed to Marcus. She hadn't seen or heard from him since Sunday night, when he'd driven her home from the airport. During the two-hour flight, he'd seemed a little withdrawn, making no attempt to seduce her as they'd joked about earlier in the day. And when they reached her house, he'd quietly declined her invitation to come inside, citing an early meeting in the morning.

That was when she knew something was *definitely* wrong. Every woman on the planet understood that when a man used the "early morning meeting" excuse, he was as good as history. Now, thinking back on it, Samara realized the kiss Marcus had given her at his father's house—the one that nearly knocked her off her feet—had been the kiss of death. In his own way, he'd been telling her goodbye.

Oh, girl, stop being so melodramatic. You don't know what was going through that man's mind when he kissed you like that.

The bottom line was, she didn't know Marcus Wolf as well as she would've liked. Although they'd spent an entire weekend together, talked for hours on end and connected on many levels—mentally and physically—she knew there were a lot of personal things he hadn't shared with her. She didn't know, for example, how his parents' divorce had affected him, and what kind of relationship he had with his mother, who lived in Minnesota. Because he'd seemed reluctant to discuss her, Samara hadn't pried. But she'd sensed pain in his silence, and she'd wanted to explore the source of it.

She sighed, impatient with herself. She was spending way too much time worrying about Marcus. Just because she hadn't heard from him in two days didn't mean he'd lost interest in her. But something was definitely wrong.

She couldn't help but wonder if she'd scared him off by asking that stupid question about his other relationships. Her mother and grandmother had always warned her that nothing drove a man away faster than a jealous woman. It was the one thing the two women had agreed on.

Samara scowled. If Marcus Wolf thought she was going to start acting clingy and possessive, he'd better think again. She had better things to do than chase after a man.

Even a wonderful, amazing man like him.

"I never know what mood you're going to be in when I step foot in this office."

Samara looked up and smiled at Melissa standing in the doorway. "Hey, girl. Come on in, pull up a seat."

Melissa arched an amused brow. "You're actually *inviting* me into your office? Who are you, and what have you done with the real Samara Layton?"

Samara chuckled dryly. "I missed you around here yesterday. That was probably the first time you've ever called in sick in the ten years you've worked here. I was at a meeting when you called this morning, but Diane told me you had a doctor's appointment. Is everything okay?"

"Everything is better than okay." Melissa sat down in the visitor's chair, hazel eyes gleaming. "I just found out that Gary and I are going to be parents."

Samara's eyes widened. "Oh my God! Are you saying what I think you're saying?"

Melissa grinned, rubbing her flat stomach. "I'm pregnant, Samara."

With an ecstatic squeal, Samara jumped up from her chair and rounded the desk to wrap her friend in a big hug. "Congratulations, Melissa! I'm so happy for you!"

"I met Gary for breakfast right afterward. He was so excited, Samara. You would think the man had just won the lottery!"

Samara laughed, drawing back to cradle Melissa's face in her hands. "And what about you? How thrilled are you?"

"Very. Oh, I know it's going to be a huge lifestyle adjustment. No more dropping everything and going to the movies or ballet performances whenever we want. No more sleeping in late on weekends."

Samara guffawed. "You talk as if the baby will be here tomorrow! You and Gary still have plenty of time to enjoy those things. When are you due anyway?"

"Late September." Grinning, Melissa sat down again as Samara perched a hip on the corner of her desk. "I can hardly believe it. I keep rubbing my stomach, unable to believe that a tiny life is already growing inside me. God, I'm going to be someone's *mother*!"

"And you're going to be as good at it as you are at everything else."

"I hope you're right." Melissa worried at her bottom lip with her teeth, and Samara's heart stirred at the naked vulnerability reflected in her friend's eyes. It was hard to imagine Melissa, who was used to taking charge of every aspect of her life, being daunted by the prospect of motherhood. But given the many uncertainties that came with the job, Samara could see how it was possible to feel intimidated, to question one's own qualifications.

She reached over, gently touching Melissa's knee. "You're going to be just fine. I'm betting that it won't take very long for that little boy or girl in there to realize how incredibly lucky they are to have a mommy like you."

Tears shimmered in Melissa's eyes. "I really needed to hear that. Thank you, Samara."

Samara smiled softly. "You know I meant every word." She clapped her hands together. "This calls for a celebration. I'm thinking lunch in Georgetown, a toast with sparkling cider!"

"Tomorrow," Melissa said, rising from the chair. "I have tons of invoices to be mailed out this week, and the day's almost over. Gary has already put me on notice that my days of working late at the office are numbered."

Samara grinned. "Girl, that man is going to spoil you rotten."

"Tell me about it. He's already promising foot and back rubs every night, commuting together so I don't have to drive, an unlimited supply of Häagen Dazs ice cream…"

Samara groaned enviously. "Don't rub it in."

Melissa chuckled, pausing at the door. "Before I forget, how was your weekend with Marcus?"

Samara hesitated, then answered truthfully, "It was wonderful. He showed me the time of my life."

"I'll just bet he did," Melissa said with a lascivious grin. "Over, and over, and over again."

Laughing, Samara pointed at Melissa's stomach. "See, it's that dirty mind of yours that got you in trouble in the first place."

"You know it! But, hey, I'm not the one who's in trouble here. *You* are."

"How's that?"

Melissa gave her a knowing smile. "Judging by the way your eyes light up every time you hear Marcus Wolf's name, I would say you're in serious trouble, girlfriend. It won't be long now before you're writing his name across your blotter and drawing little hearts around it."

Heat stung Samara's cheeks. "Don't be silly. I didn't even do that kind of stuff in junior high school."

Melissa's smile widened. "Well, you know what they say. There's a first time for everything."

Long after Melissa left, her parting words echoed in Samara's mind.

There's a first time for everything.

Including a first time for falling in love.

Samara froze, shaken by the thought.

Could it be true?

Had she been foolish enough to fall in love with Marcus, a man who was about as attainable as a pot of gold at the end of a rainbow?

After years of avoiding serious romantic entanglements and carefully safeguarding her heart, had she finally allowed the unthinkable to happen?

Closing her eyes, Samara leaned her head back against the chair and groaned softly. She didn't have to look too deep within herself to find the answer.

God help her, she already knew. And Melissa was absolutely right.

Samara was in serious trouble.

Across town, Marcus had just hung up the phone with a client when the intercom on his desk buzzed. "Mr. Wolf, you have a visitor," announced his receptionist.

Marcus frowned, his hand stilling over the legal pad he'd been making notes on. It was after five o'clock, and he knew he didn't have any other appointments that day.

Unless…

"Her name is Celeste Rutherford, sir."

The blood drained from Marcus's head. Not Samara, as he'd briefly hoped. Instead, the visitor was the *last* person on earth he would have expected.

Slowly, unsteadily, he rose to his feet.

"Mr. Wolf?"

He took a long, deep breath. "Please send her in, Laura."

He didn't trust his legs to carry him out to the reception area to meet her. Not after all this time.

Moments later, his mother stepped into the office almost tentatively, and Marcus's heart clutched painfully in his chest. Ten years. That was how long it had been since he'd last seen her. *Ten years.*

Celeste Rutherford looked the part of a prosperous doctor's wife in a mauve silk blouse tucked into pale cashmere slacks, her tiny feet covered in matching designer pumps. Her black hair was cut in short, stylish layers that accentuated her oval-shaped face. After all these years, her creamy skin remained smooth and unlined. But not even the expensive cosmetics she wore could conceal the faint lines of strain around her cinnamon-brown eyes and soft mouth.

A fine-boned hand lifted self-consciously to touch the pearl necklace clasped around her throat. "Hello, Marcus," she said quietly. Her expression was guarded as she watched him, as if she fully expected to be met with a barrage of angry accusations.

Marcus inclined his head coolly. "Mother." He remained planted behind his desk, wanting the physical barrier between them—*needing* it. "Would you care for something to drink?"

"No, thank you. Your secretary already offered."

He nodded slowly. "How've you been?"

"I'm fine. I don't know whether or not your father told you that I was coming to town with Grant—"

"He told me."

She nodded. "Grant is giving a surgical lecture at a medical convention at Johns Hopkins, so I wanted to take the opportunity to see you. It's been so long. At least ten years."

"At least."

She bit her bottom lip as if she were trying to decide what to say next. "Marcus, I *am* truly sorry for missing your law school graduation. Grant and I never intended for our honeymoon to coincide with that date. It's just that we weren't able to go right after the wedding because Grant was needed at the hospital, and I—"

"You don't have to explain, Mother." The corner of his mouth lifted sardonically. "It was Greece. Who could blame you for not passing up on such a trip?"

"Marcus—"

"How *is* your husband, by the way?" He still couldn't bring himself to utter Grant Rutherford's name aloud. It felt like blasphemy against Sterling Wolf.

Celeste hesitated before answering evenly, "He's doing well. One of his recent studies on stem cell research is being published in the *New England Journal of Medicine*. The Mayo Clinic has received even greater publicity and financial contributions as a result of Grant's research work."

"Congratulations, to both of you."

"Thank you." She cast an appreciative look around the large office. "You've done extremely well for yourself, Marcus. We're all very proud of you."

His mouth curled in a mocking half smile. "Nothing but the best, right, Mother?"

Her eyes returned to his. "Maybe this was a mistake, my coming here like this. I assumed since your father told you in advance that I would be in town…" she trailed off, nervously stroking the pearl necklace again. "I suppose I just thought—"

Marcus arched a cynical brow. "What? You thought I would welcome your visit with open arms?"

"And would that be so terrible?" she asked, her voice rising on a shrill note. "I'm your mother, Marcus. Nothing you say or do will ever change that fact. *Nothing*."

"I'm well aware of that," he said coldly.

She turned away from him, facing the mahogany-paneled wall of books so that he wouldn't see the sheen of tears in her eyes—too late. When she spoke, her voice was husky with emotion. "How long will you punish me for what happened between me and your father?"

Marcus was silent, his fisted hands jammed into his pants pockets. Anger pumped hard through his veins, as raw as ever.

"I don't know how many times I can apologize to you for the way things happened," Celeste continued.

"Things didn't just happen, Mom. You *made* them happen."

She spun around. "You have *no* idea what you're talking about! You were just a child, Marcus. You knew nothing about my true relationship with your father!"

"I know he loved you more than life itself," Marcus said in a low, controlled voice, "and you betrayed him in the worst possible way. I don't need to know much more beyond that."

"Don't you?" she cried.

Marcus's expression hardened. "Are you about to tell me that Dad abused you, cheated on you, or mistreated you in any kind of way?"

Her moist eyes softened. "Of course not. You know better than that, Marcus. Your father was—*is*—the most decent man I've ever known."

"And you repaid his 'decency' by cheating on him."

"It's been twenty-five years, Marcus! How much longer are you going to carry this grudge against me? Your brother has forgiven me. We speak to each other quite often, did you know that? When he agreed to attend my wedding, we had a long heart-to-heart talk and resolved everything between us. He was just as hurt by the divorce as you were, but he was willing to put the past behind him and move on. Even your *father* has forgiven me, Marcus! Why can't *you*?"

"I guess I'm not as magnanimous as Michael and Dad," Marcus said mockingly.

"I don't believe that! You are one of the most generous people I know. I haven't forgotten the way you were as a little boy, defending your classmates from bullies, running errands for the elderly people in our neighborhood who couldn't get around on their own. You always had such a big heart, so much love to give. I

131

wasn't at all surprised when you became the kind of attorney that would help others. It was like you were answering a calling." Her voice broke as a single tear escaped from the corner of her eye. She sniffed and dabbed at the errant drop without looking at him. "You're not a cruel person, Marcus. I *know* what it must be doing to you to hold on to this much hatred. Even if you don't care what it's doing to me, at least think about yourself."

"Don't you *dare* pretend to care about my well-being!" Marcus roared. "You haven't cared since the day you walked out on us without a backward glance. You didn't even fight for custody—you didn't want us!"

"That's not true! Of course I wanted you and Michael—you're my *children*, for God's sake! The only reason I didn't push for custody was because I knew your father was hurting enough. The last thing either of us needed was a bitter custody battle. I couldn't do that to him. Besides," she added, her voice lowering, "in those days, I knew that no judge would look favorably upon my behavior."

"Your *infidelity*, you mean."

"Yes, my infidelity," she hissed, her eyes suddenly flashing. "I have many regrets about what happened, Marcus. I regret that I felt desperate enough in my marriage to cheat on your father. I regret that you had to walk in on me with Grant that afternoon. I regret that all of you were devastated by my reckless actions, and that our family was torn apart as a result. Believe me, I will carry those regrets to the grave. But I do *not* regret meeting Grant Rutherford." She didn't falter at the dangerous look that filled Marcus's face, but bravely continued, "I fell in love with Grant almost from the moment we met at the hospital. I know it was wrong of me, a married woman, to have such strong feelings for another man. But sometimes, baby, we have no control over who we fall in love with or why. All we know is what the heart dictates."

"Don't give me that crap," Marcus said caustically. "You knew damn well what you were doing when you got involved with a doctor from the hospital. You wanted an *out*, Mother. An out from a marriage that kept you from having all the material possessions you wanted, things that Dad could never give you. Why don't you just admit it?"

Celeste closed her eyes and held a trembling hand to her mouth. When she spoke, her voice was barely above a strained whisper. "If you can believe such a thing about me, then I guess I should abandon any hope of reconciliation between us once and for all."

Marcus turned away from her to face the window. He couldn't believe how badly shaken he was. He felt like that ten-year-old boy again, wanting his mother's comforting arms around him at the same time he wanted to push her away for good. His chest hurt from the internal struggle raging through him, his emotions warring against one another.

She's your mother. It's time to forgive her, pleaded one voice.

She hurt you, countered the more cynical side of him. *You know you can't trust her. Don't be a fool.*

He closed his eyes. "I just want to know one thing," he said quietly.

"What is it, Marcus?"

"Did you ever love Dad?"

His mother was silent for so long that he wondered if she'd left the room without saying goodbye. But he knew better. He still sensed her presence, just as surely as he'd done as a child whenever she got home from her late shift at the hospital. In those days, even before she crossed the threshold, he was already awake and waiting up for her.

Finally she spoke. "Yes, Marcus, I did love him. In my own way, I will always love your father."

Marcus said nothing, keeping his back to her.

"Grant and I will be in town for a week," she said gently. "We're staying at the J. W. Marriott. We wanted to visit some friends and do a little sightseeing before returning to Minnesota." She hesitated. "I would love nothing more than to have dinner with you, Marcus.

Just you and me. We have so much to discuss. If you're open to it, I'm leaving my card with our hotel room and phone number."

He heard her place the card on his desk, but still he didn't turn around.

"Please, Marcus. Call me."

It was only when he heard the door close softly behind her that he turned from the windows, hands thrust into his pockets, his muscles rigid. For several moments he just stared at the plain white business card she'd left on his desk. Then slowly, almost against his will, he reached over and picked it up.

The front of the card read: CELESTE W. RUTHERFORD, M.S., R.N., ADMINISTRATOR. Respectfully known as the "power duo," she and her husband served on several hospital boards, including the board of trustees at the Mayo Clinic in Rochester, Minnesota. They'd relocated there when Grant was offered a surgeon position in the clinic's internationally renowned neuro-surgery department.

On the back of the card, Celeste had written their hotel room and phone number in her graceful, distinctly feminine hand-writing—the same handwriting that once graced Marcus's field trip permission slips and report cards. He remembered the way she used to hug him and kiss the top of his head, congratulating him for getting straight A's, urging him to tell her all about the fun places he'd visited.

Marcus's heart clutched painfully at the memory. There was no denying that she'd been a good mother, incredibly nurturing and attentive to her children. Marcus had adored her, which was what made her desertion that much harder to accept.

Following the divorce, she'd attempted to remain active in their lives, attending their basketball games and school events as often as possible, showing up for her court-appointed visits. But as the years passed, her efforts waned until she disappeared completely from the picture. Once she and Grant got married and moved to Minnesota, they hardly ever heard from her. But by then, Marcus had stopped returning her sporadic phone calls and letters altogether. He was in college, old enough to make his own decisions about whether or not to have a relationship with his mother. No one could force him to see or talk to her, and he definitely couldn't be pressured into attending her wedding—which he'd refused to do.

The fact that she'd waited several years to remarry made no difference to him. As far as he was concerned, she had moved on with her life, while they'd been left behind to pick up the shattered pieces of theirs.

Abandonment was abandonment, any way you sliced it.

Frowning, Marcus looked down and saw that he'd crumpled the business card in his balled fist. He threw it into the wastebasket, then grabbed his suit jacket from the back of his chair and left the office.

Chapter Eleven

As he'd often done during law school before a big exam, Marcus drove around for the next three hours trying to clear his head and make sense of the things happening in his life. As much as his mother's unexpected visit rattled him, thoughts of Samara dominated his mind.

Since Sunday night, he'd been struggling to come to terms with his feelings for her. He could no longer deny it. He was in love with her. Completely, irrevocably, in love with the woman.

It scared the hell out of him.

He'd never been in love before. And he sure as hell never expected to fall in love so quickly. That kind of thing happened to other people, not Marcus. If anyone had ever told him that he'd find himself in this position—over a woman he'd known less than two weeks—Marcus would've laughed in the person's face.

He wasn't laughing now.

He was running scared.

As he crossed the Potomac River and headed back into the District, a light rain began to fall. Without conscious thought, he pointed the car toward southeast D.C. By the time he pulled up in front of Samara's old-fashioned house with its wide front porch, it was pouring so hard he could barely see through the windshield.

Although it was only nine o'clock, all the lights were off in Samara's house. As he waited on the porch for her to answer the door, Marcus glanced up and down the tree-lined street and realized that the entire neighborhood was pitched black. The storm had knocked out the power.

Samara came to the door a few moments later, the soft glow of a candle illuminating the surprise on her face when she saw him standing there. The surprise quickly turned to wariness.

"What are you doing here?"

He gazed down at her. "I wanted to see you," he said silkily.

She hesitated, eyeing him a moment longer before opening the door wider to let him in. As Marcus brushed past her, he caught the clean scent of shampoo and soap that clung to her skin. Her hair was wet, hanging in thick ropes over her shoulders and dripping down the front of her terry cloth robe. Imagining her warm and naked beneath the robe made lust coil inside him, just like that.

He cleared his throat. "No electricity, huh?" Unless you counted the electrical currents pulsing through his veins, heating his blood.

She shook her head. "I just got out of the shower and was about to blow-dry my hair when it went out." Stepping away from the door, she moved soundlessly through the living room, lighting fragrant candles that cast long willowy shadows against the walls.

Marcus watched her, unable to tear his gaze away from her. In the white robe, with her dark hair clinging sleekly to her face and neck, she looked like a mythical creature silhouetted against the flickering flames.

Finished with her task, she started back toward him. "Did you get wet?"

Blood rushed straight to his groin. "What?" he said hoarsely.

In the candlelit gloom, he saw her eyes glitter. "Were you caught in the downpour?" she clarified, and he wondered if he'd only imagined the breathless note in her voice. "I can get you a towel."

He shook his head, even as rainwater trickled into his ear. "I'm fine, thanks."

A streak of lightning flashed across the sky, briefly illuminating the room. Their gazes locked, crackling with awareness. His body burned. His heart pounded so hard, it threatened to shatter in half.

Samara drew a soft, shallow breath. "I'm going to put on some clothes," she told him, turning and starting away. "I'll be right—"

Reaching out, Marcus caught her arm to halt her retreat. She didn't resist as he curved an arm around her waist and pulled her against his body so that her head fell back on his shoulder. The feel of her lush, shapely ass pressed against him made his dick throb with need.

He bent his head to nuzzle her throat, brushing his lips over her silky, fragrant skin, catching droplets of water with the tip of his tongue. She trembled hard.

"I couldn't stay away any longer," he whispered huskily in her ear. "I tried, but I couldn't do it. You're in my blood, Samara."

Her breath quickened as he drew her earlobe into his mouth and gently suckled. Taking her chin between his thumb and forefinger, he turned her face toward him. Dark, heavy-lidded eyes met his. Holding her gaze, he leaned down and kissed her, slow and seductively. Her lips were warm and incredibly soft, parting for him as he swept his tongue inside the velvet nectar of her mouth. She hungrily responded, sucking on his tongue as her body strained closer. His erection swelled painfully against her buttocks. His fingers tangled in her wet hair as he kissed her harder, crushing her lips under his, stealing her breath and giving it back as they panted into each other's mouths.

With his other hand he reached inside her robe and cupped her left breast. She gasped, arching upward as he tweaked and tugged the nipple into a tight bead. She moaned and closed her eyes as he used both hands to fondle and caress her breasts until she writhed against him in mindless pleasure.

His heart thundered as he reached down to untie her robe, then slipped it from her shoulders and let it fall to the floor. He stroked his hand slowly down her side, tracing the voluptuous curves of her body, splaying his fingers across her flat belly. She shivered beneath his touch, her lids at half-mast as she gazed at him over her shoulder.

"Marcus…" Her voice was barely audible.

"I want you," he murmured thickly, bending to touch his mouth to the nape of her neck, then trailing lower, kissing between her shoulder blades and running his tongue down her spine until he felt her shaking. "I want to do unspeakable things to you," he continued, sinking to his knees behind her. "Things you can't even begin to imagine."

"*Marcus…*" she whispered pleadingly.

The breathless desire in her voice only fueled his own arousal. He wanted her so bad it hurt, but he wanted to savor every moment of the seduction, prolong their satisfaction for as long as he could.

He cupped the juicy swell of her rump and began to knead the muscles, groaning deep in his throat from the exquisite pleasure. "You have the sweetest ass I've ever seen," he uttered, low and rough. "Makes a man lose his damn mind."

She quivered uncontrollably as he kissed her buttock, the back of her knees, between her upper thighs.

"Bend forward and open your legs for me," he huskily commanded. When she obeyed, he pressed his mouth to the hot, pulsing mound of her sex. She groaned sharply and arched her back.

Lust raged through his body, throbbing in his groin. Grabbing her hips, he rasped his tongue over her slippery feminine lips, murmuring hoarsely, "Damn, you taste like honey."

"*Oh God, oh God…*" she whispered brokenly as he licked, nibbled and suckled her, filling his mouth with her essence. He tortured her until he thought she might explode, her hips undulating against him, her breath loud and gasping.

He brought her to the brink of fulfillment, then pulled away and lurched to his feet, drawing a protesting moan from her. Hands shaking, he unzipped his pants, almost breaking the zipper in his haste. He removed a condom from his wallet and quickly sheathed his engorged penis, so stimulated he nearly came from the pressure of his own hand.

Taming the Wolf

As a rumble of thunder shook the house, he led Samara into the candlelit living room, bent her over the arm of the sofa, then entered her from behind. She cried out wildly, clasping him in her tight, wet heat. Too ravenous to be gentle, Marcus thrust hard and deep, taking her roughly and possessively. She moaned loudly, holding her bouncing breasts as he rammed in and out of her, showing her no mercy.

"Marcus...*I'm coming!*" she cried as her inner muscles contracted around his dick and her body trembled violently beneath him.

Moments later he exploded inside her with a force that tore a raw expletive from his throat. He gripped her waist and shuddered against her, rocked by one of the most intense orgasms he'd ever had. Fitting that it should be with Samara, the first and only woman he'd ever fallen in love with.

It was several minutes before he could even attempt to move. As he slowly withdrew from her body, a rush of warm liquid seeped out and slid down her inner thighs. He'd never been with a woman who came as hard and freely as Samara did. It was unbearably erotic.

He turned her around and lifted her onto the arm of the sofa, then wiped some of the slick moisture from her thigh. As she watched in heavy-lidded arousal, he put his fingers in his mouth and sucked her nectar from his hand.

"Delicious," he pronounced huskily.

Her eyes rolled back in her head as a ragged moan escaped. Without another word, Marcus lifted her into his arms and started from the living room, in search of a bed for round two.

He was inside her, her legs wrapped around his waist, before they even made it to the hallway.

Hours later, they lay spent in each other's arms, listening to the rain lashing against the windows, drowsily counting the number of times lightning arced across the night sky.

"Aren't you glad you didn't stay away?" Samara murmured, sprawled on top of him, her thick hair spread across his bare chest.

Marcus smiled lazily in the darkness. "Mmm, most definitely."

She hesitated, then admitted, "I was beginning to think you'd lost interest."

Hearing the wistful note in her voice, Marcus felt a sharp pang of guilt. He kissed the top of her head. "I don't even think that's possible."

He felt her smile against his chest, and it filled him with warmth. "Before I forget," he drawled wryly, "my father and brother send their regards."

"Yeah?" There was unmistakable pleasure in her voice. "Well, tell them I said hello. I really enjoyed meeting them."

"Believe me, the feeling's mutual. Dad called me this morning wanting to know when you'd be returning for another visit."

Samara chuckled softly. "I didn't think he'd welcome me into his home again after the way I beat him and his friends at poker."

Marcus grinned. "Where'd you learn how to play like that anyway?" he asked, angling his head to get a better look at her face. "I meant to ask you on Sunday."

"I worked as a bartender during college. One of the other bartenders was a diehard poker player, so he thought it'd be fun to teach me."

Marcus chuckled. "Let me guess. You became greater than your master."

"You know it." A flash of lightning revealed her satisfied grin. "I beat him so many times that he finally dared me to sign up for one of those national poker tournaments. Naturally, I couldn't resist the challenge. A bunch of us rented an RV and drove cross-country to Vegas for the tournament and…" she trailed off, lifting one shoulder in a modest shrug.

"You're kidding me. You're a national poker *champion?*" When Samara nodded sheepishly, Marcus threw back his head and roared with laughter.

She lifted her head and glared playfully at him. "What's so funny about that?"

Shaking his head, Marcus wiped tears of mirth from his eyes. "You never cease to amaze me, Samara Layton. A humanitarian executive by day, a blues-singing poker guru by night."

"I wouldn't exactly say I'm a guru."

"You beat Sterling Wolf. Trust me, you're a guru."

She grinned. "He took it pretty well though."

"That's because he likes you. Come to think of it, you seemed to have *all* of his buddies wrapped around your finger when it was all said and done."

"I liked them. A few of them even reminded me a little of my grandfather—or at least how I'd always imagined him to be. He died in a car accident before I was born, but my grandmother told me so many stories about him that I felt like I knew him personally. I always wished I did." She paused, then added a little forlornly, "I envy you and your family, Marcus. The three of you seem very close."

"We are," he soberly agreed. "We had no other choice."

Silence lapsed between them for a few minutes. Thunder rumbled in the distance, signifying that the storm was finally moving off.

"I saw my mother today," Marcus said quietly. He hadn't planned to tell Samara about his mother's visit, but the moment the words left his mouth, he knew it was the first of many private things he'd be sharing with her.

Samara grew very still against him, understanding the import of his announcement. "Where did you see her?"

"She showed up at my office late this afternoon. She and her husband are in town for a medical convention at Johns Hopkins."

"Your mother remarried?"

Marcus flinched in the darkness. "Yeah, she did."

"How long has it been since you've seen her?" Samara asked gently.

Marcus drew a long, deep breath. "Ten years. I've stopped counting the days and months," he added, a shadow of cynicism twisting his mouth.

"It must have been very hard for you to see her again, after all this time," Samara murmured.

He nodded, then surprised himself by quietly admitting, "I didn't know whether to ask her to leave, or beg her to stay."

He could feel Samara's compassionate gaze on his face. "What did you do?"

"Neither. She left her card for me to call her at the hotel where she's staying."

"And will you?"

Marcus stared up at the darkened ceiling, his gaze unfocused. "I honestly don't know, Samara. A part of me knows I should forgive her for cheating on my father and causing the divorce. I'm thirty-five years old, too damn old to be holding grudges from childhood. But any time I see her, or just think about her, all I see is her betrayal. And for the life of me, I can't get past it. Know what I mean?"

"I know exactly what you mean," Samara murmured, and Marcus remembered she *did* understand where he was coming from. Understood it better than anyone he'd ever known.

He couldn't remember whether that was a good or bad thing.

Shoving aside the unsettling thought, Marcus rolled her onto her back and pinned her beneath his body.

"I have just one question for you," he said, smiling down at her, wishing he could see her beautiful face better.

Lazily she rubbed the sole of her foot along the length of his calf. "What's that?"

"Do we have a game of strip poker in our future?"

Samara threw back her head and laughed.

Chapter Twelve

When Marcus strode through the door of the conference room the next morning—fifteen minutes late to a meeting with his senior associates—three pairs of eyes regarded him in surprise.

"Sorry for being late," he said as he took the seat that had been left vacant for him at the head of the conference table. Someday he'd like to shake things up a bit and see what would happen if he sat somewhere else.

"How's everyone doing this morning?" he asked, opening a thick manila folder crammed with notes and filings he'd brought to discuss during the meeting.

When his query was met with silence, he glanced up from the table. Donovan, Timothy and Helen Whitlaw were staring at him as if they'd never seen him before.

Marcus frowned. "What?"

Donovan spoke first, hitching his chin toward Marcus's open collar. "You forgot something."

Marcus glanced down and saw that, in his haste to get dressed that morning after leaving Samara's house, he'd forgotten to put on a tie. It was an uncharacteristic oversight, but he didn't think it warranted the strange looks he was getting from his colleagues.

"I've got some extra ties in my office," he said briskly. "I'll grab one after our meeting. Now—"

Timothy discreetly cleared his throat. "Uh, boss?" When Marcus looked at him, he pointed to his jaw. "You've got a little shaving cream…No, right there."

Marcus wiped the dab of foam from his face and reached inside his breast pocket for a handkerchief. When he didn't find one, he swore softly under his breath.

"Don't worry about it," Timothy said, an amused note in his voice. "You got all of it."

"Anything else?" Marcus demanded, looking around the table. "Do I have toothpaste on my chin? Is my fly open?"

Donovan, Timothy and Helen exchanged startled glances. And then, without warning, they burst into laughter.

Even Marcus felt a smile tugging at his lips.

The conference room door opened, and Laura stuck her head inside. "Sorry to interrupt—" She broke off, staring at the three laughing attorneys.

"What's up, Laura?" Marcus asked, since he seemed to be the only one capable of speech at the moment.

"There's a phone call for Ms. Whitlaw," Laura said. "I wouldn't have interrupted, but the caller said it was very important."

"Who is it, Laura?" Helen asked, sobering.

"It's your realtor. She said she tried to reach you on your cell phone, but—"

Helen jumped up from the table. "I'll take it in my office. We're engaged in an intense bidding war over my house in Atlanta," she explained to Marcus as she hurried to the door. "I'll be right back."

"Take your time." As Marcus poured himself a cup of coffee from the carafe on the table, Donovan and Timothy continued grinning at him.

"That must have been one helluva night you had, boss," Timothy remarked.

"Uh huh," Donovan chimed in. "Coming in here all disheveled. No tie, shaving cream on your face…"

"How is that such a big deal?" Marcus muttered.

Donovan laughed. "If we were talking about anyone else, it *wouldn't* be a big deal. But we're talking about *you*, man, so that changes the whole conversation. Marcus Wolf doesn't show up fifteen minutes late to meetings not wearing a tie, with shaving cream still on his face. It just doesn't happen. I knew him in college," Donovan explained to Timothy, "and even on the days when he was slumming, he *still* managed to be Mr. Smooth. Those Spelman chicks *loved* it."

Timothy laughed. "Well, he's not hurting with the ladies, that's for sure. We heard you brought a beautiful one to your brother's club on Saturday night. They said her name was Samara. Would she happen to be the same Samara you met at Georgetown last week?"

"So what if she is?" Marcus said.

A knowing gleam filled Donovan's eyes. "Things must be getting mighty serious if you're taking her home to meet the family."

"Maybe." Marcus took a sip of coffee, idly wondering if he'd made a mistake in handpicking Donovan and Timothy to help him establish the D.C. office. The two men weren't just employees; he considered them good friends, especially Donovan, with whom he shared a long history. But that was part of the problem. Friends were too damn nosy, and Marcus wasn't ready to share his news yet.

He was still getting used to the idea of being in love himself.

A white Rolls Royce limousine was staked out in front of the office building when Samara emerged that evening. It sat in the *No Parking* zone as if daring anyone to enforce the law. Samara's heart plummeted as soon as she spied the luxury vehicle.

She knew who was inside.

And she was struck by the irony of the timing. First Marcus's long-lost mother had paid him a visit yesterday at his office. Now it was Samara's turn.

As she walked past the Rolls, the tinted window in the rear of the limousine rolled halfway down. Her mother's face appeared, her eyes concealed behind an expensive pair of sunglasses.

"Samara."

For a moment Samara considered walking on, pretending she hadn't seen her mother or heard her voice. She stood stiffly with her back facing the limo.

"I called your office earlier," Asha spoke calmly, "but the receptionist said you were out for lunch. I didn't leave a message because I knew you wouldn't return my call."

Samara turned slowly around. "Why are you here, Mother?"

"I'm in town for the grand opening of my Georgetown boutique." She paused. "I was hoping we could talk."

"I believe we covered everything the last time we spoke."

"Samara…"

"I have nothing to say to you, Mother. Now if you'll excuse me, it's been a long day, and I'd really like to get home."

She turned and strode purposefully toward her car, furious with her mother for showing up unannounced and expecting Samara to drop everything to accommodate her.

So what else is new? She fumed as she tossed her briefcase across the passenger seat. Some things just never changed.

The good mood she'd enjoyed all day had evaporated when Asha appeared. This, too, was nothing new. Whenever things began to improve in Samara's life, her mother had always shown up out of the clear blue, sending her world tilting on its axis, demolishing what bit of progress she'd made.

A tap on the window startled her. She looked up in surprise to find her mother's longtime personal assistant, Pierre Jacques, standing outside the car.

Samara hesitated, then rolled down the window. Folding her arms across her chest, she regarded Pierre with one cynical brow arched. "Please don't tell me she sent you over here to get me."

"No, dearest, that was completely *my* doing." Pierre Jacques was medium height and slender, with spiky mousse-sculpted blond hair. He had delicate, almost effeminate features to include long eyelashes, high cheekbones and a generous poet's mouth. He wore tight black leather pants under a flowing white shirt.

Hands planted on narrow hips, he cast an appraising look over the Avalon through critical blue-gray eyes. "Interesting transportation you have here. Very 'working girl.' "

"Pierre, you didn't come over here to talk about my car."

He issued a dramatic sigh. "Dearest, you must come over at once and speak to your mother. I *implore* you."

"Why?"

"Because she has been an absolute nightmare to work with over the last two weeks! You would think after having such a successful spring collection and being the toast of town she would *finally* be happy, but alas, such is not the case. She's been screaming at everyone, issuing unreasonable demands and making life a living hell for the rest of us. Two of the wardrobe assistants have already quit, and I fear that if your mother's impossible behavior continues much longer, she won't have anyone left in her employment."

Samara couldn't help but grin. Pierre's predilection for melodrama could always extract a smile from her. "She'll always have *you*, Pierre. You're not going anywhere."

"That's because *I* am a glutton for punishment, *chère*. Why do you think I pop Prozac like candy? Listen, I don't know what you and your mother argued about after the premiere, but she hasn't been the same since you left New York."

"Why would this time be any different from any of our many other arguments?" Samara asked wryly.

"I haven't the faintest idea. Perhaps she's getting sentimental in her old age—although you didn't hear that from me. *Merde!* Asha would kill me if she ever heard me utter such a thing. Anyway, the point is, she came here hoping to speak with you. It may be that she feels bad about the last argument and wants to kiss and make up."

"Doubtful."

"At least hear what she has to say!" Pierre cried, waving his elegant hands in consternation. Leaning through the window, he gently but firmly grasped her upper arms. His expression was beseeching. "If you have an ounce of compassion left in that big heart of yours, Samara, you will go over there and talk to your mother, even if it's just for a few minutes."

"Pierre, I'd really rather not."

"Please, *chère*, I beg of you." He paused. "If not for yourself or Asha, then do it for me."

Samara hesitated, torn between warring loyalties. On one hand, she owed it to herself to finally be happy, a feat that could only be achieved through little or no interaction with her mother. If she climbed into that limousine and they argued again, Samara knew she would be back to square one, an emotional wreck.

On the other hand, Pierre *had* once come to her rescue against André Leclerc, her mother's spurned ex-lover who'd decided to get revenge by seducing Asha's sixteen-year-old daughter. When Samara rejected his advances, he'd become enraged and started beating her up. Pierre had, in all likelihood, saved her life by arriving when he did and driving her to the hospital.

Samara shuddered at the horrific memory. Yeah, she owed Pierre big time. The least she could do for him was talk to her mother, especially if he felt that it would improve Asha's disposition.

"All right," she reluctantly consented. "But I'm only doing this for you, Pierre."

"*Merci beaucoup, chère.*" Relieved, he kissed both of her cheeks. "I thank you, as will all of your mother's employees when we return to New York."

"I'm not promising any miracles," Samara grumbled as Pierre grabbed her hand and hastened her from the car.

A uniformed chauffeur emerged from the limousine to open the back door for Samara. Giving her a thumbs-up sign, Pierre climbed quickly into the front seat and closed the door before she could change her mind.

Asha was effortlessly sleek in a chic dark dress that subtly accentuated her voluptuous figure and the shapeliness of her crossed legs.

Her black hair was swept back into an elegant chignon that accented her high cheekbones and slanted dark eyes and the sensuous fullness of her mouth.

She was speaking tersely to someone on her cell phone and didn't look up as Samara climbed into the limo. "I know we've been selling well in the Midwest markets, especially after our last fall collection. It was the most conservative line we've done to date." She paused, drumming manicured fingertips against her knee. "René, we're long past the days of giving department stores the maximum discount on the clothing while eating our own advertising and overhead expenses. You *do* realize this? Then please act like it. Now, on to the next item." Another clipped pause. "*Bien*. We'll discuss it at the next strategy meeting on Friday. If anything else comes up, you know where to reach me. *Au revoir.*"

Asha disconnected and slid the phone inside the sleek black sachet at her feet. Smiling congenially, she leaned across the plush leather seat and kissed Samara on both cheeks. "Sorry about that shop talk, darling. That was the VP of Operations—my people never give me a moment's peace, even when I'm out of town."

"You've always been in demand, Mother," Samara said without inflection.

Asha laughed humorlessly. "After months of conducting extensive market studies, we're preparing to launch a perfume line. You know it's always been part of my vision to enter the cosmetics and perfume industry, but I wanted to establish the clothing line first. Our marketing division is currently working on concepts for the ad campaign—the market study revealed the sheer importance of package design, both in the bottle containing the perfume as well as the package in which it is sold." She paused, a whimsical smile teasing the corners of her mouth. "But then, I'm not telling you anything you don't already know, with your marketing background. I wonder what kind of creative ideas *you* would come up with for the new perfume."

Samara stiffened. "Mother—"

Asha held up a hand. "Relax, darling. I'm not trying to recruit you for the ad campaign. I think I've finally learned my lesson in *that* regard. Anyway, that's not why I'm here. I thought we could have dinner together."

"I'm not very hungry. I had a late lunch."

"All right, then. We'll just take a scenic drive around town." She pushed a button to roll down the tinted glass window separating the front and back seat. She gave instructions to the chauffeur before raising the glass partition again. As the limo glided forward, she gave her daughter an assessing look. "You're looking rather well. Lavender—that's a nice color on you. Not everyone can wear it. The cut of the suit is quite flattering, too."

"I'm glad to hear that my appearance passes inspection," Samara murmured dryly. She found it ironic that while she was irritated by her mother's words, there were many who would kill for such a compliment from the esteemed Asha Dubois.

After years on the modeling circuit, Asha had received a rare opportunity to study fashion design at the prestigious *Académie de Couture* in Paris—a dream come true. She'd trained under some of the best in the business, honing her raw talents while rubbing elbows with the world's most prominent couturiers. Upon graduating from the *Académie* she'd gone to work for Givenchy. After years of paying her dues and establishing a name for herself as a promising up-and-coming designer, Asha had left Givenchy to launch her own couture house—a gamble that paid off major dividends. After building a base in Paris using her hard-earned connections, she'd returned to the States to expand operations, acquiring boutiques in principal money markets and buying interests in major department stores. Through hard work and persistence, she'd proven to be an astute business-woman as well as a talented designer. Last month marked almost fifteen years to the day House of Dubois made its official U.S. debut at a spring collection in New York and was met with rave reviews. Her signature clothing line was selling exceptionally well across the country, aided by an aggressive marketing campaign. At the age of forty-seven, Asha Dubois was on the brink of making fashion history as one of the first African-American couturiers to cross international lines.

Despite their estrangement, Samara had never stopped being proud of her mother's accomplishments. Asha had overcome tremendous hardships in order to see her dreams fulfilled, and the fact that minorities were still greatly underrepresented in the fashion industry made her success much more admirable.

Samara turned her head to stare out the tinted window as the limousine followed Pennsylvania Avenue as it merged from the northeast to the northwest quadrant of the city, winding past such tourist favorites as the J. Edgar Hoover FBI building, the White House, the Blair House and the Old Executive Office Building.

"I owe you an apology, Samara."

Startled from her musings, Samara swung her head around to stare at her mother. "Excuse me?"

Asha winced. "Don't sound so incredulous, darling. It's not as if I have never apologized to anyone in my life before."

Samara was silent, and Asha laughed ruefully. "Perhaps it's something I should practice more often. All right, then. It's never too late to add items to my New Year's resolution list."

"I didn't know you kept a list. It never occurred to me that you, of all people, would have need of one."

"Because it seems like such a frivolous thing to do?"

"Not so much frivolous. Normal."

"You've been reading too many tabloid stories about me, *chère*. You'd be surprised to hear the many 'normal' things your mother does." When Samara said nothing, Asha cleared her throat discreetly. "As I was saying, I owe you an apology. You were right to be angry with me for not giving you the donation I had promised. I regret that I reneged on our deal."

Samara grew still, shocked into momentary silence by her mother's unexpected words. "Then why did you do it?"

Asha stared at the diamond twinkling on her right hand, her expression remote and reflective. "I suppose I hoped if the Institute did not survive its financial turmoil, you would consider coming to work for me. I now realize this was wrong of me. I felt even worse when I learned that the organization was bailed out by an anonymous donor that should have been me."

Samara fell silent again, absorbing her mother's words. She couldn't remember the last time Asha had been so transparent with her. She honestly didn't know what to think.

She turned in the seat to face her. "Let me ask you a question, Mother. Why is it so hard for you to accept that I enjoy my work, even if it's not associated with your company? We haven't been close in years, so please don't say you want me there for sentimental reasons. Plenty of your designer friends have grown children that aren't involved in the business. Why is this so unacceptable for *your* child?"

Asha bristled. "I don't think there's anything abnormal about a parent wanting their child to take an active role in their business. Do you honestly believe that everything I'm building is for my *own* legacy—the clothing lines, the perfume? Will I care about being mentioned in the annals of fashion history once I'm dead and buried? Don't get me wrong, Samara. I'm loving every minute of my success. I worked hard for it; I deserve to enjoy it. But don't think for one second that you aren't part of the equation, that you aren't a motivating factor behind everything I do. When I leave this earth, I want to leave with the assurance that you are financially set for life. I never, *ever*, want you to suffer the way I did, or have to depend on any man for your survival. And I make no apologies for that."

"I'm not asking you to apologize for that, Mother! God knows I appreciate the many sacrifices you've made for me. If I've ever given you the impression that I'm even remotely ungrateful, allow *me* to apologize because that was never my intention. But Mother, there's so much more…" Her voice caught on a tremor, and she closed her eyes against the predictable sting of tears.

You will not *cry,* she mentally ordered. *Pull yourself together and see this through.*

She drew a deep breath that burned in her lungs before continuing, "There is so much more to being a parent than providing financial security, You have far more to offer than that."

Asha turned her head to stare out the window, but not before Samara detected moisture in her own eyes. Asha's profile was stony. "I don't know what you want from me, Samara."

"I want you to be my mother again!" Samara cried. "I want to enjoy being your daughter again! I want to know you'll be there for me when I need you, and that you'll turn to me whenever *you* need someone to lean on. We're all each other have left in the world, yet we're keeping a world of distance between us. *Why?*"

Asha was silent for so long that Samara feared she wouldn't respond. "You know," Asha said distantly, keeping her face averted, "I actually believe things were better between us when we were poor and down on our luck, moving from one place to the next. Perhaps my modeling career was the worst thing that could have happened to our relationship."

"How can that be," Samara countered softly, "When it was the best thing that ever happened to *you?*"

"Ah, that is the $64,000 question, is it not?" Asha lifted her shoulders in an elegant, dismissive shrug. "*C'est la vie.* Life is a paradox, *chère.* One we're not meant to understand or examine too closely."

Samara hated it when her mother resorted to riddles and clichés to avoid serious discussions. What was she running from? *Would the real Asha Dubois please stand up?*

Samara suddenly felt very tired and emotionally drained. She glanced at her watch. "It's getting late. I really need to get home and catch up on some paperwork."

Asha looked at her then. "No special evening plans? That's rather surprising."

"Why?"

"Because when I first saw you this evening, I swore you had the look of a woman deeply in love."

Samara faltered, at a loss for words. Was she *that* transparent, or had her mother added clairvoyance to her exhaustive list of talents?

"So I wasn't mistaken." Asha's lips curved in an intuitive smile. "A mother knows these things, darling. Who is he?"

"You wouldn't know him," Samara mumbled, then felt compelled to add, "Besides, it's not that serious."

"What a shame. You looked quite blissful. Flushed, even."

Heat flooded Samara's cheeks as she remembered the long hours of lovemaking with Marcus in the dark, rainy night. "Do you think you could ask the driver to turn around and take me back to my car?"

Asha sighed in resignation. "*Certainement.*"

Hours later, Samara was still trying unsuccessfully to put her mother's visit out of her mind. Asha's sudden appearance, and her unexpected apology, had thrown Samara for a loop. Asha had *never* apologized to her before. Not for abandoning her as a child, not for repeatedly disrupting her life. She'd never apologized for not accepting Samara's decision to pursue her own career path.

And to this day, Asha had never apologized for accusing Samara of seducing André Leclerc, thereby inviting his brutal attack.

Samara had more than enough reasons to sever her mother from her life. But try as she might, she couldn't.

Beneath all the pain and resentment, she was still the same little girl who'd sat at her mother's dressing table the night of her very first fashion show in Philadelphia, giggling hysterically as her mother tickled her. She was still the same reclusive teenager who'd kept a secret collection of clippings from every magazine and newspaper Asha ever appeared in, dreaming that one day her mother would climb down from her mountaintop and realize how much she missed her daughter.

No matter how many times Asha disappointed her, a tiny part of Samara always held on to the hope that all was not lost between them, that someday they *could* have a healthy mother/daughter relationship.

What had Pierre called himself earlier? A glutton for punishment? He wasn't the only one. Samara was a glutton for punishment if ever there had been one.

Needing a distraction, she set aside her paperwork and popped in a *Sex and the City* DVD. She was sitting around in her bra and panties, giggling through the famous episode about Charlotte's boyfriend with the uncircumcised dick, when Marcus called.

"Hey, beautiful," he said, his deep voice pouring into her ear like honey. "What are you doing?"

When she told him, he chuckled softly. "I heard that episode pissed off a lot of people. Someone even contacted me about filing a defamation lawsuit against the producers of the show."

"Hmm. Well, I guess it's a sensitive issue." Realizing what she'd said, she started laughing at the same time as Marcus.

When their laughter subsided, he said huskily, "I miss you. What are you going to do about that?"

Samara smiled into the receiver. "I don't know. What *should* I do about it?"

"Let me come over and show you."

Her toes curled inside her furry pink bedroom slippers. "You could," she murmured. "Or I could come over there, since I've never been to your place before."

"Mmm, sounds like a plan. I'll order Chinese."

"And I'll bring dessert."

"Sweetheart, you're all the sugar I need," Marcus drawled in those dark, velvety tones of his.

Samara's nipples hardened. "Give me thirty minutes."

Chapter Thirteen

Twenty minutes later, a smiling Marcus opened the door and gestured Samara inside his penthouse.

The private foyer was bathed in warm buttery light that spilled across the Italian tile floor and into a large sunken living room.

"Nice," Samara murmured appreciatively.

"Thanks. You had no trouble finding the place?"

"None whatsoever. I grew up here, remember? I know this city like the back of my hand." Her spiky heels sank into luxuriant Berber as she crossed the endless expanse of empty space to a wall of glass windows, which overlooked a wide balcony that provided a stunning view of the Potomac River. It would be spectacular to watch the sunset from there, or to recline in lounge chairs on a sticky July evening to take in the fireworks display on the National Mall.

"Great view," Samara remarked, turning away from the window before her imagination could roam wild. She had to remind herself not to assume that she and Marcus had a future together—just because she now wanted it more than her next breath.

"It is," Marcus agreed, approaching her from behind. She marveled that such a powerfully built man could move with so little sound. Stealthy as a panther—or wolf. "Maybe tomorrow morning we can sit out here and watch the sun rise," he bent low to murmur in her ear.

She felt a slow, hot tingle of anticipation. "Assuming I spend the night," she said offhandedly, knowing good and well she wasn't going anywhere.

The roguish glint in Marcus's eyes told her he knew it, too.

Sidestepping him, she wandered over to a row of crates on which stood an elaborate stereo system. The only other items of furniture were a cherry bistro table and two matching chairs in the dining room. "Where's the rest of your furniture?"

"Stayed with the house in Atlanta. The renters paid extra to keep it furnished."

"So when are you going to furnish the penthouse?"

"Eventually. I haven't spent much time here yet. But I've got the essentials."

"Essentials, huh?"

"The barest. A bed, too, if you'd like to see it."

She grinned. "Nice try, Slick."

Marcus chuckled as he headed from the living room. "It was worth a shot."

Samara hung up her jacket in the foyer closet before following him into the gourmet kitchen. More Italian tile, stainless steel appliances and an island in the center of the floor. A cardboard box sat unopened on the counter near the Sub-Zero refrigerator. It was labeled KITCHEN in black magic marker.

"Let me guess. Dishes?"

Marcus glanced over his shoulder as he rummaged through the cabinets. "There might be a few in there. My housekeeper packed that box for me before I left Atlanta."

"Marcus," Samara said, unsure whether to laugh or scold, "you mean to tell me you've been living here a whole month and haven't unpacked any of your kitchen items yet?"

"Haven't gotten around to it." Triumphantly, he held up a new package of paper plates. "That's why these were invented."

Samara rolled her eyes. "Bachelors," she said in mock disgust. "God forbid you should take a few minutes to open the box and actually begin using *real* plates—oops, but then you'd have to load them into the dishwasher, too!"

Marcus grinned unabashedly. "My point exactly."

Working together, they piled fragrant helpings of lo mein and vegetables and Szechuan chicken onto the plates, grabbed cold sodas from the refrigerator and settled down at the small dining room table. While they ate, they listened to slow jams and talked about anything and everything. Samara considered, then decided not to tell Marcus about Asha's unexpected appearance at her office. Although he'd told her about his own mother's visit yesterday, Samara didn't want him remembering how much baggage *she* had.

"I just remembered another one of your hidden talents," Marcus drawled when he'd finished teasing her about singing at his brother's restaurant.

"What?"

"The fact that you're a tiger tamer."

For a moment Samara was confused. And then she remembered the premiere in New York and laughed. "I do *not* tame tigers."

"Sure as hell looked like it to me. You were the only one in that showroom not scared out of your mind when that tiger stepped onstage."

"As I told you and Walt, Pandora and I are old friends. She remembered me."

Marcus took a sip of Pepsi, catching a stray drop from his bottom lip with the tip of his tongue. Samara couldn't look away, suddenly reliving all the ways he'd pleasured her with that incredibly talented tongue of his.

"How'd that happen, by the way?" Marcus asked. At her blank look, he clarified, "How'd you come to befriend a tiger?"

"I agreed to accompany my mother on a photo assignment in Johannesburg the summer before I graduated from college." She grimaced. "Let's just say the best part of the trip was being there for Pandora's birth."

Marcus looked faintly amused. "Africa didn't agree with you?"

"No," Samara grumbled, "being around a bunch of prima donna supermodels didn't agree with me. Anyway, the animal trainers took pity on me and let me hang around between photo shoots. It was really cool. When Pandora was born, they allowed me to name her."

"Why'd you choose the name Pandora?"

"Nothing deep." Samara paused, distracted by the sight of a long noodle sliding between Marcus's juicy lips. God, she envied the lo mein on his plate right now. "It was my favorite Greek mythology tale in high school. What was yours?"

Marcus chuckled. "That would have to be Bellerophon and Pegasus. I admired Bellerophon's gutsy arrogance when he challenged the gods and stormed Mount Olympus, even though it cost him in the end. And, hey, what can I say about Pegasus? A winged horse—what better mode of transportation could a guy ask for?"

Samara laughed. "That was my second favorite Greek tragedy. I even wrote a short story about it for English class."

Marcus grinned. "Where have you been all my life, woman?"

Although he was only teasing, Samara's heart thumped just the same.

When they'd finished their meals and the plates were cleared away, Marcus casually announced, "I have a brand-new deck of poker cards waiting to be broken in. That is, if you're up for a friendly game?"

Samara grinned. "Oh, Marcus, I'd feel really bad about taking your money. Which is ridiculous, considering you have more than enough to spare."

"Is that a yes or no?"

She shrugged. "Sure, why not? It's not like you don't already know about my *championship* poker skills," she said smugly. "I have no reason to feel guilty if you're still willing to take me on."

Marcus chuckled. "Confident, aren't we?"

"I think I have reason to be," she said as he disappeared into the kitchen and returned with a deck of playing cards. Samara rolled her eyes in exasperation. The man couldn't unpack a simple box of kitchen supplies, but he had a readily available deck of poker cards. For that reason alone she'd have fun beating him.

She dug into her jeans pocket as he began setting up at the small bistro table. "We'll have to keep the ante low. I'm not sure I brought enough cash—"

"We're not playing for money."

"What?"

"You heard me. Yesterday you promised me a game of strip poker, remember?"

"I did not! You asked me if we had a game of strip poker in our future, and I just laughed. I *never* promised anything."

"What's the matter, Samara?" Marcus challenged, a wicked gleam in his eyes. "Afraid you might lose?"

She lifted a haughty chin. "Of course not." She sat down decisively at the table. "Deal."

"Before we start, I'd like to establish some ground rules. When you lose a hand—"

"*If*, you mean."

"I get to decide which article of clothing comes off." His mouth twitched in amusement. "Considering that I'm way out of my league here, I think it's only fair to spot me at least one advantage."

Samara hesitated, her eyes narrowed on his face. "Well, I suppose that wouldn't be a problem."

She had no intention of losing a game of strip poker to Marcus.

An hour later, she was eating some serious humble pie—in spades.

"Read 'em and weep." With a look of smug satisfaction, Marcus displayed his cards on the table with a flourish.

Samara's heart sank when she saw his hand. An ace high straight-flush. His third royal flush. He was beating the pants off her—literally.

Marcus leaned back in his chair with an air of relaxed confidence. "Perhaps *I* should consider entering a poker tournament. I never realized just how good I am."

Samara scowled darkly. "I'm having an off night," she muttered.

"Hmm. Well, speaking of 'off'..." He looked pointedly at her angora sweater. "I believe you have some stripping to do."

Samara groaned in protest. "Not my sweater! Couldn't I just remove my other sock?" She'd already lost her boots and one sock in the course of the competition. Marcus had been generous thus far, picking her slowly apart the way a hunter methodically stalks his prey. Now he was closing in for the kill.

He shook his head slowly from side to side. "No deal—the sweater goes."

Pouting, Samara stood and pulled off the sweater, tossing it impatiently aside. "If I catch a cold because I'm sitting around in *your* air-conditioned penthouse with no clothes on..."

The words died on her lips at the look on Marcus's face. He was staring at her satin-covered breasts with blatant hunger. Even as her knees wobbled traitorously in response, she knew she'd just found her ace in the hole. It was so simple she wanted to kick herself for not thinking of it earlier. She should have lobbied to remove the sweater the first time she lost, then used her partial nudity as a way to distract him from the game. After all, poker was as much a mental game as one of skill and chance. If one had difficulty concentrating on the game...

Ah, strategy was such a beautiful thing.

Smiling demurely, she lowered herself back down into the chair, causing her breasts to bounce just a little as she sat. She made an exaggerated show of leaning way across the table to retrieve the cards so that she could deal the next hand. She noted, with triumph, the way his dark eyes fastened on the swell of her cleavage. She half expected him to lick his lips he was so riveted.

Men are so predictable.

Her ploy worked. Marcus lost the next hand.

"Guess you'll have to lose your other boot," Samara said blithely. He'd lost one boot when she won the first hand, not knowing it would be her last taste of victory.

But instead of toeing off his boot, Marcus removed his gray pullover, the muscles in his wide chest bunching and rippling with the fluid movement. Samara's stomach flipped over, and her mouth went dry. All that glorious mahogany skin. The flat, dark nipples she loved to suck every time they made love. The taut, beautifully sculpted abdomen she braced her palms against as she straddled him, climbing toward one climax after another.

"W-What are you doing?" she managed hoarsely. "You're supposed to remove your *boot*, not your shirt." No way was he going to turn the tables on her with the distraction game!

"I never said *you* could tell *me* which articles of clothing to remove. Besides," he said, smiling rakishly, "isn't the whole point of strip poker to get your opponent 'stripped' down to the last stitch of clothing?"

Samara swallowed with difficulty. "Fine. Have it your way."

"Oh, I fully intend to," Marcus said, his voice husky with promise. He looked so incredibly male and virile that she had to drag her gaze away from him.

Despite the fact that she kept her eyes carefully trained on her cards, she lost the next hand. Without saying a word, Marcus leaned back in his chair and stretched out his long legs, watching her expectantly.

Suppressing her frustration, Samara rose to her feet and unsnapped her jeans. Holding his gaze, she slid the tight denim slowly, provocatively, over her waist and down her legs. She even rotated her hips for good measure and was rewarded when Marcus's eyes grew hooded, darkening with desire.

"Come here," he said huskily.

His words sent hot shivers through her whole body. She shook her head, a naughty smile playing at the corners of her mouth. She stepped carefully out of her jeans and kicked them aside, along with the remaining lone sock she wore. "We're not finished with our game yet."

"Yes we are. You lost."

"Is that right? Then I suppose I owe you some type of reward."

"There's only one thing I want right now, Samara," Marcus said in a voice roughened with need, "and it has nothing whatsoever to do with poker."

"Mmmm," she purred. "I wonder what *that* could be."

Despite her teasing tone, it was with a combination of nerves and anticipation that she stood trembling before him. He sat silently with his hands clenched at his sides, and she could tell how much of a struggle it was for him not to pounce on her. The knowledge filled her with immense feminine power.

He ran his eyes over her body as if it were his first time seeing her. Samara just stood there, erect nipples pressing painfully against her satin bra, allowing him to drink his fill of her.

"You are so beautiful," he finally murmured.

Her legs quivered. "You'll say anything to get what you want," she tried to joke, but her voice was too throaty, too tight with arousal to successfully deliver the line.

With a muffled groan, Marcus leaned forward and wrapped his arms tightly around her waist, burying his face against her belly and rubbing back and forth. Her eyes closed and her head tipped back as his hands roamed up her spine to unclasp her bra, sliding the straps from her shoulders and sending the scrap of lace to the floor. She felt only a moment of cool air upon her exposed flesh before his large hand gently covered one breast, his warm mouth enveloping the other. He licked the left nipple, circling the tight point with his tongue before catching it between his teeth and applying delicate pressure. At the same time, his other hand teased and tormented her nipple until she thought she would explode.

"No, wait," she gasped, stepping quickly out of his embrace.

Marcus swore raggedly under his breath. "Please don't make me beg."

"Shhh." Samara laid a finger to his lips. "I'm not going to make you beg. Just sit back and relax."

Chest heaving, Marcus watched as she knelt between his legs. She ran her hand invitingly down his chest before leaning forward and placing her lips to his heated flesh. His breath quickened as she rained hot kisses all over him.

Next she reached for the zipper of his jeans, and he sucked in air sharply as her fingers slipped inside and grasped his hardened penis, freeing him. Holding his gaze, she took him deep into her mouth. She laved and suckled him until he flung his head back against the chair, groaning in sheer ecstasy.

"Samara, I don't think I can take much more."

Filled with pleasure at the raw need in his voice, Samara straightened from her kneeling position and smoothly straddled his lap.

"Wait," Marcus whispered hoarsely. He dug into his pocket for his wallet, his fingers somewhat clumsy as he withdrew a condom. Samara took it from him and raised herself above him so that she could tug his jeans and briefs off. He lifted his hips, helping to facilitate the swift removal.

He groaned as she sheathed him with the condom, smoothing it over his engorged shaft with deliberate slowness. Then, as he stared in helpless fascination, she slipped her fingers beneath the waistband of her panties, leisurely dragging the black satin off her hips and over her legs before tossing it aside.

As she climbed into his lap again, he lifted his head to receive her kiss, letting her explore his mouth with deep, languid strokes of her tongue that made him moan. She took his throbbing penis in her hand and guided it into her body. As he entered her, she inhaled sharply and bit her lip to keep from screaming at the exquisite pleasure of it. They both closed their eyes and sighed deeply as she continued lowering herself until he filled her completely. His hands came up, grasping her hips as he prepared to begin thrusting into her.

But Samara had other plans. After taking just a few moments to savor the sensation of him embedded inside her, she raised herself up until he almost slipped from her body. Then, slowly undulating her hips, she lowered herself again, never taking him completely into her.

Marcus went insane with lust as she repeated the motion again and again. With a low, guttural oath, he arched and dug his fingers into her buttocks, trying to hold her in place so that he could bury himself deep inside her. But Samara resisted his desperate attempts and raised herself once again. She captured his agonized groans in her mouth, telling him in sultry whispers to be patient.

But as she felt her own body begin to convulse around him, she wondered how much longer she could keep up the slow, maddening pace. Especially when she wanted nothing more than to have him deep inside her, thrusting and possessing her.

She lowered herself a little more, then clenched her inner muscles as she rose up one final time. They both moaned at the deeply erotic sensation. Marcus slipped his fingers beneath her buttocks until they found what they were searching for and plunged inside. Samara paused in mid-stroke, shocked into crying out as he caressed her wet vagina.

Arching against him in surrender, she pushed her breasts into his face, wanting to be filled with him until she soared into blissful oblivion. His mouth covered one erect nipple, suckling greedily and nearly sending her over the edge. She arched again to take him all the way into her body and wrapped her legs tightly around his waist, shaking violently with need. She began moving on him, faster and faster, until they were both breathless, until their bodies slapped noisily together over the sound of John Legend crooning softly in the background.

"I'm…almost there," she gasped. She threw back her head and panted Marcus's name until the last of his restraint snapped.

Grabbing her hips, he thrust deep and hard, devouring her, literally screwing her brains out. She cried out wildly as she erupted, burying her face in the crook of his shoulder to absorb the violent shudder that swept through her.

Marcus controlled his own urges and slowly rebuilt her desire, stroke by stroke, until she climaxed once again, rhythmic cries tearing from her throat. Only then did he let himself go, gripping her back tightly and moaning with his own explosive release. They clung to each other as their racing heartbeats gradually steadied and their ragged breaths quieted.

Marcus held her in place, stroking a hand down her slick back. His lips brushed her cheek and grazed her moist mouth, kissing her slow and deep. When they at last parted, they could do no more than lean their damp foreheads against each other's.

"Samara."

"Yes, Marcus?"

He chuckled softly. "I haven't even asked yet."

"Asked what?"

He ran his fingers down the smooth column of her spine. "Will you marry me?"

Samara stiffened for a moment before lifting shocked eyes to his face. "*What?*"

He looked her straight in the eye. "Will you marry me?"

Tears rushed to her eyes. "Oh my God! Are you *serious?*"

"As serious as I'll ever be. I'm in love with you, Samara. I want you to be my wife."

Her hand flew to her mouth. A tear slipped from her eye, followed by another and another, until she was openly weeping.

Marcus attempted humor. "You're crying. That can't be a good thing."

She laughed softly through her tears. "Of course I'll marry you, Marcus. I love you so much, and I wasn't sure whether you felt the same."

Marcus leaned forward and caught her lips in a deep, possessive kiss. "Does this feel like I don't feel the same?" he whispered against her mouth. He kissed her again and again like he couldn't get enough. "Does this?"

"Oh, Marcus." Samara's arms tightened around his neck. He tenderly kissed away her tears, one by one, before reclaiming her mouth. They held each other tightly, their heartbeats pounding in unison.

As the kiss intensified, Marcus rose from the chair with her legs still wrapped around his waist. "Let's finish this in the bedroom," he growled, already striding purposefully down the corridor.

He kicked the bedroom door shut behind them, and minutes later their exultant cries penetrated the walls as they loved each other long into the night.

When Samara awoke the next morning, the first thing she remembered was Marcus's marriage proposal. In the pale light of day, she didn't know which was more shocking to her: the proposal itself, or her swift response. She could hardly believe she'd accepted—and yet she knew no other response would have been possible.

She was hopelessly in love with Marcus. She wanted to spend the rest of her life with him.

"What's going through that beautiful head of yours?"

Samara looked over and found Marcus awake and watching her quietly. The room's predawn shadows enhanced the faint growth of stubble along his jaw, making him look roguishly sexy.

"Good morning," she murmured.

"Mmm. It is, isn't it?" he drawled, his voice a deep, husky rumble she felt in the pit of her stomach.

As he raised himself up on one elbow to gaze down at her, Samara felt her breath catch in her throat. In his eyes she could easily become lost, carried away in those infinite pools of onyx. And in that instant she realized the enormity of her situation. It was dangerous to have allowed herself to fall so hard for Marcus. She'd spent years avoiding serious relationships in order to protect herself from heartache. In less than two weeks, Marcus Wolf had infiltrated her ironclad defenses and invaded her heart.

And there was no turning back.

Almost tentatively, Samara reached up and cradled his lean cheek in her hand. Her eyes searched his. "Marcus, about last night…" she trailed off uncertainly.

Marcus turned his head and kissed the center of her palm, his expression serious. "The answer is yes. I meant to propose to you last night, and I don't regret it this morning." His solemn gaze traced her features. "Do you regret accepting?"

Samara shook her head against the pillow. "No."

He smiled, then bent his head and kissed her gently on the lips. Hope bloomed in Samara's chest. Maybe it was finally time to let go of her fears. Maybe everything would be all right from now on.

She curved a hand around Marcus's neck, holding him closer as she deepened the kiss. He murmured his approval against her mouth. Before she could draw another breath, he swept her into his arms, swung his long legs from the bed and carried her into the adjoining bathroom.

She had only a glimpse of gleaming brass faucets and black marble tile before steam enveloped them inside the glass shower stall. She stared up at Marcus as he stood before her, naked and fully aroused, water sluicing down his powerful body. Her throat went dry as desire flooded her, a pulsing ache between her legs.

Dark eyes smoldering, Marcus lifted a bar of soap and began lathering his hands instead of a washcloth. Samara swallowed with difficulty as he slowly massaged the froth of bubbles into her shoulders.

"You know," she managed huskily, "I can wash myself."

His eyes flickered with a devilish glint. "Of course you can."

She gasped as deliciously callused hands covered her sensitive breasts and slathered soap onto the swollen mounds. "As a matter of fact," she continued thickly, "I've been washing myself for a long time now. And I think—" Her voice broke as his slippery hands made their way down her torso. She quivered uncontrollably when he caressed her thighs.

"Marcus…"

"Shhh. Just relax." He knelt and focused his attention on the curve of her calves, then the delicate arch of her feet. Samara closed her eyes as his hands glided up her legs once again. He paused for a moment, and Samara swore she could feel the heat of his gaze scorching her wet flesh. She held herself rigid until his hand reached her feminine triangle. He massaged soap into the silken tuft of hair before one finger slipped beyond and began caressing her intimately. Samara moaned and grasped his shoulders.

Before she could recover from the erotic ministrations, he drew his head toward her body. His finger was replaced by the warm stroke of his tongue.

Samara cried out sharply and threw back her head. Need pounded furiously through her. Her legs parted of their own accord, allowing him greater access. She cradled the back of his head as his wet tongue probed deep inside her. Her moans of ecstasy escalated, piercing the steamy shower stall. Marcus's expert tongue glided over the swollen folds of flesh, back and forth, in and out, suckling lavishly, until Samara could take no more. She screamed his name as her body began convulsing.

Marcus caught her in his arms as he straightened from his kneeling position. Flesh met flesh as his mouth took hot possession of hers, sharing her taste with her. He pressed his firm erection against her stomach and deepened the carnal kiss until it grew wild and fiery, their tongues mating frantically. He backed Samara against the shower wall and gripped her hips, lifting her from the floor. She clung to his shoulders and wrapped her legs around his waist.

Marcus groaned softly as he entered her. Samara arched her back, and he plunged deeper within her, their bodies moving in perfect unison as they quickly found their rhythm. Warm water caressed their limbs, adding to the sheer sensuality of their coupling. Marcus cupped her buttocks as he thrust harder and faster, his smoldering gaze boring into hers.

"Talk to me," he huskily commanded above the shower's roar and their mingled moans. "Are you all right?"

"I'm good," came her breathless reply. He increased the tempo and she groaned. "Better than good."

She was on the verge of shattering when Marcus rocked his hips one final time and stiffened against her, his grip tightening on her buttocks. Their loud cries blended as they climaxed together in a violent rush.

Minutes later a weakened Samara emerged from the steamy bathroom and collapsed on the bed while Marcus finished showering. She was completely exhausted from their lovemaking marathon, and it was barely six in the morning. She couldn't imagine returning to her house to get dressed for work. For the first time in a long time, *work* was the last thing on her mind.

She sat up as Marcus stepped from the bathroom with a bath towel draped around his waist and strode across the large room to the walk-in closet. As she watched, he opened the doors to reveal an enormous closet filled with an arsenal of business suits. All of them were Italian and professionally pressed, lining the cavernous closet with military precision.

Samara whistled softly through her teeth. "So *that's* where your fortune is going." Marcus merely grinned at her over his shoulder.

She lay down again and snuggled deeper into the downy softness of the cotton bath towel she was wrapped in. The towel was so big it hung well past her knees. She sighed languidly. "I don't think I can move, Marcus. You might come home this evening and find me in the exact same position."

Marcus chuckled, eyeing her in the huge bed with her damp hair spread across the pillow. "I'd have no objections to that. Matter of fact," he drawled wickedly, approaching the bed, "It would make it a lot easier to pick up where we left off."

"That works," Samara replied sleepily, "because I'm going to need about ten or twelve hours to get my second wind."

Marcus sat down on the edge of the bed near her. Lovingly, he caressed her smooth bare shoulder. "I know we've been other-wise…occupied, but have you given any thought to possible wedding dates?"

That instantly rejuvenated her. She pulled herself up to a sitting position and looked at him. Her voice was soft with surprised wonder. "You mean you're ready to discuss details?" *So he was serious about this.*

"Of course." Marcus traced the soft shell of her ear with a lazy finger. "Don't tell me. You're surprised because you assumed most men leave all the planning to their fiancées and just show up on the appointed day."

Samara grinned sheepishly. "Well…"

"I'm not most men, Samara." He smiled at her to soften the mild censure in his tone. "I was actually thinking about an early September wedding."

"*This* September? But it's already April."

Marcus was nonplussed. "Does it take longer than six months to plan a wedding?"

"It depends on how elaborate the ceremony will be. You have to take so many things into consideration, like reserving a place for the reception, securing a caterer, ordering invitations and flowers." She ticked off the items on her fingers while Marcus tried not to reel from information overload. "And then there's my wedding gown, which I suppose could be bought off the rack for the sake of time—"

Marcus shook his head. "No. I want something special made just for you. A wedding gown you would cherish for years to come, maybe pass along to our daughter someday."

"Oh, Marcus." Samara was deeply touched by the sentimentality of his words. She reached out, laying a gentle hand across his cheek. She suddenly felt foolish for running off at the mouth like that. She'd never imagined she would become one of those obsessed bridezillas whose constant companion was a monstrously thick binder filled with wedding details from A-Z.

Come to think of it, she'd never imagined getting married. Period.

"None of that other stuff matters," she said softly to Marcus. "As long as we're together, I don't care what I wear. I would marry you in a burlap sack if you didn't object."

He chuckled softly. "Sweetheart, I would still think you were the most beautiful bride I'd ever seen." He leaned close and kissed her gently on the lips. "I love you."

"And that's enough for me," Samara whispered against his warm mouth. She draped her arms around his neck, and they shared a long, deep kiss.

When they drew apart, Samara wore a shy smile. "I *have* thought of the perfect place to hold the wedding though. It actually occurred to me while we were there—not that I was expecting *us* to get married at the time or anything," she hastened to add.

Marcus smiled softly. "I know what you meant. Now where's this perfect place?"

"The garden at your father's home in Stone Mountain. It's breathtaking."

"You're right, it is." His smile deepened. "I think that's a wonderful idea, baby girl."

"You do?" She threw her arms around his neck excitedly. "It's going to be beautiful, Marcus! Just wait and see."

"I can't wait."

"Marcus?"

"Hmm?"

She pulled back, her eyes twinkling with sudden mischief. "Let's play hooky today. The weather's supposed to be gorgeous. We could go down to the Tidal Basin to see the cherry blossoms before they're gone. Then we can act like tourists and do a little sightseeing around D.C., maybe have lunch on a ferry."

"Sounds good, but…"

"I finished all of my important meetings yesterday. What about you?"

"I don't have any meetings today. But I do have a few conference calls scheduled."

"Okay…maybe next time." Samara tried not to sound too disappointed. She understood how incredibly busy he was, especially since he was trying to get his new office established. She didn't want to interfere with his work.

"One of those conference calls could be postponed until next week," Marcus said slowly, thinking aloud, "and my senior associates can handle the other two for me. I just need to call and bring them up to speed."

"Only if you're absolutely sure it won't be a problem."

"It's no problem." His gaze softened on her face. "I'd be a fool to pass up on the opportunity to spend an entire day with my bride-to-be."

She warmed with pleasure. "We'll have a great time, I promise."

Marcus used the phone on the side table to call the office. Samara stared at his handsome profile as he gave instructions to his secretary.

While he spoke on the phone, he never stopped touching Samara. He stroked her hair and ran his finger down her arm. Without missing a beat, he reached beneath the towel and found her breast. Samara gasped as he cupped her breast in his warm palm before brushing the pad of his thumb across the nipple, making it tighten in response. Marcus met her aroused look with a slow, knowing grin.

Two can play that game, thought Samara. She shifted her body away from his marauding caresses and knelt on the bed beside him. As he watched her, she leaned close, lightly nipping his earlobe with her teeth. A faint shudder passed through him. Emboldened, Samara opened her mouth and flicked her tongue against his ear. She heard his breath escape on a soft hiss. But he continued speaking calmly with his secretary.

Slowly, seductively, Samara danced her fingertips across his collarbone. She ran her hand down the broad expanse of his chest, caressing hard, muscled flesh before trailing lower. Marcus's breathing quickened as she spread her hand across his taut abdomen and traced a rhythmic circular pattern. She slipped her fingers beneath the waistband of his towel and roamed until she found just what she was looking for. Marcus's erection strained against the cotton. She wrapped one hand around the hard, throbbing length and gently squeezed.

Bingo.

Marcus made a strangled noise, half grunt and half groan. On the other end of the phone, his concerned secretary must have asked him what was wrong.

"Nothing, Barbara," he mumbled hoarsely. "I-I'm fine, don't worry."

Grinning now, Samara nibbled on his earlobe while stroking the granite-smooth hardness in her hand. Marcus's breathing grew ragged.

"Listen, Barbara, I need to go. Just have Donovan, Timothy or Helen give me a call when they get in the office. Thanks." He hung up and turned to Samara. His dark eyes smoldered dangerously. "You must be trying to bankrupt me, woman."

"What do you mean?"

Marcus reached for her towel. "Because if this is what I have to look forward to every morning, I'll never go to work."

Taming the Wolf

Samara's laughter was short-lived as Marcus stripped the towel from her body and tossed it aside before discarding his own. Pushing her back onto the mattress, he covered her naked body with his. The exhaustion she'd felt only minutes before evaporated. She tugged his head down to hers for a greedy kiss. Marcus captured her wild cry in his mouth as he thrust deep inside her.

Chapter Fourteen

W hat do you think of this one?"

Melissa lifted her head from the clothing rack she'd been sifting through. Samara held up a maternity dress in a soft shade of green for her to examine.

"Nice," Melissa murmured, reaching for the dress. "Very nice."

The two women had taken an extended lunch break that Monday afternoon and headed to Pentagon City Shopping Mall in northern Virginia. Just eight weeks pregnant, Melissa was already complaining that her clothes didn't fit anymore.

Melissa added the green summer dress to the growing pile on her arm and sighed. "I'm going to have to put something back on the rack. I promised Gary I wouldn't go on a mad shopping spree today, but I can't seem to help myself. Everything is just too cute for words."

"Except for that floral-print number on the rack over there. The one that looked like a housecoat."

Melissa made a face. "And let's not forget that tacky skirt and halter set that's designed for the stomach to protrude. I'm sorry, but I just don't see anything attractive about pregnant women waddling around in public with their bellies hanging out—I don't care what *Marie Claire* says."

Samara laughed. "I agree, but then I've never been one to follow fashion trends anyway."

"Your mother should seriously consider designing maternity wear. If anyone can make pregnant women look sexy, Asha Dubois can."

"I'll pass along the suggestion," Samara said dryly.

"Just as soon as the two of you discuss how she's going to design your wedding gown. I know it's going to be spectacular."

Samara fell silent.

Melissa stared at her. "Don't tell me. You're not going to ask her, are you?"

"Melissa, I haven't even told my mother about Marcus, let alone that I'm engaged."

"When do you plan to tell her?"

Samara shrugged, sifting through more maternity outfits. "I don't know. It's not like my mother and I are close, the way you and yours are. I'm not even sure how Asha would react to the news. Definitely not the way Marcus's father reacted when we called him on Sunday. He was genuinely thrilled for us. And so were you. But my mother…that's an entirely different story."

"Samara," Melissa said quietly, "despite the strain between you and your mother, I honestly believe she cares about you and wants to see you happy."

"I wish I shared that belief, Melissa, but I just can't. And the last thing I want is to call her with my wonderful news and hear a bitter lecture about how men are not to be trusted. I've been listening to that lecture my entire life. Nothing's changed."

"You never know. She might surprise you with tears of joy."

"Highly unlikely." Not for the first time, Samara found herself lamenting the state of affairs between her and her mother. Of course she wanted nothing more than to pick up the phone and relay the news of her engagement to Asha like a giddy bride-to-be. But she had to face reality, and reality reminded her that their relationship was not one that invited shared confidences and "girl talk."

Wanting to erase the mournful expression on Samara's face, Melissa grabbed her arm and started for the nearest checkout counter. "Come on, girl. Let's go have lunch. All this shopping has worn me and Junior out."

"Junior?"

"Gary and I are hoping for a boy first. We figure if we refer to the baby as 'Junior' often enough, we just might get our wish. Don't look at me like that. It's no crazier than what the women of old used to do to determine the unborn child's sex. You should hear some of my mother's stories."

Samara chuckled dryly. "Don't worry, I seem to recall some of my grandmother's wild anecdotes. And you're right, there's absolutely nothing wrong with calling your baby Junior. I'll even hop on the bandwagon if it helps any."

Melissa grinned. "I knew you'd make the perfect godmother." As she dumped all the outfits onto the countertop, it was obvious she'd decided not to part with a single item. Samara smiled inwardly. Pending motherhood was already changing Melissa's frugal ways.

"Let me pay for a couple of those," Samara offered. "That way you can keep your word to Gary about not overspending."

Melissa waved her off with a grin. "Just buy lunch and we'll call it even."

As they left Macy's a few minutes later, Melissa said, "By the way, is there any chance that you and Marcus might consider pushing up the wedding date?"

"Why?"

"By the time September arrives, your matron of honor might need to be rolled up the aisle in order to fulfill her duties."

Samara laughed and curved an arm around her friend's shoulders. "I'll run the idea past Marcus."

Late that afternoon, Marcus had just gotten off the phone with his father when his receptionist buzzed his extension. "Mr. Wolf, Antoinette Toussaint is here to see you."

Taming the Wolf

Marcus frowned in puzzlement. What was Antoinette Toussaint doing at his office? He'd had a meeting with her father earlier that day. Maybe William Toussaint had forgotten something and sent his daughter to retrieve it.

"Please send her in, Laura. Thanks."

Marcus saved the file he'd been working on before his father called and exited the program. He stood just as Antoinette appeared in the doorway.

"Ms. Toussaint," he greeted her. "Please come in."

Antoinette Toussaint didn't merely enter the room. She *glided* into the office with a seductive feline grace that reminded Marcus of an animal intent on cornering its prey. It seemed appropriate that she wore a skintight black leather body suit that molded her voluptuous curves like a second skin. A dangerous-looking pair of stiletto heels completed the femme fatale look and accentuated her statuesque build. Her lustrous ebony mane was swept back from her dark face and tumbled past her shoulders. Marcus would have to be dumb and blind not to notice what a strikingly beautiful woman she was, or that way she oozed sexuality seemed as natural to her as breathing.

Her sultry amber eyes were fixed on his face as she approached his desk. "Hello, Marcus," she said in a low, throaty voice. "It's so good to see you again."

Marcus inclined his head in a slight nod. "That's quite an outfit you're wearing."

She glanced down at herself and laughed huskily. "I just came from a photo shoot across town. I had nearly forgotten I was still in costume. No wonder I received so many interested looks on the way over here!"

Likely story. "What can I do for you this evening, Ms. Toussaint?"

She waved a hand tipped with red talons. "Oh, please. Call me Antoinette. Ms. Toussaint is my mother."

"All right, then. What brings you here, Antoinette?"

"Actually, I was hoping to catch my father before he left. But when I got here, your receptionist informed me that my father's appointment was this morning." She gave an elegant shrug. "I must have gotten my times mixed up."

"It happens," Marcus murmured. He didn't buy her explanation for one second.

"Since I was already here, I thought it wouldn't hurt to say hello. This is quite an impressive office you have, Marcus." Antoinette turned and walked over to a mahogany-paneled wall of books. Marcus knew the maneuver was meant to give him an unobstructed view of her tight, shapely ass.

He lowered himself slowly into his chair. He knew without a doubt that if he'd met Antoinette a month ago, they would already be lovers. And when the affair was over, they would've gone their separate ways. No hard feelings, no empty promises. No mess.

But he hadn't met Antoinette a month ago. He'd met Samara first, and she had ruined him for all other women.

Marcus paused, momentarily startled by the realization that his bachelor days were behind him. He would never make love to another woman again. His wife would be his only lover for as long as they both lived.

Antoinette turned at that moment and sashayed toward him. "My father thinks the world of you, Marcus. You should hear the way he brags about you to all his friends and colleagues. One would think you were his own son."

Marcus propped his elbows on the desk and steepled his fingers. "Your father is a generous man."

"He is," she purred. "But I certainly don't think his glowing accolades are unwarranted. You *are* a remarkable man, Marcus Wolf." She came around the desk and stopped mere inches from his chair. He watched in bemused silence as she rested a curvaceous hip against the desk. "Do you find me attractive, Marcus?"

His mouth twitched humorously. "That's a ridiculous question if I ever heard one. But whether or not I find you attractive is moot."

"And why is that?"

"Because I don't intend to do anything about it."

"Even if I give you permission?"

Marcus chuckled softly. "Believe me, Antoinette," he drawled as he rose to his feet, "if I wanted to initiate something between us, I wouldn't need your permission."

Antoinette's amber eyes flickered with excitement. She slid onto the desk and crossed her long legs. "You're right. I doubt any woman in her right mind would ever resist you, Marcus."

Before he could respond, Antoinette tugged on his loosened tie and pulled him toward her. Caught off guard, Marcus braced his palms on either side of her to steady himself. He had only a fleeting glimpse of the wicked satisfaction in her eyes before her hand grasped the back of his head and drew his mouth down to hers.

Samara was on her way home that evening when she remembered she still had Marcus's laptop. She'd borrowed it over the weekend to get some work done while her own laptop was on loan to Brianna Lynch.

Samara glanced at the clock on her dashboard. It was five-thirty. She knew Marcus was still at the office; he'd told her earlier he planned to stay late to catch up on some paperwork. If he decided to take the work home instead, she didn't want him to be without his laptop. She already felt guilty for monopolizing so much of his time. After playing hooky on Thursday, they'd spent the entire weekend together, alternately making love and watching old Blaxploitation flicks. The only time they'd ventured outdoors was to have lunch at a popular Foggy Bottom restaurant and visit a few jewelers.

As much as Samara enjoyed spending time with Marcus, she didn't want to become dependent on his presence. She had to keep reminding herself that they were both busy professionals with many responsibilities. She didn't want FYI to suffer any more than she wanted his practice to suffer.

"I don't have to guess what *you* were up to on Thursday," Melissa had teased her when Samara arrived at the office that morning. "I know exactly what 'personal time off' means when there's a gorgeous man in the picture."

Melissa had applauded Samara for putting pleasure before business, for once in her life. Samara didn't plan to make it a habit.

At least not until after the wedding.

She made a U-turn at the next traffic light and headed back toward Marcus's office building.

Minutes later she climbed out of the car and retrieved the laptop from the trunk. She wouldn't stay long, she told herself firmly. No more than ten minutes.

Her steps were jaunty as she entered the building and rode the elevator to the tenth floor. The thought of seeing Marcus always filled her with breathless anticipation, much as it had that night when she'd showed up at his office wearing nothing but lingerie beneath her trench coat.

The reception area was empty when she arrived. Samara glanced around in search of Marcus's receptionist, who didn't get off until six. Seeing that Laura's computer was still on, Samara decided she was probably in the restroom.

She waited around for another minute before heading down the corridor to Marcus's office. He hadn't mentioned any evening appointments, so she should be safe.

As she approached the door she heard the low murmur of voices. Marcus's deep timbre was followed by a woman's low, sultry drawl.

For some reason, the woman's voice struck Samara as familiar. A foreboding sensation crawled over her and settled in the pit of her stomach. It was the sort of feeling one got before receiving bad news. A second before she stepped through the doorway, she remembered whom the sex-kitten voice belonged to.

She came to a dead stop.

The sight that greeted her would be permanently etched into her brain. It was the sight of Marcus and Antoinette Toussaint locked in a passionate kiss. Antoinette sat on his desk, one hand curved possessively around his neck as he stood between her legs.

Samara blinked in stunned disbelief for a moment, not wanting to accept what she was seeing. Her stomach twisted violently and nausea surged upward.

At that moment, Marcus glanced up and saw her standing in the doorway. He jerked his head back from Antoinette's and stepped away from the desk.

But it was too late. Samara had seen enough. Trembling with outrage, she set the laptop down on the floor and spun on her heel. She couldn't get out of there fast enough.

As she stood at the bank of elevators furiously pressing the down button, she heard Marcus in the reception area.

"I didn't know she was here, Mr. Wolf," the receptionist was apologizing. "I stepped away for a minute to use the restroom and—"

"Don't worry about it, Laura." Marcus pushed through the door and approached Samara.

Before he could open his mouth, she said icily, "Save it, Marcus. I don't want to hear it."

"Let me explain—"

"What's to explain? Now I know what *really* goes on when you're 'working late' at the office!"

"Come on, Samara, you know it isn't like that."

She whirled on him. "I saw you, Marcus. Do you think I'm dumb *and* blind?"

Over his shoulder, she saw Antoinette Toussaint appear in the reception area. The sight of the woman in a stunning leather body suit only fueled Samara's wrath. She spun around and started for the stairs, refusing to wait around for the elevator with Marcus and his lover.

Marcus was right on her heels as she yanked open the stairwell door. "Samara, wait! Just listen to me."

"No!" She hurried down the steps, cursing her high heels for slowing her escape. On the next landing, Marcus grasped her upper arm and pulled her to a stop. She struggled against him, pummeling his broad chest with her fists. "Let go of me!"

"Not until you calm down and listen!"

"*Calm down?* You want me to calm down? God, I'm such an idiot. I trusted you, Marcus. I trusted you!" Her voice broke and tears stung her eyes.

Marcus pulled her closer to him. "I wasn't kissing her, Samara. You have to believe me."

Her chest heaved as she glared up at him. "Wait, let me guess. Antoinette was kissing you, but you weren't kissing her back. Is that about right?"

"*Yes*," Marcus answered, sounding annoyed that she made the scenario sound so implausible.

"Oh, please! Do you take me for a fool, Marcus?"

"It's the truth!"

"She was sitting on your desk, Marcus. What were you doing while she sat her ass down on your desk, huh?"

"I'll admit it looked bad, but nothing happened, Samara. I swear to you."

"I don't believe you. You were kissing her, Marcus. I saw you!"

"Maybe you shouldn't believe everything you see."

"Don't give me that!" By now Samara was trembling violently, and she feared that any minute she'd start crying. But she refused to give Marcus that satisfaction. She yanked her arm free and started down the stairs again. "Leave me alone, Marcus. Go back to your sexy supermodel in her *Catwoman* suit."

Marcus swore viciously as he followed her. His Southern accent was more pronounced in his anger. "I don't want Antoinette Toussaint, I told you that before!"

"You told me a lot of things before, none of which matter now."

"What the hell is that supposed to mean?"

Samara halted mid-step, turned and glared up at him. "It means that it's over between us, Marcus. We're finished."

He grimaced at the finality of her words, then tried to reach for her again. "Come on, Samara, you don't mean that."

She twisted out of his grasp. "Don't touch me! Don't ever touch me again, or so help me God I'll kill you!"

Stunned by the force of her anger, Marcus stared at her. "I can't believe you're willing to throw everything away on a simple misunderstanding."

"*I'm* not the one who threw everything away, Marcus. *You* are."

"No, sweetheart, you are. You've completely misconstrued the entire situation, and you're too proud and stubborn to see that."

"Go to hell, Marcus."

His expression hardened. "Maybe it's better it happened this way, before we both made the biggest mistake of our lives by getting married."

"Amen to that." Samara's legs were shaking so badly she was afraid she would collapse. She hoped Marcus couldn't tell. "Thanks for doing us both a favor, Marcus."

His scowl was ferocious. He gave a terse nod of farewell, turned and marched back up the stairs. Samara stood where she was, listening to his receding footsteps above the roar of her hammering heart. Only when she heard the stairwell door clang shut on the tenth floor did she allow a tortured sob to escape.

She took the elevator down to the lobby and rushed outside to her car. She sped out of the parking lot and got as far as the next street corner before the tears spilled, fast and bitter. She stopped at a red light and banged her fist against the steering wheel.

Oh God, what have I done?

What the hell just happened?

Marcus shook his head as he returned to his office. He couldn't believe how quickly things had escalated out of control. One minute he'd been discussing wedding plans with his father, the next minute he was having a heated argument with his fiancée.

Ex-fiancée, he corrected himself. And all because she didn't trust him.

Trust. When all was said and done, that's what it boiled down to. Not Antoinette's thwarted seduction attempt. Not the seemingly compromising position Marcus had been caught in. Samara's inability to trust him was the *real* issue. On some level he'd always known her insecurities would come between them. He hadn't known, of course, that it would happen so soon. And he'd hoped when the time came, they could work through it together.

So much for that idea.

Marcus paced the floor angrily as he replayed the whole scene in his mind. Samara hadn't even given him a chance to explain himself. She'd tried and convicted him without a trial, hurling accusations and insults. But what hurt Marcus the most was her total lack of faith in him. Under the circumstances, he knew he would have been just as furious if the shoe was on the other foot. God knows he had his own share of trust issues to work through. Stumbling upon Samara in the arms of another man would've felt like déjà vu, thrusting him back to his childhood and that fateful afternoon he'd walked in on his mother and her lover.

But if the shoe was on the other foot, *he* would have given Samara a chance to explain! *She* hadn't bothered to grant him even that.

It was better this way, he told himself.

No one should have to go through life trying to prove their trust-worthiness to another. If he and Samara had gotten married, that's exactly how it would've been. How long could he have put up with constantly looking over his shoulder, wondering if his wife was waiting for him to mess up so that she could walk out on him?

Hell, no. He needed her unconditional trust. If she couldn't give him that, then there was no point in going through with marriage. A relationship built without trust was doomed for failure.

With a savage oath, he kicked at the trash container and took no satisfaction in spilling the crumpled paper contents. He sat down at the computer and reopened the case brief he'd been working on before Antoinette interrupted.

He couldn't concentrate on a single word.

Shutting off the computer, Marcus grabbed his suit jacket and briefcase. He paused in the doorway and regarded the laptop Samara had returned. Who told her he needed the damn thing back anyway? He had two others!

Cursing a blue streak, Marcus picked up the laptop and shoved it inside the mahogany armoire where the others were stored. He strode from the room without bothering to lock up the bureau. If the cleaning people wanted to help themselves to his office equipment, they were more than welcome to it.

If Marcus never saw another laptop again, it'd be too soon.

Chapter Fifteen

Y ou look like hell."

Samara didn't look up as Melissa appeared in her doorway the next morning. She pretended to be totally engrossed in her paperwork—although her mind hadn't processed a single thing.

She'd cried herself to sleep the night before and awakened with the grit of insomnia in her eyes. Images of Marcus and Antoinette Toussaint had plagued her dreams all night and kept her tossing and turning. Somehow, she'd managed to get dressed and drag herself to the office by seven. But she couldn't stop staring at the phone. She vacillated between hoping Marcus would call, and wanting him to drop off the face of the earth.

She was a complete and utter wreck.

"Seriously though." Melissa stepped into the office and closed the door. She held a steaming mug of herbal tea in her hand. Her obstetrician had restricted caffeine from her diet since the women in her family had a history of developing hypertension during pregnancy. Melissa hated herbal tea.

But she had bigger concerns that morning. "What happened last night, Samara?"

"I don't want to talk about it."

"That bad, huh?"

Samara stared at the report in her hand. The words and figures blurred in her vision. She didn't realize she was crying until Melissa hastily set down her mug and knelt at her side. She rubbed Samara's back in soothing circular motions.

"Shhh. Just take deep breaths. That's it, just like that."

"I'm such an idiot, Melissa," Samara blubbered. "I should have known it was too good to be true! I kept thinking that it was, but I went along with it anyway. I'm such a fool. My mother's right about men. They *can't* be trusted—well, except for Gary and Richard Yorkin. And my old friend Walter Floyd. But that's about it!"

"What happened between you and Marcus?" Melissa asked gently.

"What you *should* be asking is what happened between Marcus and Antoinette Toussaint."

Melissa frowned. "Who in the world is Antoinette Toussaint?"

Samara wiped her tears and told Melissa the whole sordid story. Melissa was livid by the time she finished.

"I can't believe he did that to you," she raged.

"Believe it. He did."

Melissa rose and began pacing before Samara's desk. "It doesn't make sense, Samara. From what you've told me about Marcus, settling down was the farthest thing from his mind before he met you."

Samara sniffled. "And your point is?"

"Meeting you changed him. He asked you to *marry* him, for God's sake! Men like Marcus Wolf don't take that kind of step unless they're absolutely certain they've met the right woman. Why would he just throw it all away on some bimbo?"

"You haven't seen this particular bimbo," Samara grumbled. "She's drop-dead gorgeous. An Amazon. Sex on stilts."

"And I suppose *you're* chopped liver?" Melissa sounded exasperated. "Come on, Samara, you know it takes a whole lot more than good looks to snare a man like Marcus Wolf. Give him more credit than that."

Samara glared at her friend. "Whose side are you on anyway?"

"Sweetie, you know I'm always in your corner. But I just don't want to see you make a huge mistake that you might regret someday—when it's too late."

"I think it already is. I told him to go to hell and thanked him for doing us both a favor by cheating."

"Ouch." Melissa cringed. "Well, you were rightfully upset. People say things in the heat of the moment they don't always mean."

"Oh, I meant it."

"Are you sure about that?"

"Look, Melissa, I know you mean well. But you weren't there. You didn't see what I did." Samara closed her eyes as if to shut out the painful memory of Marcus's betrayal.

Melissa's expression softened. "And you're absolutely sure it looked like he was kissing her back?"

"It did to me. And even if he wasn't, what was that hussy doing on his desk in the first place? *Something* was definitely going on between them." Her mouth curved in a mirthless smile. "You know what's so ironic? The first time Marcus and I ever made love was in his office. Afterward I teased him about being the proverbial boss that fools around in his office right under his employees' noses. We got a good little chuckle out of it. I guess the joke's on me, huh?"

"Oh, Samara," Melissa said sadly.

"It's all right, Melissa. I don't want you worrying about me. Stress isn't good for you or the baby. I'll be fine. I'm in a lot of pain right now, but I'll get over it eventually. I have no other choice."

Melissa looked unconvinced. "Can you promise me one thing?"

"What's that?"

"If Marcus calls and wants to talk, will you at least hear him out? Give him a chance to better explain himself?"

Samara knew that the odds of Marcus ever calling her again were one in a million. The final look he'd given her had been lethal and filled with contempt. It was nearly her undoing.

"Promise me?" Melissa pressed.

"I promise." But beneath the pile of paperwork on her desk, Samara's fingers were crossed.

Over the next two weeks, Samara threw herself into work like never before. Each day she worked for thirteen hours straight, from sunrise to sundown. By the time she crawled home, she was too exhausted to do much more than eat a solitary meal, shower and hit the sack. Her body ached almost as badly as her heart, which worked to her advantage. She was so physically drained that she actually managed to grab more than a few hours of sleep.

She checked her voice mail messages on a nightly basis, hoping to hear Marcus's voice.

He didn't call.

On her first weekend without him, Melissa invited her over for dinner. Samara knew her friend's hospitality had more to do with pity than a burning desire for Samara's company. Samara hadn't *been* much company since she and Marcus broke up.

She accepted the invitation out of politeness, then wished she hadn't.

Gary and Melissa Matthews lived in Adams Morgan, an upscale Washington, D.C. neighborhood. Their spacious apartment was filled with more than contemporary furnishings and the original African oil paintings they enjoyed collecting. Their home was filled with *love*.

Throughout the evening, Gary treated Melissa with the utmost affection and concern. He was attentive to her needs—adjusting the thermostat if she were cold, retrieving her bedroom slippers when her feet began to ache, refilling her juice to ensure that she got her daily recommended fluid intake. When they smiled at each other, no one else seemed to exist.

The couple's obvious contentment was an excruciating reminder of Samara's own loss. Although she didn't begrudge her friends their happiness, she found it hard not to envy them.

She wanted to go home.

"Have you decided what you're going to wear to the community fund-raiser in two weeks?" Melissa asked after dinner. Gary had disappeared into the kitchen to wash the dishes. Sounds of an NBA basketball game poured from the small color television tucked into a corner.

Samara groaned loudly. She'd almost forgotten about the mayor's biannual fund-raiser banquet. Richard Yorkin had attended without fail as the Institute's representative. As the new executive director, it was Samara's responsibility to continue the tradition. When the invitation arrived several weeks ago, she'd stuck it inside her desk drawer and forgotten all about it.

She sent Melissa a hopeful look. "I don't suppose you'd be willing to go in my place?"

"I knew you would ask, and the answer is no. You know how important it is for the Institute to be represented at these functions. If there are ever any extra funds in the city budget, we want to be seriously considered as recipients. And Mayor Williams expects to meet and greet FYI's executive director, *not* their accountant."

"I know, I know." Samara sighed gloomily. "It's just that I'm not feeling very sociable these days."

"All the more reason to get out there and mingle. You never know, Samara. Dressing up and attending some black-tie affair might do you a world of good."

"If you say so. Will you at least go with me in case I need a little handholding? You know I'm not very good at these social mixers."

"You'll be fine. But, yes, I will accompany you. Gary, too. Maybe Paul Borden could even come as your date." When Samara opened her mouth to protest, Melissa rushed on, "Don't worry, it won't be like a real date! It's common for friends to escort each other to formal affairs. No one likes to show up at these things without dates."

"I don't mind," Samara countered grumpily.

"You will if Marcus Wolf shows up with that bimbo on his arm. Sorry," she added when Samara flinched, "but it's the truth. If you want to show him that you've moved on with your life, this is as good a start as any."

Samara reflected on that conversation the entire ride home. As much as she hoped Marcus didn't show up at the banquet with Antoinette Toussaint, she knew it was highly possible. If the two hadn't been involved before last week, they were definitely an item now. Men like Marcus Wolf didn't skulk around licking their wounds. And women like Antoinette Toussaint didn't wait long to go after what they wanted. Samara had cleared the path for the other woman to move in for the kill. If Marcus's ego was feeling the slightest bit bruised, he'd be Antoinette's for the taking.

Sickened by the thought, Samara parked her car and trudged inside her house.

As soon as Marcus got home from work on Monday evening, he stripped out of his suit and changed into sweats, then left the penthouse and drove to Rock Creek Park for a run. He needed to clear his head, and his nightly workout with the weight equipment at his place wasn't going to cut it.

He headed onto one of the narrow trails and joined the steady flow of joggers, runners and power walkers jockeying for position. The air was still damp and humid from the showers that had pelted the city that afternoon. The surrounding trees dripped and the grass at the edge of the footpath was muddy. The clouds hung low and heavy, making the night appear later than it was, and threatening more rain.

Marcus's thoughts raced a mile a minute as he ran. He'd been operating on nothing but sheer adrenaline for the past week. Sleep eluded him at nights, and eating had become little more than a mechanical function. He had to keep reminding himself that without nutritional sustenance, he couldn't operate at his maximum capacity. And if that happened, his clients suffered. If his clients suffered, business suffered.

Marcus didn't need any more suffering in his life. Losing Samara was more than enough for him to handle at the moment.

Donovan and Timothy had been trying, unsuccessfully, to get Marcus to open up about his feelings. They'd heard about what happened that evening and didn't need more details. All they wanted to know was what Marcus planned to do about the situation.

Marcus hadn't decided.

Between endless meetings and conference calls, he'd found himself staring at the phone. On several occasions he'd contemplated calling Samara. He'd even gotten as far as picking up the phone and dialing nine digits. But before he could bring himself to punch in the final number, his pride kicked in and he hung up in disgust. Why should *he* make the first move? *She* was the one who'd ended their relationship, not him. *She* was the one who'd ruthlessly told him to go to hell. The ball was in her court. If she opted out of the match, so be it.

Besides, he hadn't decided whether or not he was ready to forgive her.

Marcus was so absorbed in his musings that he didn't notice when it started to rain. It was only when another runner jostled him as she scurried off the footpath that Marcus became aware of his surroundings. He reversed direction and started for his car, in no particular hurry.

As he walked, he saw a young couple with a small red-haired child in tow. They'd been enjoying an evening stroll in the park when the showers started. Instead of dashing for cover, they continued their leisurely pace. Laughing, they held their faces toward the sky and collected rainwater in their open mouths.

Marcus's steps slowed as he stared at the little family. As he watched, the couple grabbed both of the child's hands and hoisted her between them. She giggled and squealed in delight as they swung her high in the air.

Marcus's heart constricted painfully in his chest. He came to a complete standstill, hands braced on his hips as the rain soaked him to the bone. He didn't care. In that moment he realized what he wanted more than anything. A family of his own. A wife and child to return to at the end of each workday.

A family to make his house a home.

But these things weren't meant to be. Not unless he settled for someone other than Samara.

Marcus closed his eyes and lifted his face to the warm spring rain.

The only woman he wanted *was* Samara. But maybe it was time to accept the possibility that he might never have her. And if that was the case, he'd have to learn to move on.

He walked back to his car and drove home.

No sooner had he peeled off his drenched sweatshirt and turned on the faucet for a hot shower did the doorbell ring.

For a moment he wondered if Samara had been conjured up by his thoughts. His pulse accelerated.

He grabbed a towel and went to answer the door, mopping at his damp head as he walked.

But it wasn't Samara who waited on the other side of the door.

Antoinette Toussaint stood there looking vastly different from the way he'd last seen her. She'd traded in the leather body suit for a snug pair of denim jeans and a simple white shirt knotted at the waist. Her long black hair was pulled back into a ponytail that made her appear more youthful, almost vulnerable. And she wore a lot less makeup—not that she needed much to begin with.

The transformation was like night and day.

Marcus propped a shoulder against the doorjamb and regarded her lazily from beneath his eyelashes. "Don't tell me. You were in the neighborhood and decided to stop by my house."

Antoinette smiled winsomely. "Actually, Marcus, I came out of my way just to see you," she admitted. "I wanted to apologize for what happened last week. I was way out of line for coming on to you like that, and I'm sorry if I messed things up between you and your girlfriend. If you want, I could talk to her and straighten things out between the two of you."

His mouth twitched. "Thanks for the offer, Antoinette, but I think you're the *last* person Samara wants to hear from. Next to me, that is."

"I'm really sorry. I've been feeling incredibly guilty ever since it happened."

And pigs could really fly. "How'd you get up here? Wait, let me guess. You charmed your way past the security guard."

"There are times when it pays to be a fashion model."

"Hmm. I suppose I should be grateful you're not a serial killer."

Antoinette grinned. "Does that mean I'm forgiven?"

"As long as it doesn't happen again," Marcus said evenly.

"You have my word." She swept an appreciative look across his bare, muscled chest. "Mind if I come inside for a minute?"

"Don't push your luck."

She pouted. "Have you had dinner yet?"

"No. And if it's all the same to you, I have an appointment with a hot shower that shouldn't be kept waiting much longer." He started to close the door.

Antoinette sighed dramatically. "It's just as well, I suppose. I don't trust myself not to sneak into the shower while you're in there and have my way with you."

Marcus chuckled in spite of himself. "Good night, Antoinette. Go home." He closed the door on her sultry laughter.

He waited until he'd reached the bathroom before removing his sweatpants. And just in case Antoinette had sweet-talked a spare key to his penthouse out of the security guard, he locked the bathroom door.

Chapter Sixteen

The mayor's biannual community fund-raiser banquet was held at the opulent Omni Shoreham Hotel in Washington, D.C. Crystal chandeliers glistened from vaulted ceilings as white-jacketed waiters served exotic hors d'oeuvres on silver trays. Linen-covered tables with elegant centerpieces were arranged in a semicircle, leaving the middle of the floor open for dancing, milling around and the all-important networking. Receiving a formal invitation to the event was considered a major coup in most social circles. Ticket prices were astronomical, and the closer one sat to the mayor, the more one paid. Proceeds from the fund-raiser were donated to various charitable and community organizations.

All of D.C.'s movers and shakers were in attendance. Local businessmen, politicians, and civic and community leaders milled about in formal attire. Armed with business cards and plastic smiles, they worked the room making contacts and vying for the television news cameras, hoping their rehearsed sound bites would make the eleven o'clock broadcasts.

It was exactly the sort of pretentious gathering Samara detested.

Melissa nudged her as they made their way around the ballroom. "Stop fidgeting. It makes you look bored."

"I wonder why," Samara murmured.

"Even if you *are* bored, you're not supposed to show it. Here comes Alberta Graves. Smile."

Samara assumed the appropriate expression and exchanged pleasantries with the D.C. Council chairwoman. When Alberta Graves moved off to greet other guests, Melissa sent Samara an approving nod.

"You're getting better at this. There's hope for you yet."

"Gee, thanks."

"How're you holding up?"

Samara didn't have to ask what her friend meant. She'd heard through the grapevine that Marcus was expected to be in attendance that evening. He'd been invited as one of the mayor's personal guests.

So far he hadn't arrived. She hoped she could duck out before he did.

"Just relax," Melissa reminded her for the umpteenth time. "You look fabulous. But I've already told you that."

Samara glanced down at herself. She wore a black chiffon creation from her mother's spring collection. Provocative, sleek and sophisticated, the gown accentuated the firm roundness of her breasts and sleek torso. One shoulder was left completely bare before the silk material skimmed down to her shapely waist and flared from the knees. After much deliberation, she'd decided to wear her hair loose and parted down the center. The front edges had been bent with a flat iron to achieve a trendy feathered look. She told herself the decision to wear her hair down had nothing to do with Marcus liking it better that way.

She'd never been a very good liar—not even to herself.

She smiled at Melissa, who was understated elegance in black crepe. "You don't clean up too bad yourself, Mrs. Matthews."

Melissa grimaced. "My feet are killing me in these heels. I swear, I don't know how I'm going to get through the next seven months of this swollen-ankle business."

"Do you want to sit down?"

"Nice try. Once we greet Mayor Williams, we can take a break."

Samara peered through the crowd to see a line of people waiting to talk to the mayor. Her heart sank.

"On second thought," Melissa said as she spied the long procession, "we can catch up to him later. Gives me a good excuse to keep you here longer. Don't think I haven't noticed the longing stares you've been sending toward the exit. Let me repeat myself. We're not leaving this shindig until you've formally introduced yourself to the mayor. And definitely not until I've gorged myself on that scrumptious-looking food."

Samara followed the direction of her friend's hungry gaze. Long serving tables were laden with everything from succulent prime rib au jus to smoked salmon. Unlike Melissa, the sight of all that food didn't make Samara want to stuff herself. If anything, she felt slightly nauseous. She looked away with a mild shudder.

Gary and Paul Borden stood in unison as the two women returned to the table. Both men looked handsome and debonair in black tuxedoes, their wingtips polished to a shine. They helped the women into their seats.

Paul smiled warmly at Samara. "We were just saying how lucky we are to have accompanied two of the most beautiful women here tonight."

Melissa beamed with pleasure. "Isn't that sweet?" she said to Samara.

Samara had misgivings about inviting Paul to the banquet for fear of leading him on. But so far he'd been nothing but a gentleman. Since he hadn't called her after their last lunch together, she wondered if he'd finally lost interest in her. She hoped so. She didn't want to hurt his feelings.

About the time Samara was beginning to relax, she glanced up and froze.

There, standing across the room with the mayor and several city councilmen, was Marcus. He was dressed in a tailored black tuxedo that fit his tall, muscular frame to mouthwatering perfection. He looked like he had just stepped from the cover of *GQ*, right down to the hand thrust carelessly into one pocket. With little or no effort, he was the epitome of masculine power and raw magnetism.

The sight of him took her breath away. She didn't know how on earth she'd missed his arrival, but now that he was there, she couldn't take her eyes off him. And she didn't have to look around the crowded ballroom to know that she wasn't the only woman with that problem.

Samara willed him to look her way but was afraid of what would happen if he did.

And then it happened.

As if in slow motion, he lifted those fathomless black eyes and looked right at her. Her heart thudded as hard as if he'd actually reached out and touched her. The moments that passed while they stared at each other seemed like an eternity.

A flash of color to his right drew Samara's eye. Her heart plummeted at the sight of Antoinette Toussaint, resplendent in gossamer gold satin. As Samara watched, Marcus bent his head toward hers so that the woman could murmur something into his ear.

Samara looked away quickly, but not before Melissa caught her eye. Her expression was sympathetic. *Are you okay?* she mouthed.

Samara nodded jerkily. She was *not* okay, but she saw no point in broadcasting her misery to everyone else at their table.

Paul snagged a fluted glass of champagne from a passing waiter's tray. He looked sullen.

Dinner followed the mayor's opening remarks. Samara couldn't force down more than a few bites of the lavish offerings. When she excused herself to use the ladies room, Melissa stood as well.

Samara laughed in spite of herself. "No, sit and finish your dinner. Let's dispel the myth that women always have to go to the bathroom in pairs."

Melissa scowled at her but complied.

Only a few other women occupied the luxurious marble bathroom. Samara walked to the sink, moistened a paper towel and pressed it to her flushed cheeks. She felt like she was coming down with the flu. As soon as she got home, she would take something and hopefully nip the virus in the bud. It was her own fault for not taking better care of herself.

When she raised her eyes to the mirror, her reflection was joined by Antoinette Toussaint's.

Taming the Wolf

Oh, great. Just what she needed—a cat fight.

Cool amber eyes assessed her. "Samara, right? Imagine us running into each other again. This is—what—the third time in less than three weeks?"

"Something like that," Samara answered in a tight, controlled voice.

Antoinette eyed her critically. "You don't look too good, Samara. Is everything all right?"

"Everything is fine." She knew this bitch was *not* pretending to be concerned about her!

"Listen, Samara." Antoinette's voice lowered to a discreet murmur. As if she wanted to protect their conversation from eavesdroppers. "I feel a bit awkward in light of what happened a few weeks ago. Despite what you may think, it was *never* my intention for you to walk in on me and Marcus that way. I can only imagine how difficult that must have been for you."

Anger and humiliation tightened Samara's chest. "No more difficult than it must have been for you," she countered with stinging sweetness.

Antoinette's eyes narrowed. "What do you mean?"

"Oh, you know. That whole 'other woman' thing." It was Samara's turn to discreetly lower her voice. She leaned closer to Antoinette for added effect. "I can only imagine how difficult it must be for you to feel that you're second best. You know, because you're always reduced to being the other woman. It must take a terrible toll on your self-esteem."

Antoinette's expression hardened. "I wouldn't worry about my self-esteem if *I* were you. Your time would be better served figuring out how to keep *your* man happy so he doesn't have to go looking for the 'other woman.'"

Samara flinched. She couldn't help it. Antoinette's cruel taunt struck too close to home. She took a deep, steadying breath. "Look, Antoinette, I'm not going to stand here and argue with you. We

202

could do this all night and, frankly, I have better things to do with my time."

She started to move past the woman when Antoinette spoke again. Her voice dripped with triumph. "As long as we're being so honest with each other, Samara, I'll let you in on a little secret. Prior to that day you walked in on us, Marcus and I weren't involved. But thanks to your childish insecurities, that's about to change." She touched an elegant hand to her coiffed hair. Her full lips curved into a temptress's smile. "And unlike *some* women who shall remain nameless, *I* know how to keep a man happy. Enjoy the rest of the evening, Samara. You can be sure Marcus and I will."

Samara left the bathroom without another word. If she'd felt ill before, she felt even worse now. Antoinette's snide revelation confirmed what she'd already known deep down in her heart: Marcus *had* been telling the truth. She'd wrongly accused him of kissing Antoinette, and now it was too late to take back her angry words or undo the damage she'd caused to their relationship.

Needing some fresh air, Samara headed for the private lobby outside the ballroom. A pair of French doors was open for guests to enjoy the warm night breeze. She stepped onto the terrace and stood at the decorative banister overlooking Rock Creek Park.

God, what a royal mess she'd made.

"I thought I'd find you out here."

Samara turned to see Paul Borden standing in the door. She managed a wan smile. "Just getting some fresh air."

He joined her at the banister. "It's a beautiful night, isn't it? Half moon, glittering starlight." His gaze met hers. "It's a night for lovers."

"Hmm." Samara glanced away, suddenly feeling uncomfortable.

"Is something wrong, Samara? You've been preoccupied the entire evening. I don't even think you've noticed how many male heads you've turned—but then, that's nothing new for you." He chuckled. When she remained silent, he grew sober. "Anything you want to talk about? I'm a good listener."

"I have a lot on my mind. Nothing for you to worry about though."

Music from the ballroom drifted through the open terrace doors. Paul held out his hand to her. "Dance with me?"

"Oh, I don't think—"

"Come on, Samara, don't be a spoilsport." Ignoring her protests, Paul drew her into his arms and began swaying gently to the music. His breath was peppered with alcohol. Samara's stomach recoiled.

She tried to pull away, but his arms were a steel band around her waist. "Paul—"

"Don't worry, he's not going to see us dancing together. That's what you're worried about, isn't it?" He drew back to observe her stricken expression. His mouth curled into a mocking sneer. "You think I haven't noticed the way you've been watching him all night like a lovesick puppy? You think I don't know why Melissa's been monitoring you as closely as if you're about to slit your wrists?"

"Paul," Samara said, striving for composure, "I think you've had a little too much to drink."

"I'm not drunk, I'm frustrated! There's a big difference." His laughter was a thin, harsh sound. "What is it with you women? I've spent the last two years playing Mr. Nice Guy, hoping you would give me just *one* chance to prove that we could be good together. *Two* whole years, Samara. And what do you do? You fall for the first good-looking thing to come along. Never mind that guys like Marcus Wolf never settle down with one woman. Never mind that he can't make you happy!"

Samara wrenched herself free. "I'm going back inside."

Paul grabbed her arm. "The truth hurts, doesn't it?"

"Get your hand off me, Paul."

"I'm a decent guy, Samara. I work hard, pay my taxes, handle my responsibilities. I'm smart, attractive and I've even been told that I'm a great dresser. But I guess that's not good enough for you.

Women like you never settle for the nice guys. You prefer to be used and discarded at whim." He tightened his painful grip and leaned closer, his face twisted scornfully. "Just like a whore."

"You bastard!" Furious, Samara struggled to free her arm from his grasp.

"Is there a problem here?" said a low, deadly voice from across the terrace.

Samara and Paul looked over in unison to see Marcus standing in the entrance. Slowly he stepped from the shadows, as dark and forbidding as an avenging angel.

Paul released Samara's hand. His tone was coldly mocking. "Well, well, well. If it ain't Prince Charming to the rescue."

Marcus's expression was so ominous that Samara instinctively stepped in front of Paul. Her eyes beseeched Marcus. "Please don't make a scene."

He looked down at her, lethal fury smoldering in his eyes. "Go back inside, Samara."

She shook her head. She didn't want to be the cause of any bloodshed. "Please don't do this, Marcus. Think about all those people inside. Think about your reputation."

"Besides, this is none of your business," Paul blustered from his safe position behind Samara.

Marcus took another menacing step forward. Samara put her hand to the solid wall of his chest. His muscles were rigid, primed for a fight. "All right, I'll go inside. But not without you. *Please*, Marcus."

"Get your things," he said tersely. "I'm taking you home."

"*I* drove her here!" Paul sputtered in protest. "She's leaving with me."

"I don't think so." Marcus's tone was low and formidable.

Desperate to prevent a violent clash between the two men—a clash in which she knew Paul would come out the loser—Samara grabbed Marcus's hand and started quickly from the terrace. His eyes didn't leave Paul until they were back inside the lobby.

He followed Samara to the table to retrieve her purse. Melissa and Gary looked up in surprise at their approach.

"Hey, Marcus," Melissa greeted him, then took one look at Samara's strained expression and frowned. "What happened? Where's Paul?"

"Out on the terrace. Marcus has, uh, offered to take me home since I'm not feeling well. Could you guys make sure Paul gets home safely? I think he's had one too many glasses of champagne."

Melissa nodded as understanding dawned. "I'll call you tomorrow."

Marcus and Samara walked to his Bentley in silence. Out of the corner of her eye, she stole glances at his stony profile. Controlled rage rolled off his body like heat waves. He was holding his temper with an iron will, but Samara knew it was only a matter of time before he would unleash it.

It would not be pretty.

She waited until they were out of the parking lot and safely away from the hotel before she ventured to speak. "You didn't have to drive me home."

"I sure as hell wasn't letting you go home with that drunken bastard."

"Melissa and Gary could have taken me home."

A solitary muscle ticked in his jaw. He said nothing.

Samara plucked a piece of imaginary lint from her gown. "You know, I could've handled Paul myself back there."

"Before or after he succeeded in hitting you?"

"He wasn't going to hit me. He was just blowing off steam."

Marcus's mouth curved cynically. "Where I come from, Samara, that's called abuse."

She sighed heavily. She couldn't deny that Paul's volatile behavior had alarmed her. For a moment she'd had flashbacks of Paris. She saw André Leclerc's face contorted with rage as he beat her.

She shuddered at the memory and rubbed her sore arm.

"So is that what you want, Samara?" Marcus growled. "A man like Borden?"

"Of course not. Anyway, what do *you* care? You were there with Antoinette."

Marcus shook his head in disgust. "Still jumping to conclusions, aren't you?"

"What's that supposed to mean?"

"Did you see me arrive with Antoinette?"

"Well…no."

"Because I didn't. She was there with her parents. When you saw us, she'd just walked over to say hello."

"Oh." Samara felt foolish—for the second time that evening. She dropped her eyes to her lap. "I'm sorry."

Marcus's tone was cynical. "So am I, Samara. So am I."

They rode the rest of the way in strained silence. Samara's nerves were stretched perilously thin. Nausea burned at the base of her throat. All she wanted to do was go home and bury her head beneath the pillow. And forget about this nightmare that had become her life.

When they arrived at her house, Marcus parked at the curb. He climbed out of the car and came around to open her door.

"For what it's worth," Samara said as she stepped out, "I do thank you for not making a scene at the hotel. I'm not sure the Institute could handle the negative publicity if word got out that its executive director was indirectly responsible for a brawl at the mayor's fund-raiser banquet."

Marcus didn't even crack a smile. He skirted the fender and climbed back into the Bentley, prepared to leave.

Samara thanked him for the ride and started up the walk. Suddenly she was struck by a wave of nausea so violent that she gasped. She clamped a hand over her mouth and ran to the shrubbery that lined the driveway. She almost didn't make it in time.

With a muffled curse, Marcus got out of the car and strode to where she knelt on the ground, vomiting into the bushes. He crouched beside her and held her hair back.

When she had finished, he helped her gently to her feet. "Are you all right?" he demanded gruffly.

She bobbed her head quickly, embarrassed beyond belief. "I don't think my gardener will be too pleased in the morning though."

Marcus frowned. Without another word, he swept her into his arms and strode purposefully toward the house. Samara was too weak to protest.

Once inside, he carried her into the bedroom and set her down gingerly on the bed, then knelt in front of her. Silvery moonlight from the window illuminated his worried expression as he peered into her face. "Do you feel like you're going to be sick again?"

"Not yet. Marcus, what're you doing?"

He ignored her startled tone as he began to undress her. He removed her gown and high heels before reaching for her sheer pantyhose. She stopped him. "I think I can manage from here."

Guided by moonlight, he stood and crossed to the dresser, opening drawers until he located a nightgown for her. If Samara weren't so weak, she would have been mortified at having a man rummage through her lingerie. Of course, Marcus wasn't just *any* man. He was the only man she'd ever loved. If she hadn't messed things up so badly, he would have been her future husband.

Marcus returned to the bed and helped her into a cotton nightshirt, then drew back the covers and made her lie down. He left the room and returned moments later with a glass of cold water. She sat up and forced herself to take a few sips.

"Thank you, Marcus," she mumbled.

He sat on the edge of the bed. "How do you feel?"

"A little better. I think I'm coming down with the flu. I felt kind of feverish at the banquet."

Marcus reached over and felt her forehead.

"I always catch a bad cold whenever I'm under a lot of stress. Let's face it, the past two weeks haven't exactly been a picnic." She hesitated, then reached over and switched on the bedside lamp. She wanted Marcus to see her face for what she was about to say.

"I owe you another apology, Marcus. I shouldn't have jumped to conclusions about you and Antoinette when I saw the two of you…Well, when I saw what *appeared* to be the two of you kissing. I should have given you a chance to explain the situation. I owed you that much."

Marcus stared down at his hands clasped between his legs. He didn't utter a word.

Samara's heart sank. "You have every right to be angry with me, and I'll understand if you choose not to forgive me. I hope that…" Her voice hitched. She turned her head on the pillow, averting her face from his as she blinked away tears. "I hope that, in time, we can be friends."

Marcus got slowly to his feet. His expression was impenetrable as he gazed down at her. "I'm going to stay for a while in case you get sick again," he said without inflection. "I'll be in the living room if you need me."

Samara nodded mutely. She turned onto her side and closed her eyes. She jumped a little when she felt Marcus's warm fingers on her arm followed by a low, savage oath.

She looked up at him and watched the cold fury return to his eyes as he examined her arm. Her skin bore an ugly purplish bruise where Paul's fingers had gripped her. Slowly, carefully, Marcus lifted her hand and noted the same discoloration on her wrist.

"It doesn't hurt," Samara tried to assure him. "I just bruise easily, that's all."

Marcus said nothing. He didn't have to. The lethal expression on his face spoke volumes. He leaned over and switched off the lamp.

"Get some sleep, Samara," he said brusquely.

He turned and walked out of the room, closing the door quietly behind him. Samara sighed heavily into the darkness. Within minutes, she was fast asleep.

Out in the living room, Marcus paced up and down like an enraged animal. He wanted blood.

Samara's leather address book caught his eye. He walked over, picked it up from the sideboard table and flipped to the B section. Sure enough, Paul Borden's address was scrawled across the page in Samara's bold, feminine handwriting.

Marcus memorized the address and closed the book.

He left Samara's house just before dawn and drove northwest to Wisconsin Avenue. He had stayed with Samara longer than he'd intended, but when she woke up at midnight spilling her guts— *literally*—he couldn't bear to leave her alone.

He fed her ice, mopped her fevered brow and put her back to bed. At her softly spoken request, he remained at her bedside until she fell asleep. In the silence of the night, he'd watched her slumber as he'd done countless times before. But this time he had to force himself not to touch her, not to trace his fingers lightly over the delicate arch of her eyebrow or the lush fullness of her lips.

He had a lot of deliberating to do over the next several days. He couldn't afford to succumb to his emotions or the lure of Samara's vulnerability.

Nonetheless, he'd already decided that if her illness persisted through the weekend, she was going to see a doctor—even if Marcus had to drive her there himself.

It was probably for the best that he'd remained at her house all night. It had given him a chance to cool off.

But as he approached Paul Borden's Wisconsin Avenue address, the simmering anger resurfaced, fueled by the memory of Samara's bruised arm.

Marcus parked at a meter and crossed the street to the garden apartment building. There was no security guard posted at the front entrance, so he had no problem entering the building and riding the elevator to the third floor.

Paul Borden answered the door after several minutes, sounding annoyed at the early-morning intrusion. "It's freakin' Saturday morning," he grumbled as he unlocked the deadbolt. He didn't even ask who was at the door.

His bloodshot eyes widened in shock at the sight of Marcus. "What the—"

Marcus's voice was chillingly soft. "You didn't think this was over, did you, Borden?"

Paul staggered backward as Marcus casually stepped into the apartment and closed the door behind him. Paul's frantic gaze swung around the cluttered living room in search of a crude weapon.

"How're you feeling, Paul?" Marcus inquired in a mild tone. "Hung over?"

Paul swallowed hard and shook his head. "I wasn't drunk last night."

"Good. Because I want you clear-headed when I talk to you. Just so that there's no misunderstanding."

"Y-You shouldn't be here. I could have you arrested for breaking and entering."

"How's that? I knocked, you opened the door and let me in. No B and E here." At Paul's dubious look, Marcus smiled mockingly. "Take my word for it. I'm a lawyer, remember?"

Paul reddened. "Look, Wolf, what happened last night was between me and Samara. You should've stayed out of it! It was nobody's business but ours, man."

Marcus's jaw clenched. "I suppose if you'd started using her as a punching bag, that would be nobody's business as well. Right?"

Paul looked uncertain. Again, he glanced quickly around the room for a blunt object to use to defend himself. Finding nothing, he planted his feet and faced Marcus squarely. "Samara needed a little sense talked into her. I considered it my duty as her *friend* to enlighten her."

"Is that right? Well, allow *me* to enlighten you, Borden." Marcus stopped just inches from the man's face. Borden's breath still reeked of alcohol.

Marcus said in a low, lethal tone, "If you ever lay a hand on Samara Layton again, I'll kill you. If you even *think* about touching her, I will kill you. Do I make myself clear?"

Paul blanched. "I-I could see to it that you never practice law again. How do you like that, Mr. Hotshot Attorney?"

"Do your worst, Borden. I've made my fortune. I could retire today and not think twice about it. Don't touch Samara again. You've been warned." He turned and started for the door.

"I don't want her anymore!" Paul called out scornfully. "As it turns out, I don't particularly find pathetic women very attractive."

At the door, Marcus turned to look at him. His expression was one of grim amusement. "From the way it looked to me, Borden, you were the only pathetic one on that terrace last night. The fact that you're so pathetic is probably one of the many reasons Samara has never wanted you."

Paul flushed with anger and humiliation. "She's nothing more than a pretty face and body! Women like her are a dime a dozen — a flavor of the month. And I bet she's not even good in bed. Frigid as damn January snow!"

The fury that hardened Marcus's eyes was as lethal as the slice of a well-honed sword. "Do you really want to continue down this road, Borden?"

But Paul was too far gone to heed the deadly warning in Marcus's eyes. "I can't believe I wasted so much time on her. If you think I feel bad about last night, think again, Wolf. I should've done it a long time ago. She's lucky I didn't *really* knock some sense into her like she deserved. Now *that—*"

In a heartbeat Marcus crossed the room and landed a vicious right hook that sent Paul's head snapping backward. Paul cried out sharply and grabbed at his face. When his fingers encountered blood, he slid weakly to the floor on his knees.

Swiftly, Marcus knelt over him. He grabbed Paul's face with one hand and gave a ruthless squeeze. "You punk-ass bastard," he said through gritted teeth. "You ain't a man. You handle rejection like a spoiled little brat who didn't get his way. She doesn't want you—get the hell over it."

Paul's Adam's apple bobbed when he gulped. "M-My nose. I-I think you broke my nose."

Marcus sneered contemptuously. "Send me the bill." He stood, towering over Paul's huddled form. His smile was narrow, a blade turned to the sharpest edge. "As for Samara's performance in bed. Well…a gentleman should never kiss and tell. I *will* tell you that she's got me whipped, and you know that doesn't happen very often with 'guys like me.' A shame you'll never know for yourself though."

Paul didn't utter another word as Marcus turned and strode out of the apartment, slamming the door behind him.

Marcus was gone when she awakened.

Samara told herself she was a fool for being disappointed. She couldn't have expected him to crawl into bed with her and remain the entire day. They no longer had that kind of relationship. Last night she'd apologized for not trusting him, but it was too late. Marcus wasn't going to forgive her. His dead silence had made that abundantly clear. It was time for her to stop feeling sorry for herself and get on with her life.

Grim with determination, Samara climbed out of bed and stood. So far, so good. She walked gingerly to the bathroom and flipped on the light switch, then nearly bolted from the room when she caught her reflection in the mirror. She looked like death. Disheveled hair everywhere, deep bags underneath her eyes, a sickly pallor to her skin.

Had *Marcus* seen her this way?

Shaking her head, Samara bent over the sink to splash cold water on her face and brush her teeth.

She was heading to the kitchen for a glass of water when the nausea returned, sending her right back to the bathroom.

After emptying what little remained in her stomach, she flushed the toilet and sank down weakly onto the cool tiled floor. She closed her eyes and leaned her head back against the wall. She could no longer dismiss the suspicion that had whispered through her mind during the night. Her illness had nothing to do with the flu virus.

She was pregnant.

Pregnant.

Samara groaned as the word hammered through her brain. No, this couldn't be happening to her. She *couldn't* be pregnant. Not now, and not by a man who no longer wanted her.

But even as her mind rebelled against the notion, Samara knew better. Her period was two days late. Although her cycle was sometimes erratic, she instinctively knew this wouldn't be one of those months when her period arrived unexpectedly after a brief delay. She and Marcus had made love more than a few times without protection. They'd known the risks and had taken them anyway. And now she was pregnant.

Pregnant.

She was a walking cliché—a woman who'd risked it all for love, only to lose everything in the end. God, what was she going to do?

Samara's eyes snapped open. First, she needed to confirm her suspicion before deciding on her next course of action. If there was even a remote possibility that she *wasn't* pregnant, she had to know.

Pushing herself to her feet, Samara undressed and took a quick shower. Praying for a reprieve from the nausea, she threw on clothes and rushed out to the nearest drugstore.

Half an hour later, she had her answer.

Three different home pregnancy tests confirmed that she was pregnant.

Numb with shock, Samara stared back and forth between each plastic applicator. Different brands, same results.

She was going to have a baby.

She, who'd always prided herself on being too smart to let such a thing happen. She, who mentored teen mothers like Brianna Lynch and taught other girls to practice safe sex. She, who had vowed not to become a single parent like her mother.

Samara would have laughed at the sheer irony of the situation—if there were anything even remotely humorous about it. She was pregnant, alone and scared.

Her gaze dropped to her flat waistline. A tiny life was growing inside her. A life she and Marcus had unknowingly created together. Did she dare tell him? How would he react to the news? Would he be angry or elated?

Samara scraped her hand through her hair. She didn't have to tell him. If they never saw each other again, he'd be none the wiser. Just like her parents. Samara's child would be raised as she herself had been raised—without a father.

She shook her head as tears burned her eyelids. She didn't want to raise her child alone. Not because she wasn't capable, but because she knew the emotional toll it would take on both of them. She had only to look at her own life to know how painfully true this was.

She loved Marcus. She wanted him in her life. She wanted him in their baby's life.

But if he no longer wanted to be with her…what was she going to do?

Chapter Seventeen

Marcus got the surprise of his life that morning when he arrived home to find his brother waiting for him in the lobby of his apartment building. Michael Wolf stood at the security desk, laughing and conversing with the security guard as if they were old buddies.

"What are you doing here, Mike?" Marcus asked, dumbfounded. "And when did you get in?"

"I flew in late last night. I knew you wouldn't be home, so I crashed at a hotel for the night. Came over first thing this morning." Michael eyed his brother's rumpled appearance, taking in the wrinkled white shirt that hung over his black tuxedo pants and the jacket slung carelessly over Marcus's arm.

Michael grinned. "Must have been one helluva party you attended last night. Where've you been all night?"

Marcus grunted in response. He inclined his head toward the grinning security guard. "Morning, Mr. Parker."

"Good morning, son. You gonna answer your brother's question? Inquiring minds wanna know."

"I plead the Fifth." Marcus headed for the elevators. A cab arrived almost at once.

Michael followed him. "Seriously, Little Man, where did you spend the night? Wait a minute. What happened to your hand?"

Marcus glanced down, calmly acknowledging the trace of blood on his fist. He hadn't even noticed it while he drove home. He removed a handkerchief from his tuxedo jacket and wiped his hand. "It's nothing. What're you doing here, Mike?"

"I came to rescue you from yourself. And from the looks of it, I got here just in time." Michael grabbed his hand and examined it. "That blood wasn't yours. Whose was it?"

"Nobody's. Don't worry about it." Marcus propped a shoulder against the wall and closed his eyes. He was drained—mentally and physically. All he wanted was a hot shower and a magical elixir to make him forget the past two and a half weeks.

Michael studied him shrewdly. "It's even worse than I thought. Let me guess. You saw some guy coming onto Samara at the party and you went ballistic."

"It's a little more complicated than that." Marcus stepped off the elevator. "Let's just say he had what was coming to him, and then some."

Michael chuckled and drew an arm around his brother's neck. "Defending your woman's honor, ATL style. That's my boy."

Inside Marcus's penthouse, Michael filled a large bowl with ice and passed it to Marcus. "You know the routine. Keeps the swelling down."

Marcus leaned against the counter and stuck his fist inside the bowl. It was like old times again. The Wolf brothers had always looked out for each other when it came to fights. Growing up in a rough neighborhood, brawls had been like a rite of passage. You either learned how to defend yourself, or you got the crap beat out of you on a regular basis.

Marcus was glad to see his brother, although he wasn't sure he would feel the same once he discovered the reason for Michael's surprise visit. He eyed him suspiciously. "What did you mean about rescuing me from myself?"

"Glad you asked." Michael folded his arms across his broad chest. "We've all decided this thing between you and Samara has gone on long enough."

Marcus raised an eyebrow. "We?"

"The Atlanta contingent—me, Dad, your employees at the firm who, through no fault of my own, caught wind of what happened.

No doubt from talking to folks at the D.C. office." At Marcus's scowl, Michael grinned. "Even the most loyal servants will gossip, Marcus. Anyway, I've been sent here as an emissary to broker peace between the two warring factions known as Marcus and Samara."

"I hate to break it to you," Marcus groused, "but this isn't the U.N. Samara and I can handle our own problems without outside interference."

"Which would explain why you're both so miserable."

Marcus set down the bowl with a thud. "Stay out of this, Mike."

"I can't. I'm not allowed to return home until you and Samara get back together."

"And what about the restaurant?"

"It's in good hands. Being the boss means I can do whatever I want, remember? I'm long overdue for a vacation anyway." Michael clasped his hands behind his head with a smug grin. "So it looks like I'm in for the long haul, Little Man."

Marcus shrugged, feigning nonchalance as he started from the kitchen. "Stay as long as you want. I could use some good home-cooking anyway. I've been eating out too much."

Michael snorted. "I'm not here to be your personal chef."

"But you will be. You won't be able to stop yourself. Matter of fact," Marcus drawled, "feel free to make breakfast while I'm in the shower."

"Actually, I was thinking about going to see Samara."

Marcus stopped cold in his tracks. His tone was flat. "What for?"

Michael shrugged. "I'm in town. Why not?"

Marcus didn't want Michael talking to Samara. After watching her at the table with Paul Borden last night, he'd realized he didn't want to see her with *any* man—not even his own brother.

"I don't think that's a good idea," he said in a low voice.

"Why not?"

"She's not feeling well. She was throwing up all night."

Michael was silent. If Marcus had been facing him, he would have seen the sharp, discerning look that filled Michael's dark eyes. "She was throwing up?"

"Yeah. I told her to stay home and get some rest. So leave her alone."

"Yes, sir."

Satisfied, Marcus left the kitchen. "After breakfast," he called on his way down the hallway, "I'll drive you to the hotel to pick up your things."

"I told you I'm not making breakfast!" Michael called after him. There was no response.

Muttering under his breath, Michael opened the refrigerator and surveyed the meager contents. Bottled water, a few takeout containers, some overripe apples in the vegetable tray.

Michael shook his head in disgust. His brother lived like the stereotypical bachelor. If he weren't a multimillionaire with the means to feed himself, he would probably starve to death.

Michael hoped fatherhood would improve Marcus's eating habits.

Marcus finished eating and sat back in his chair with an approving nod. "Not bad. Not as good as something *you* could make, of course, but it definitely hits the spot."

While Marcus showered, Michael had gone across the street to the Foggy Bottom Deli and bought a few croissants filled with ham and egg. They ate outside on the balcony to enjoy the mild spring morning.

Michael's mouth curved cynically. "Even if I'd wanted to fix breakfast, I had nothing to work with. Your refrigerator is so empty I can hear an echo."

"Yeah, well, grocery shopping hasn't really been one of my priorities."

"Funny you should mention that. What *are* your priorities, Marcus? Does getting your life back in order appear somewhere on that list?"

Marcus scowled. "Don't start with me, Mike. I told you before that I don't want to talk about this."

"Come on, Marcus, this is me you're talking to. I used to change your diapers and wipe your snotty nose. Open up the vault and tell me what *really* happened between you and Samara."

"As I told you and Dad over the phone," Marcus said tersely, "Samara and I decided not to get married. End of story."

"What prompted the decision?"

"We had an argument."

"That must have been one hell of an argument. What was it about?"

Marcus stretched out his long legs. He'd forgotten how relentless Michael could be when he wanted something. Like a pit bull on steroids. He couldn't begrudge him though. It ran in the family.

Marcus pushed out a deep, ragged breath. "She thought I was cheating on her with a client's daughter."

Michael raised an eyebrow. "And what gave her that idea?"

"She walked in on us kissing and drew her own conclusions. She didn't give me a chance to explain that Antoinette had caught me by surprise, and I was about to pull away right before Samara walked through the door." Anger roughened his voice. "She stormed out of the office, we argued, and the rest is history."

Whistling softly through his teeth, Michael picked up his bottled orange juice and took a long swig.

Marcus waited. He knew what his brother's next question was.

"Has she given you another opportunity to explain what happened?" Michael asked.

"Better than that. Last night *she* apologized and asked my forgiveness." Bitterness edged his words.

Michael studied his stony profile. "You didn't accept the apology." When Marcus remained silent, Michael shook his head incredulously. "I don't believe this. Not even *you* can be that cold."

"What's that supposed to mean?"

The shift in the tension between them was subtle, but there just the same. "It means that this is your modus operandi, Marcus. When someone hurts you, you punish them for it. You kill them with your silence. No matter how repentant they are or how many times they try to make amends, you don't relent. You lord your anger and disappointment over them like it's a source of power. How do I know this? Because you've been doing it to Mom for the past twenty-five years!"

Marcus grew very still. "We're not talking about her. Leave her out of this discussion."

Undaunted by the lethal fury that hardened his brother's tone, Michael leaned across the table. "Don't you see the pattern, Marcus? Mom made a mistake and spent the next twenty-five years of her life doing penance for it. Now it's Samara's turn. She's been tried and convicted in the Supreme Court of Marcus Wolf. Her sentence is to spend the rest of her life blaming herself for what happened and wishing the man she loves could find it in his heart to forgive her. She and Mom have become cellmates."

Marcus scowled. "It's not the same thing and you know it."

"Why isn't it?"

"Because Mom betrayed us!" Marcus roared. He shoved to his feet and began pacing up and down the balcony. "Don't talk to me about her as if she's the victim here. She's not!"

"No, because everyone knows *you're* the only victim of what happened. Poor little Marcus who walked in on his mother and her boyfriend in the middle of their afternoon tryst. Poor disillusioned Marcus who would be scarred for life."

Marcus stopped pacing and glared at his brother. "What the hell's going on here? Where is this coming from?"

"Ever since Mom and Dad got divorced, you've been brooding through life like a wounded little boy. Everyone made allowances for your temper tantrums when you were a child because we understood you were hurting and needed to work through your pain in your own way. But here's a news flash, Marcus: You aren't the only one who was hurting. Dad was hurting, Mom was hurting and *I* was definitely hurting. Did you think you were the only one who cried behind closed doors, or wiped away tears when you thought no one else was looking?"

Marcus's chest heaved as he fought to control his labored breathing. "Are you calling me self-absorbed, Michael?" he asked in a low, quelling voice. "After all the late-night conversations we had? After we would talk for hours on end about never having children because we didn't want to put them through the same bullshit we were going through? Are you saying your feelings never mattered to me?"

"What I'm *saying*, Marcus, is that we all suffered—you, me, Mom and Dad. But twenty-five years later, *you're* the only one still carrying a grudge! When are you going to cut the Wounded Martyr act and let go of the past once and for all?"

"Just pretend it never happened, right? Bury my head in the sand and act like everything's fine and dandy, like Mom never violated our trust?"

Michael slammed his fist down on the table. "Listen to you! You act as if you're perfect, like *you've* never made a mistake in your entire life!"

"I never cheated on my spouse and left my kids to fend for themselves!"

Michael bounded to his feet. His tone was low and scathing as he approached Marcus. "Do you even know why Mom and Dad got married in the first place? Of course you don't. You're too full of your righteous anger to hear what anyone has to say on the matter."

"What difference does it make? It doesn't change what happened."

"No, but it sure as hell sheds some light on a few things. For starters, did you know that Mom and Dad weren't dating at the time they got married? Mom was actually involved with someone else, someone she planned to marry right after high school. He got killed in a drunk driving accident. Mom and Dad were good friends, so naturally she turned to him for consolation. One thing led to another, and they wound up sleeping together. It was something they both regretted immediately afterward, but it was too late.

"Four weeks later, Mom found out she was pregnant. She was devastated. Her father—our esteemed grandfather who would take the belt to *us* if we stepped out of line—was one of those strict do-it-by-the-book Baptist ministers. She was scared of what he'd do if he found out she was pregnant. Having a child out of wedlock wasn't an option, and neither was abortion. When she told Dad she was pregnant, he was crushed. He wasn't any more prepared for parent-hood than she was. But being the honorable man he's always been, he offered to marry her. Mom reluctantly accepted. She felt she had no other choice. But there was something else." Michael paused and took a deep breath. "She didn't think the baby she was carrying was Dad's. She had slept with her boyfriend two nights before he was killed. She was with Dad three nights later."

Marcus stared at his brother in stunned disbelief. "What are you saying, Michael? That we're half-brothers?"

Michael watched him through narrowed eyes. "Would it matter?"

"Of course not. Are we?"

"Mom and Dad got married without knowing the answer. Dad was determined to raise me as his biological son, whether or not I really was. And he did. Mom said he was the most devoted father she'd ever seen, and she loved him for that. But she wanted to know for sure. I think she believed, on some subconscious level, that if they found some closure regarding my paternity, it might help other areas of their troubled marriage. Make no mistake about it,

224

Marcus," Michael added somberly, "their marriage was on shaky ground long before Grant Rutherford entered the picture."

"So what about the paternity test?"

"Well…" Michael said slowly, "the results confirmed that… Drum roll please!"

Marcus swore impatiently. "Damn it, Mike—"

Laughing, Michael clapped a hand to his brother's tense shoulder. "Relax, man. Sterling Wolf has very potent sperm. He's one-hundred percent my father. Look at us, Marcus. We both look just like him!"

Marcus sat down at the table and scrubbed a hand over his face. He didn't think he could've handled any more shocking revelations. "What happened after that?" he asked wearily.

"Naturally they were both ecstatic about the news. But it didn't cure their other problems. See, Mom and Dad cared for each other a whole lot. But they were never in love. I think in many ways they both felt trapped by the situation. It was like they were living a lie for everyone else—her parents, Dad's parents, their friends." Michael sat down. "After about five years, Mom decided she couldn't go through the charade anymore. She was about to ask Dad for a divorce when she found out she was pregnant. She knew she couldn't leave Dad after that."

"So I was her ball and chain," Marcus said bitterly. "Having me sealed her fate in a loveless marriage."

"Yes, and no. She freely admits she initially resented the pregnancy. But by the time you were born, Marcus, she'd resolved those feelings. Without an ounce of jealousy, I can tell you that I've always known you were her favorite." He chuckled wryly. "She said it was love at first sight with you. She loved you so much that she wanted to name you after her first love, the one who died. Be grateful she didn't, by the way—his name was Wendell. Anyway, things seemed to get better between Mom and Dad after you were born."

"But it didn't last."

"No," Michael said softly. "It didn't last. You know the rest."

Marcus stood and walked over to the balcony. He stared down at the light Saturday morning traffic on the street below, his mind racing. So much made sense now. So many pieces of the puzzle had been put into place. He didn't know how to describe the emotions swirling through him. Relief? Remorse? Sadness?

Michael spoke quietly behind him. "While nothing I've told you excuses what Mom did, it does provide a better explanation for it. And it also explains why Dad was so willing to forgive her, to set her free to find her own happiness, even if it meant with another man." He paused. "I hope one day you, too, can find it in your heart to forgive her."

Marcus squeezed his eyes shut, saying nothing.

After a minute his brother appeared beside him at the railing. "If you can't forgive Mom, then you're never going to forgive Samara. And if that happens, you're going to spend the rest of your life alone and bitter. Or worse yet, you'll end up married to some woman you don't even love, and you'll spend your days and nights wondering about the one who got away. Don't let that happen, Marcus. If not for yourself, do it for Samara. Do it for the poor sap *she* may end up marrying someday, the man she won't be able to give her heart to because she lost it to you."

Michael paused, then gently grasped his brother's shoulder. "Do it so that you won't repeat the legacy of our parents' loveless marriage."

Samara felt like a prisoner in her own home. Nausea kept her confined to her bedroom for the rest of the day.

On Sunday morning she managed to drag herself out of bed and take a shower. Feeling a little stronger, she ventured out to the kitchen and poured herself a small glass of fruit juice. She nibbled on a piece of dry toast while she listened to her voice mail messages.

Melissa had called twice. "Samara, it's me. Just wanted to check up on you and make sure everything was all right. Gary and I are supposed to be going furniture shopping for the nursery today, but if you need me to come over, I will. Call me."

Her next message was laced with urgency. "Samara, you are *not* going to believe what happened! This morning Gary went over to Paul's apartment to check up on him—you know, just to make sure he wasn't too hung over from last night. When Gary got there, he found Paul with a black eye! Apparently Marcus went over there first thing this morning to take care of some unfinished business. Girl, what happened out on that terrace last night? Anyway, you'll be relieved to know that Paul doesn't plan to press charges. He was too humiliated. Gary said he looked real bad though. Call me as soon as you get this message—*please!*"

While Samara was still reeling from shock and confusion, the next message rolled on. "Hey, Samara, it's me." Her heart thudded at the sound of Marcus's deep timbre. "Just wanted to see how you're doing. Hope you're feeling better." He paused, and Samara thought she detected a hint of quiet uncertainty in his voice. But then he continued more briskly, "You're probably sleeping, so I won't disturb you again by calling. If you need anything, give me a call. If you can't reach me at home, you have my cell."

Tears filled her eyes as she hung up the phone. *Oh, Marcus. I don't want your pity or protection. I want your love.*

As soon as the toast hit her stomach, the nausea returned. She bolted for the bathroom.

She had just finished brushing her teeth for the second time when the doorbell rang. She groaned. It was probably Melissa. Samara wasn't in the mood for company, not even her best friend's. And she feared that Melissa would take one look at her and know her secret. Pregnant women had an uncanny knack of detecting pregnancy in other women, or so she'd always heard.

Samara scraped her wild hair into a ponytail and splashed cold water on her face before going to answer the door. She groaned inwardly at the sight of her mother standing on the doorstep. She would have preferred Melissa.

"This really isn't a good time for me, Mother."

Asha arched a perfectly sculpted eyebrow. "Is it ever?"

Samara left her mother standing in the doorway and stalked into the living room. She was too sick and miserable to practice good manners. She flopped down on the sofa and hugged a throw pillow to her chest.

Asha closed the door and crossed the room to her. As usual, she looked effortlessly sleek in a cream silk blouse and cashmere slacks. Samara felt like a ragamuffin in the black sweatshirt and leggings she'd worn the day before.

She eyed Asha warily. "What're you doing in town, Mother? Checking on one of your boutiques?"

"I came to see you. I heard about you and Marcus Wolf."

Samara stiffened. "There *is* no me and Marcus Wolf. We broke up, or didn't your informant tell you?"

Asha's mouth tightened. "What are you talking about?"

"Which part do you need clarified? My busted love affair or the fact that you've been having me followed for the last ten years, ever since I left you in Paris and went to college? Don't look so shocked, Mother. I've known for quite some time now. At first I dismissed the 'photographer' as paparazzi, which made sense given my mother's fame. But then you always seemed to know what was happening in my life before I had a chance to tell you. I've even seen your informant on a few occasions—an older guy, short graying hair, a bit overweight. Who is he, Mother? Another one of your discarded lovers? He doesn't seem like your type. And he's not very good at being covert."

"All right. I won't deny it." Asha sighed. "After what happened in Paris, I wanted to make sure you were always safe. So I hired an old friend of mine to keep tabs on you. He runs his own security company and offered to do the surveillance himself as a personal favor to me. And I trusted him not to leak anything potentially sensitive to the tabloids. He knew I would destroy him if he did." She frowned. "I'm firing him first thing in the morning."

Samara stared up at her. "Why would you do something like that?"

"What on earth do you mean? I'm firing him because—"

"No, that's not what I meant." Samara sat up straighter. "Why would you hire a security professional to keep an eye on me when you did nothing to André? You let him get away with what he did to me. Did you think I forgot, Mother?"

"Oh, Samara." Asha joined her on the sofa. Samara recoiled from her mother's attempt to touch her. Lips pursed, Asha folded her elegant hands in her lap. "I see."

"Do you, Mother?" Samara hissed. "Do you *really* see? Do you have *any* idea how devastated I was when you showed up at the hospital in Paris and asked me what I had done to deserve André's brutality? You didn't care that your ex-lover had beaten me to within an inch of my life! All you wanted to know was what *I* had done to bring it upon myself. My own mother. How *could* you?"

"I cared, Samara," Asha cried. "Believe me when I say that I cared!"

"I don't believe you! Why didn't you do something?"

"Because I panicked! I thought the same thing had happened to you that—" She broke off abruptly and clapped a trembling hand to her mouth. She rose unsteadily and walked to the window.

Samara stared at her in wild-eyed silence. Her heartbeat was a deafening roar in her ears. "You thought what, Mother?" she asked faintly. "What did you think had happened to me?"

Asha kept her back turned to her, her arms folded tightly around herself. "I thought he raped you. And in that moment it felt like history was repeating itself."

Samara felt dangerously lightheaded as comprehension slowly dawned. "You…were raped?"

"It was a long time ago, Samara. I didn't come over here to rehash ancient history."

"Who raped you?" Samara demanded. When Asha remained silent, she snapped. "For God's sake, Mother, stop shutting me out! For once in your life, *talk* to me! I want to know who raped you."

Asha whirled around. "It was your father!"

Stunned, Samara could only stare at her. Asha's beautiful face was ravaged with grief and outrage. A thick, tense silence hung between both women for several moments.

"My...father?" Samara finally managed in a choked whisper. "*He* raped you?"

"We met during my freshman year in college. He was in med school at the university. I was pre-med, so we often saw each other on campus or in the laboratory. Nathaniel was smart, handsome and so sure of himself and what he wanted out of life. I was young and glad to be away from my domineering mother for the first time in my life. Nathaniel seemed so wise and mature. I was in awe of him, and he immediately discerned that. One night he invited me to dinner, then back to his off-campus apartment to help me study for an upcoming physics exam. I detested physics and needed all the help I could get."

She stopped and shook her head ruefully. Her eyes grew luminous with the sheen of tears. "He raped me, Samara. You don't need to know the gory details. I got pregnant and he told me to get an abortion. I couldn't go through with it. My mother had always drilled into me that life was precious and not to be taken for granted. When I refused to have an abortion and threatened to go to the dean about being raped, Nathaniel panicked and proposed to me. I married him knowing that he didn't want me or my child. That was a mistake. Once I realized how miserable we would both be in the long run, I asked for an annulment. He didn't put up a fight." Asha's laugh was low and brittle. "He was so eager to escape, in fact, that he packed his bags in the middle of the night and left without saying goodbye."

Samara shook her head slowly. "But I don't understand. You've always told me what a kind, decent man my father was."

"I didn't want you to grow up knowing what a complete bastard he was. His absence was indictment enough."

Samara swallowed a hard lump in her throat. "It all makes so much sense now," she whispered. "You were thrust into motherhood before you were ready. And that's why you jumped at the first opportunity to get away from it all. To get away from me."

Asha's expression softened, but she offered no denial. "It doesn't mean that I never loved you, Samara. I was young and terribly immature. I went to school in Pennsylvania to escape from my mother, to chart my own territory. I never knew how drastically my plans would be altered. I wasn't prepared for that."

Tears blurred Samara's vision. "I'm sorry, Mother. I'm so sorry about what happened to you."

"Oh, darling. No more sorry than I am for what André did to you." Asha sat down on the sofa and drew a comforting arm around Samara's shoulder. Samara didn't pull away this time. "I thought you were a little infatuated with André. He was a virile, worldly man who seemed to take a genuine interest in your welfare. I trusted him, and he betrayed that trust." Her voice hardened. "When your father raped me, I was so ashamed. I blamed myself for a long time, asking myself over and over again what I could have done to invite such a violation. In time I learned to stop blaming myself, learned to stop asking what I should have done differently. But a small part of me still held on to those old insecurities. When I saw you in that hospital room looking so battered and helpless, I lost it. I felt that I had failed you. I hadn't protected you like I should have. So I lashed out at you, although I know it was horribly unfair of me." Her voice caught, tears filling her eyes. "I am sorrier than you will ever know, Samara."

Samara was silent, trying to absorb the enormity of her mother's horrendous revelations. Asha had been raped. Nathaniel Layton, whose name Samara bore, was a rapist. As a child Samara had daydreamed about her father, wondering what he looked like, where he lived, what he did for a living. Of all the things she'd imagined about him, being a rapist was *not* one of them. She felt betrayed all over again.

But more than anything, she ached for her mother. No wonder Asha had always found it difficult to forge a relationship with her daughter. Samara must have served as a constant reminder of the violent act that led to her conception.

"Have you ever seen my father again?" she whispered.

"No." Asha hesitated. "He contacted me a long time ago to congratulate me on my successful modeling career."

"Did he…ask about me?"

Asha's prolonged silence gave Samara her answer even before she spoke. "No, baby. He wanted to know if we could have dinner together. I told him to go to hell." She looked at Samara with a solemn expression. "Perhaps I should have told you at the time. You were old enough. I should have given you an opportunity to meet him and decide for yourself whether or not you wanted him in your life."

Samara shook her head firmly. "I don't. I never really did, to be honest with you. I was more curious about him than anything. And now that curiosity has been satisfied." She took a deep, decisive breath. "I think I'm going to change my last name. You and Mama Tess always told me that I'm a Dubois at heart. Maybe it's time to make it legal."

"You could do that. But something tells me your last name will be changing soon anyway." Asha stroked errant strands of black hair from Samara's face and kissed her forehead. "Darling, I know what happened between you and Marcus Wolf."

Samara winced. "Your informant is good, I have to give him that."

"He isn't the one who told me. I spoke with Antoinette Toussaint myself. She called me several weeks ago when she returned from overseas. She wanted to know if I needed another haute couture model."

Samara angled her head to look at her mother in surprise. "She wanted a job?"

"*Oui*. It seems that she lost her modeling contract with her agency in New York. Antoinette always did have a horrible attitude. A rather warped sense of entitlement. It was the reason I stopped working with her years ago. Physically she makes a fabulous couture model, but I simply cannot tolerate her nasty disposition." Asha chuckled. "There's only room for one diva at the House of Dubois, and you're looking at her."

Samara smiled. "So what happened when you talked to her?"

"She must have 'conveniently' forgotten the fact that I terminated our relationship years ago. I suppose she was too desperate to care at that point. She'd probably been rejected by every other couturier in the business before she came crawling back to me. It's a small circle, Samara, and designers talk. No one can afford to burn bridges. Needless to say Antoinette was not pleased when I turned her down, but she politely thanked me for my time and asked me to keep her in mind for future assignments. I thought I'd heard the last of her until she called me out of the blue last week, presumably to ask my 'advice.' She was thinking about getting out of the modeling business altogether. Seems she met a man she'd fallen madly in love with and had set her sights on settling down with. She was only too happy to provide his name and specific details about him, perhaps assuming I would pass along the information to you. But here's the frightening part: That silly girl actually fancies herself in love with your Marcus."

"That's not hard to imagine," Samara mumbled dispiritedly. "Marcus has that effect on women."

"Present company included?"

"Unfortunately."

"I see. And what are you going to do about it?"

"Nothing. I blew it. I accused him of cheating on me and wouldn't listen when he tried to explain what really happened. By the time I realized I'd made a terrible mistake, it was too late. He didn't accept my apology."

"I see." Asha pursed her lips thoughtfully. "He's an attorney. Surely he can understand your rush to judgment was based on extenuating circumstances and therefore not your fault."

Samara frowned. "What I walked in on looked bad," she agreed, "but if I really trusted Marcus, I would have given him the benefit of the doubt. If I had stumbled upon him leaning over a dead body, I would've given him a chance to explain the situation before accusing him of murder. Why should this have been any different?"

"You misunderstood what I meant by 'extenuating circumstances.' You have a family history of trust issues, darling. By virtue of your birth, you were born with a predisposition not to trust members of the opposite sex. Throughout your life, I painted a portrait of men as the big bad wolves. Wolves in sheep's clothing. It was only natural that you inherited my cynicism, my flawed inability to separate the good ones from the bad ones."

Samara slanted her mother a dubious look. "That sounds like a cop-out."

Asha shrugged elegantly. "It's the truth. You know it as well as I do. Besides, Marcus is an attorney. Defense attorneys, for example, have used far less substantial arguments in getting their clients acquitted. If you go to Marcus and explain your background, I'm sure he'll see the merits of your case."

"Marcus already knows my background. In fact, my 'trust issues' are probably the main reason he's keeping his distance. He doesn't want to spend the rest of his life walking on eggshells around me. Can't say that I completely blame him, either."

But a tiny part of her *did* blame him. She'd made a bad judgment call. Didn't she at least deserve a second chance? Was *he* so willing to throw everything away on a simple misunderstanding, as he'd accused her of doing?

Samara leaned her head back against the sofa. She remembered the impression she'd had of Marcus when she first met him. She'd thought he would be dangerous and formidable if ever crossed. She'd known he hadn't gotten where he was in life without having a street fighter in him.

Her mouth curved ruefully when she recalled Melissa's urgent voice mail message about Marcus and Paul Borden. Marcus had proven Samara right on both counts. He was ruthless *and* a street fighter.

"So that's it?" Asha demanded. "You're just going to walk away from the only man you have ever loved—the only man you will *ever* love—without a fight?"

"I'm too tired to fight, Mother. And in case you haven't noticed, I'm not exactly feeling in top form."

Asha gave her a soft, pitying smile. "Does Marcus know you're carrying his child?" At her daughter's startled look, she laughed. "Darling, I knew the minute you opened the door! I took one look at you and could tell."

Samara chewed her bottom lip. "When I got sick last night, I told Marcus I was coming down with the flu. But if *you* could tell, then maybe—"

"He doesn't have a clue, darling, take my word for it. Men can be incredibly dense creatures at times, even men as highly intelligent as your Marcus. If you told him you have the flu, that's what he will believe until he has reason to suspect otherwise." She laid a loving hand upon Samara's cheek. "As for this sickness, *chère*, I have the perfect remedy. An old family recipe. I can send Pierre to fetch the ingredients from the store. He's been waiting patiently in the limo, no doubt spying on your neighbors like the busybody he is." She paused. "Before I call him, I must warn you that Pierre has been around women all his life. He knows the signs and symptoms of pregnancy. If I send him to get what I need, he will put two and two together. Do you have a problem with him knowing?"

"I don't care," Samara mumbled. "I'm desperate."

"Don't worry. He is the soul of discretion—at least when it comes to *my* private affairs. I trust him completely. He's one of the very few men I trust, but perhaps that's because he's more like one of *us* than…" She and Samara looked at each other and burst into laughter.

"Dear Pierre," both women murmured fondly in unison. Asha called him on her cell phone and gave him instructions.

Within minutes, it seemed, Pierre arrived with ginger ale, peppermint leaves and baking soda. Samara wrinkled her nose as Asha mixed and stirred the concoction before handing it to her.

Samara regarded it skeptically.

"Drink up, darling. You'll feel better."

"All of the other girls swear by this stuff," Pierre added coaxingly. "It's not a rare occurrence to have a model or wardrobe assistant show up at work and become violently ill on the spot—much to the absolute horror of one particular designer who shall remain nameless. He was so mortified that he had to be moved to another office down the hall, claiming that he could not think creatively while the wretched stench lingered in the air."

"Pierre," Asha said mildly, "*ferme le bouche.*"

Pierre clamped his mouth shut, but his blue-gray eyes twinkled mischievously at Samara. She made a face at him.

"Bottoms up." She downed the contents of the glass and tried not to gag.

"As long as you're able to keep the fluid down," Asha said, "it should work."

When Asha disappeared into the kitchen to rinse out the empty glass, Pierre leaned across the sofa with a conspiratorial look. "If you want the father of your baby to be brought to his senses," he whispered to Samara, "give Asha the word and she'll take care of it."

Samara laughed in spite of herself. "Pierre, I didn't get knocked up by some lowlife, if that's what you're thinking. He doesn't even know. And, no, I don't want my mother to interfere."

Pierre sniffed. "If you change your mind, let me know. You should see what Asha arranged to have done to André Leclerc after he assaulted you. She even demanded a Polaroid to ensure that the job had been done to her satisfaction. Let me just tell you it was *not* pretty." Pierre gave a delicate shudder. " 'Hell hath no fury like a woman scorned'—and don't even *think* about messing with her daughter!"

Samara's eyes widened in shock, but before she could ask Pierre to elaborate, her mother returned from the kitchen. "Pierre, dearest, I've decided to spend the night with my daughter and tend to her needs. Would you run to the hotel and retrieve my personal effects?"

"You really don't have to stay, Mother. I mean, it's not that I couldn't use the company," Samara added almost shyly, "but I wouldn't want to impose on your time."

"Nonsense. It's no imposition, and the only reason I came to town was to see *you.*"

Both women exchanged tentative smiles. A milestone had been reached in their relationship. If nothing else came out of this catastrophe, Samara knew she finally had her mother back.

"Besides," Asha drawled humorously, "staying here gives me more time to work on you. If all goes well, by morning you will realize that you simply cannot live without Marcus Wolf, and you'll be ready to do whatever it takes to win him back."

Pierre clapped his hands together gleefully. "Goody! I get to help plan a wedding!"

Asha awakened at six A.M. and sent for her limousine. While she waited, she watched Samara slumber peacefully in her bed. It had been so many years since Asha indulged in such a luxury as watching her daughter sleep. She regretted that she'd missed so much of Samara's life. She regretted so much time had been wasted.

No more.

The ginger ale recipe had worked like a charm. Samara's nausea had abated, allowing her to hold down a light meal of chicken broth and saltines. Afterward she and Asha had enjoyed a spirited poker match. It wasn't until afterward, when Asha had been beaten in embarrassing succession, that she learned Samara was a poker tournament champion. Before Samara could celebrate too boisterously, Asha suggested that she lie down to avoid "overexerting" herself.

"Want to find out the sex of your child?" Asha had asked as they settled down on Samara's bed.

Samara gave a listless shrug. "I haven't decided. I'm still trying to adjust to the idea of single parenthood."

"*If* you have to raise this child alone—note the emphasis on the word 'if'—you will do just fine. We Dubois women are survivors, always have been. And you know that I will always be here for you and my grandchild." She stopped abruptly. "Did I just say that? Am I really going to be a *grandmother*?"

Samara grinned ruefully. "Afraid so."

Asha struck a thoughtful pose, pretending to consider the notion. After a moment she heaved a dramatic sigh. "Very well. I suppose it had to happen eventually—might as well happen while I'm still young and vigorous enough to enjoy my grandchild. At any rate, what I meant before is that I know of a way to tell if you're having a boy or girl."

Samara looked skeptical. "You don't really believe that superstitious stuff, do you?"

"Humor me." Asha reached up and unclasped her gold Cartier necklace. "Lie flat and lift your sweatshirt a little."

Samara complied, then watched in wide-eyed fascination as the diamond pendant swung like a pendulum above her flat abdomen.

Before the pendant slowed to a complete stop, it suddenly changed direction and began to swing counter-clockwise.

"A boy," Asha announced. "You're going to have a boy in November."

Tears glistened in Samara's eyes. "A boy," she murmured quietly. "He's going to look just like Marcus. The Wolf men have strong genes."

Asha smiled gently. "Get some rest, darling. You've had a long day."

And now as she stood gazing down at her sleeping daughter in the pale light of dawn, Asha knew what she had to do.

"Where to, madam?" inquired the chauffeur once Asha was comfortably settled in the backseat of the Rolls Royce.

"Back to the hotel. I need to shower and change into something more appropriate."

A snowy eyebrow lifted. "More appropriate?"

"Yes." Asha gazed out the window with an enigmatic smile. "I have a very important meeting this morning. It could be a hostile takeover, and I should look the part."

Chapter Eighteen

Marcus had barely arrived at the office on Monday morning when William Toussaint called. "We missed you on Friday evening. You left rather unexpectedly."

Marcus didn't miss the veiled accusation in the man's tone. "Something personal came up."

"Yes, Antoinette was quite distraught over seeing you leave with another woman. My wife said she spoke of nothing else all weekend."

Marcus decided he'd had enough subterfuge. William Toussaint had been hinting at a possible match between Marcus and his daughter for weeks. Each time Marcus had politely changed the subject, not wanting to offend his client.

He had no such qualms now. "I have to be frank with you, William. I'm not interested in dating your daughter. Not now. Not ever. If that's going to be a problem for you, you're more than welcome to take your business elsewhere. No hard feelings."

A startled silence fell on the other end. William Toussaint coughed, then cleared his throat. "Don't be ludicrous, son! You're the best attorney I've ever had the privilege of working with. I wouldn't give that up for the world—not even for Antoinette." He hesitated uncertainly. "I'll see you next month for our meeting?"

"See you then."

After Marcus hung up, he booted up the computer to get some work done. He had a ton of things to accomplish before he left early for the day. He had a very important evening ahead of him.

He was going to get Samara back.

When his intercom buzzed, he scowled at the interruption and spoke testily, "What is it, Laura?"

"Mr. Wolf, you have a visitor in the lobby. She said she doesn't have an appointment, but she needs to see you."

"Who is it?" Ever since the Antoinette fiasco, he'd been leery about receiving unexpected visitors. He was about to instruct Laura to have the person schedule an appointment when she came back with a reply he'd never expected.

"It's Asha Dubois, sir."

Marcus froze. What was Samara's *mother* doing at his office?

He could take three guesses.

"Mr. Wolf?" Laura prompted.

"I'll be out in a minute."

Asha DuBois's appearance was causing a considerable stir in the office. When Marcus stepped into the lobby, he was met with mild pandemonium. Donovan and Timothy lounged on opposite ends of the reception desk, never ones to miss an opportunity to converse with a beautiful woman. Laura was gushing all over herself between taking phone calls. Even the more reserved Helen seemed starstruck as she stood before the fashion mogul. One of Marcus's paralegals had retrieved the latest issue of *Essence* on which Asha graced the cover. Asha graciously autographed the magazine for her.

In a tailored red power suit and matching stiletto pumps with her dark hair swept into a no-nonsense twist, Asha Dubois looked like she belonged at the head of a corporate boardroom. She was the kind of woman who kicked butt first and took names later. Marcus could always appreciate that kind of killer instinct in a person.

As long as it didn't come at *his* expense.

Asha looked up unhurriedly at his appearance. For a moment he was taken aback. The resemblance between mother and daughter was uncanny.

And people thought he and *his* father looked alike!

"Mr. Wolf," Asha Dubois greeted him in smooth, cultured tones. "I was hoping I could have a moment of your time."

As if anyone ever refused her. She had the regal bearing of a queen. At any minute he expected his employees to bow at her feet in supplication.

He inclined his head coolly. "Right this way, please."

He led Asha Dubois into his office and closed the door—in case any of his awestruck employees were bold enough to eavesdrop.

Marcus gestured Asha Dubois into a chair. "May I offer you a drink? Coffee, tea, orange juice? It's early, but I also have brandy if you're interested."

"No, thank you." Asha settled into the chair and crossed her long, elegant legs. "I know you're a busy man, Mr. Wolf, so I'll get right to the point. I'm here on my daughter's behalf."

Marcus took his seat behind the desk. "Does Samara know you're here?"

"Of course not. She would kill me if she found out. I trust you won't tell her."

It wasn't a request. It was an order. "If you'd rather I didn't…"

"I'd rather you didn't. At any rate, Mr. Wolf—"

"Marcus."

"I beg your pardon?"

"Please call me Marcus." His mouth twisted cynically. "I almost became your son-in-law. It seems ridiculous for you to call me Mr. Wolf, don't you think?"

Asha narrowed her eyes at him. "All right, then. Marcus it is. I'm here because I want to know how long you intend to continue this absurd separation from my daughter."

"With all due respect, ma'am, that really isn't any of your business."

"Of course it is. She's my daughter and I care very much what happens to her. She's heartbroken over you. It's very naïve of you to assume that I would stand by and watch her suffer needlessly." Her voice grew several degrees frostier. "You may or may not be privy to the nature of our estrangement, but before you sit there in judgment of me, I've made amends with Samara. It's your turn to do the same."

"Is that right?" Marcus asked, amused. "Do you intend to force me?"

"Don't be absurd. I would never *force* any man upon my daughter. But then, I don't have to. Surely you know that."

He inclined his head. "I do."

"However," Asha continued archly, "I'm not opposed to whisking Samara away with me for a while, perhaps introducing her to some new acquaintances during our travels. Not to advocate a rebound relationship, you understand. Just to remind her that she is a young, healthy woman with plenty of options. And if she happens to meet someone she connects with, then…" Asha lifted her shoulders in a very French shrug. "I would rather see my only child experience *some* semblance of happiness with another man than remain miserable and alone. Any mother would. You understand, don't you?"

The implication was clear. Marcus removed the metaphorical dagger from his chest and calmly set it aside. The idea of Samara meeting and falling in love with another man was unbearable. But he refused to give Asha Dubois more ammunition.

"One thing you'll learn about me," he said, deliberately even, "is that I don't respond well to threats."

"I'm not threatening you, Marcus. I want nothing more than to see you and Samara resolve your problems, because I know that would make her happy." Asha leaned forward intently. "Think real hard before you walk away from what could be the best thing that ever happened to you."

Marcus turned his head, gazing out the window for a moment. "You should know," he began softly, "that before you arrived here this morning, I was going to have a talk with Samara about us getting back together."

He felt, rather than saw, Asha stiffen in the chair. He knew exactly what she was thinking. She was afraid she'd antagonized him into changing his mind. So the Mighty Asha Dubois *could* be rattled.

Her voice was remarkably calm. "And now?"

He turned back slowly to meet her composed gaze. "I'm glad that you and Samara have worked out your differences. You mean a great deal to her, so I know how important the reconciliation was to her. Just so that we understand each other though, I want you to promise me that you will never hurt her again. Because once your daughter and I are married, I'll consider it my personal responsibility to protect her from anything or anyone that might harm her." He paused to let his meaning sink in. "Including you."

Asha stared at him through narrowed eyes. For a few moments neither spoke. And neither backed down.

And then slowly a smile crept across Asha's face. She smoothly uncrossed her legs, rose and walked to the door. She stopped and turned to him. "I think you and I are going to get along just fine, Marcus Wolf."

He leaned back in his chair with an indolent smile. "I think you might be right."

Asha started to open the door. "Oh, and Marcus?"

He raised an expectant brow.

"You and Samara should really consider an early June wedding. Before the weather gets too warm."

Another meddling parent to contend with. "Actually, we'd already settled on September."

"Mmm, September." Asha seemed to ponder this as she tapped a manicured fingertip to her lips. "I don't know...there's just something magical about a June bride. Give it some thought."

"All right," he drawled patiently. "Will there be anything else?"

"Yes, as a matter of fact. Please implore your fiancée to allow me to design her wedding gown. Samara's not very fussy about these things, which is probably one of the many things you love about her. I do, too. But her wedding day should be memorable, and I'm afraid that if left up to Samara, she might show up in a rucksack."

Marcus chuckled. "Actually, I believe it was a *burlap* sack she mentioned."

Asha shuddered before slipping out the door.

Samara exited Windows and swiveled away from her computer. Although it was only six o'clock, she was exhausted. She knew the pregnancy was responsible for her fatigue. She normally remained at the office until eight P.M. without giving it a second thought.

It was just one more aspect of her life that would be changing over the next several months.

Samara sighed deeply and reached into the bottom desk drawer for her purse. She'd scheduled a doctor's appointment for tomorrow morning, but she didn't need a blood test to confirm what she already knew. A tiny life was growing inside her, and if her mother's calculations were correct, Samara would give birth in November. So much had to be done before then.

Melissa's due date was late September, which meant that both women would be out of the office on maternity leave during the same time. Samara had to find someone to cover the office during her six-week absence. Melissa had always been her second-in-command, but if Melissa decided to stay home indefinitely with her baby—as she'd already hinted at doing—then Samara would have to explore other alternatives.

She envied her best friend for having the option to remain home with her baby. As a single parent, Samara wouldn't have that option. If she didn't work, she and her child would starve. And she'd experienced enough poverty in her past to know that she didn't want the same for her own child. Not that Asha Dubois would allow such a thing to happen. She'd already begged Samara to consider relocating to New York that summer so that Asha could take better care of her.

Taming the Wolf

"This is *not* another attempt to get you at the House of Dubois," Asha had insisted when Samara flatly refused the suggestion. "Let's face it, darling. Your situation is not the same as mine was when you were born. *I* had to work to keep a roof over our heads—you don't. You never have to work another day in your life if you decide not to. But I'm not suggesting you give up your career! Believe me, I know better than anyone how much you enjoy what you do at the Institute."

It was true. Samara would never dream of leaving the Yorkin Institute and the community work that mattered so much to her. Still, she'd always heard stories about how motherhood changed some women. Would motherhood dramatically alter her own priorities? Would she want to become a stay-at-home mom once her baby was born? How would she feel about entrusting her precious newborn to a complete stranger?

Samara paused in the middle of fishing out her keys from her purse. She hadn't decided whether or not to tell Marcus about the baby. Deep down inside she felt that she owed him the truth. He had a right to know that he was going to be a father. What he did with the knowledge was entirely his decision. But Samara didn't think she could bear it if Marcus rejected her and his unborn baby.

Just as her own father had rejected mother and child.

But Marcus was different, an inner voice reminded her. Even if he no longer wanted Samara in his life, he would never turn his back on their child. He would handle his responsibilities as admirably as he looked after his retired father. He was too honorable to do otherwise.

But Samara didn't want Marcus bound to her by honor. If she couldn't have his love, she wanted nothing else from him.

Her searching fingers brushed a glossy slip of paper inside her purse. She smiled softly as she withdrew it.

Asha had shown up at Samara's office that afternoon to take her out to lunch, insisting that Samara could no longer afford to skip meals now that she was eating for two. Over lunch at an exclusive

246

Georgetown restaurant, Asha had presented her daughter with a pleasant surprise.

"I thought you should know before next month's official unveiling."

Samara was bewildered as she accepted the slip of paper from her mother. "Know what?" But then her eyes landed on an image of a perfume bottle with the words SAMARA, FOR THE GUARDIAN OF HER SOUL printed across the glossy ad.

Her mouth fell open. She lifted incredulous eyes to her mother's face. "You...you named your first perfume after *me*?"

Asha nodded, taking a sip of cabernet sauvignon. She lifted one shoulder in an elegant shrug. "It was a strategic maneuver, really. If my venture into the *parfum* industry proves to be half as successful as the young woman for whom the launch fragrance is named, then...well, you can deduce the rest."

Tears welled in Samara's eyes. "Oh, Mom..." was all she could manage around the lump in her throat.

It was Asha's turn to get misty-eyed. "Do you realize what you just called me? You called me 'Mom.' You haven't called me that in ages."

"I know. I love you, Mom."

"Oh, darling. I love you, too."

The attentive maître d' had appeared at their table to find two weeping women. He was stricken, fearing that the service or their meals had somehow been unsatisfactory to his prestigious patrons. He began summoning waiters in rapid-fire French until a laughing Asha assured him that everything was fine.

Hours later Samara's vision blurred with fresh tears at the memory. She sniffled and dabbed at her eyes with a Kleenex. That was another thing about pregnancy. You became a human watering pot, crying at the least provocation.

She finally found her keys and left the office, meeting Melissa in the corridor.

"I was wondering if I'd have to come get you and forcibly remove you from the premises," Melissa chided her. "After the weekend you had, the *last* thing you need is to be pulling your usual thirteen hours at the office. Judging by how peaked you've looked all day, I'd say the best thing for you is to crawl into bed as soon as you get home and stay there until you feel better."

Samara had decided not to tell Melissa about her pregnancy until after the results had been confirmed—just in case she was wrong. She knew Melissa would support her no matter what.

She smiled wanly. "Bed sounds good."

"I'm going to call you to make sure that's where you are. You know, you really ought to consider getting a phone in your bedroom. That way you don't have to run out to the living room to take your calls."

"Yes, ma'am."

"Speaking of running, I'd better use the restroom before I hit the road. Not even four months pregnant," she muttered in disgust, "and already my bladder doesn't hold as much fluid as it used to."

Samara chuckled. "See you tomorrow."

She passed the employment counseling center on her way out the door. The ECC remained open until six-thirty P.M. to provide increased flexibility to its visitors. The room was empty save for Brianna Lynch, who sat at a computer terminal entering data into the resume database. She looked up and smiled at Samara's approach.

"I really enjoyed meeting your mother this afternoon. She's a lot nicer than I expected her to be." She blushed, belatedly realizing how her words might sound. "I mean, not that I thought she'd be mean or anything. It's just that—"

Samara grinned. "It's all right, Brianna. I completely understand what you meant. Just between you and me, my mother *can* be a downright diva when she wants to be. But I guess at some point, all daughters have to learn to accept their mothers as they are, and vice versa."

Brianna smiled. "I hope Lola is as understanding about me one day."

"Are you kidding? Lola's going to worship the ground you walk on, Brianna. Which reminds me, Joanne has been singing your praises. She said you're doing a fantastic job here in the center, and the customers already love you."

"Did she really?" Brianna beamed with delight. "She's been great to work with. She's really patient with me, even when I make mistakes in the database."

"You're too modest, Brianna. Joanne says you're a very quick learner. Is your mother picking you up this evening?"

Brianna nodded. "I'm saving up to buy a used car so that Lola and I can get around on our own."

"I think that's a good idea. Well, see you tomorrow, Brianna."

"Good night. Oh, Samara?"

Samara turned back with an inquisitive smile. "Yes, Brianna?"

Brianna twisted her hands nervously in her lap. "I just wanted to thank you once again for all the help you've given me. You've been a terrific role model to me. So I wanted to tell you that, um, whatever you might be going through, I know you're going to be all right."

Samara felt her throat tighten—that pesky crying thing again. She swallowed hard. "Thank you, Brianna. That means a lot to me." She paused at the door, her head tilted to one side as she contemplated the nineteen-year-old single mother for a moment. "You know, that role model thing works both ways. Have a good night, Brianna."

She stepped outside into the cool evening and took a deep, fortifying breath. Whatever happened from this day forward, she *was* going to be all right. She had no other choice.

She was a survivor.

Samara had started walking toward her car when a silver Bentley rolled to a stop in front of her. Her heart gave an involuntary leap.

Marcus.

Slowly, he climbed out of the car and stood there, his arms resting on the roof of the car. His expression was indiscernible behind the mirrored sunglasses he wore.

Samara stood completely still. Her briefcase was all but forgotten in her hand.

For several moments neither of them spoke.

Melissa emerged from the building, took one look at them and smiled slyly before heading to her car across the parking lot.

Marcus never took his eyes from Samara. As she watched, he rounded the fender and walked right up to her. She had to tilt her head backward to look up at him. Just that quickly, she'd forgotten how tall he was.

He slid off the sunglasses slowly. The piercing intensity of his dark gaze made her breath catch.

Since he didn't seem inclined to, she ventured to break the silence. "Marcus—"

"How are you feeling?" he asked quietly.

The question startled her. For one panicked moment she wondered if he knew about the baby. And then she remembered that he'd taken care of her that first night she was sick.

"I feel better, thanks."

His eyes traveled across her body as if to confirm her response. She didn't miss the way his eyes lingered on her right arm.

"See? No bruises. I told you I'd be fine." She hesitated, wondering if she should thank him for coming to her rescue against Paul Borden.

Before she could decide, Marcus took her briefcase gently from her hands. "Come with me," he said softly.

Samara nodded mutely.

Marcus helped her into the Bentley and closed the door. She stared straight ahead as he climbed in beside her and drove out of the parking lot. She didn't ask him where they were going. In all honesty, she didn't care as long as they were together.

As he steered through downtown, she noted absently that traffic was surprisingly light for a Monday evening. Night had fallen over the city, and the stone finger of the Washington Monument pointed majestically toward the sky.

When Marcus parked at a meter near the Lincoln Memorial, Samara threw him a questioning look. Without a word, he climbed out of the car and came around to open the door for her.

The night air offered a gentle breeze that whispered around them as they ascended the marble stairs and entered the interior of the monument. Only a few tourists milled around, reading inscriptions and snapping photographs.

She and Marcus walked to a private corner and faced each other.

"What are we doing here, Marcus?" Samara asked quietly.

"I want to know how you feel about me," he said huskily. "I want to know if you feel the same way you did when you first agreed to marry me."

"Of course I do. I never stopped loving you, even when I thought you'd betrayed me." She stared at a point beyond his shoulder. "I don't know how many times I can apologize for the way I acted—"

"I don't want another apology."

"Then what do you want from me, Marcus? An explanation for my behavior?" She threw her hands up in exasperation. "I could stand here and talk to you about my past, how I learned early in life not to trust many people, particularly men. But you already know all of that, Marcus. What difference would it make?"

"You think I don't understand how your past shaped your perceptions? You think that didn't occur to me after our argument? Believe me, it did." His tone softened. "But you know what else occurred to me, Samara? The fact that I had some of those same hang-ups before we met. But none of that mattered once I fell in love with you. I stopped worrying about how, or when, you would hurt me like my mother had. All that mattered was how much we loved each other, and how happy we were together."

"All right, Marcus! You've proved that you're a bigger person than I am. I get it. Did you have to bring me all the way out here, to the *Lincoln Memorial*, to further prove your point?"

He gazed at her intently. "I didn't bring you out here to berate you, Samara. But I *do* need to know where we stand."

Hot tears blurred her vision. "I don't know where we stand, Marcus. I know that I love you more than my next breath, and I want nothing more than to spend the rest of my life with you. I know I made a terrible mistake by believing the worst of you, a mistake that taught me a lot about myself and my own shortcomings. But as for where we stand—"

Marcus slanted his lips over hers, silencing the rest of her declaration with an urgent kiss. "Don't say anything else," he whispered against her mouth.

"Marcus—"

"Shh. You're not on trial here, Samara. You don't have to prove anything to me." He drew back to cup her face in his hands. His dark eyes glittered with intensity. "I'm not blaming you for what happened between us. If the situation were reversed, I probably would've reacted the same way. I don't profess to be perfect, Samara—far from it. I spent a lifetime blaming my mother for what she did to our family instead of giving her the benefit of the doubt. And I was about to make the same mistake with you, until Michael talked some sense into my thick head."

Samara stared up at him uncomprehendingly. "Your brother?"

Marcus nodded. "He's in town. Seems he was sent here by some well-meaning folks to reunite us. But that's not the point. I want us to put this whole episode behind us, Samara, once and for all. Do you think we can do that?"

She nodded slowly. "I'm willing to try if you are."

"I am." Marcus kissed her again, more gently this time. "I love you, Samara. You're the only woman I'll ever want or need. Believe me when I tell you that."

"I do," she whispered around the constriction in her throat. "I'll never question that again."

He smiled softly. "Do you remember the day we came here? When we played hooky from work and acted like tourists?"

"I remember."

"I was watching your face when the tour guide mentioned the Lincoln Memorial as a popular spot for marriage proposals. You looked ready to cry."

Samara's eyes widened as Marcus lowered himself to one knee. "It's not quite the same since I've already done this once, but in the spirit of starting over…" He removed a small velvet box from his breast pocket and opened it.

Samara gasped when she saw the exquisite diamond ring inside. "Oh my God…"

Gazing deep into her eyes, Marcus said huskily, "Will you marry me, Samara?"

"Yes," she answered breathlessly. "Yes, Marcus, I'll marry you!"

Marcus removed the ring from the satin encasement and slowly, never taking his eyes from hers, slid it onto her finger. It was a perfect fit.

Samara's eyes filled with fresh tears. "Oh, Marcus…"

He got to his feet and wrapped her tightly in his arms. Samara heard a low smattering of applause and turned her head to see the tourists watching them with pleased expressions. She and Marcus grinned and accepted the strangers' hearty congratulations.

As the people moved off to give them privacy, Samara looked down at her finger and beamed. "It's absolutely breathtaking, Marcus. I-I'm speechless."

Smiling, he leaned down to nibble on her lips. Samara shivered at the delicious sensation and curved her arms around his neck, deepening the kiss. They held each other for several long moments, silhouetted against miles of gleaming white marble.

"I'm flying to Minnesota next weekend to see my mother," Marcus said after a while. "Would you like to go with me? I know she'd love to meet you."

Samara gazed up at him, understanding the full import of his decision to visit Celeste Rutherford. He was ready to bury the hatchet and forge new beginnings.

Her heart swelled with love and admiration. "As much as I want to meet your mother," she told him, "I think it would be best if you went alone this time."

His eyes softened. "Thank you for understanding."

"You're very welcome. Besides, I don't think I'm ready to handle air travel just yet," she added, watching his face carefully. "I would hate to compound motion sickness with morning sickness. Which is an oxymoron, considering that my nausea isn't confined to morning—as you witnessed for yourself."

Marcus's brows furrowed in confusion. "Wait a minute. What're you talking about? Morning sickness?" As comprehension dawned, he stared down at her in shock. "Are you…?"

Samara smiled into his eyes. "We're going to have a baby, Marcus."

He laughed, a full, triumphant bellow that filled her with joy. Overcome with emotion, he lifted her into his arms and swung her around, and she joined in his laughter, thrilled by his response.

He set her back down gingerly, looking concerned. "Should I have done that? I didn't even think."

"Don't be silly. You can't hurt the baby that way."

Marcus grinned. "A baby," he said in quiet wonder. "We're going to have a baby, Samara. Can you believe it?"

She grimaced wryly. "My body sure does."

His expression gentled with sympathy. "Come on, let's get you home and off your feet."

She grinned. "I'm pregnant, Marcus, not an invalid."

He chuckled softly. "No wonder you were so sick. It never occurred to me that you might be pregnant." He sobered after a moment. "Wait a minute. I was so busy celebrating that I didn't even stop to ask how you felt about this."

Samara was touched by his thoughtfulness. "I'll admit that I never envisioned getting pregnant *before* marriage. I guess I'd always imagined having my husband all to myself before children entered the picture. But I'm truly happy, Marcus. I want our baby as much as you do. Nothing would please me more than to give you a child."

He stroked her cheek, gazing at her with indescribable tenderness. "You're the most incredible woman I've ever met. How can I ever repay Walter Floyd for inviting me to your mother's fashion show and bringing us together?"

"I don't know," Samara said, sliding her hands up and down his muscled back, holding him so close that her nipples puckered against his chest. "We'll have to think of something though."

"Mmmm," Marcus murmured, bending his head to lick the seam of her lips. "I'm thinking of something right now."

Heat bloomed in Samara's belly. She glanced around and saw that all of the tourists had left. She took Marcus by the hand and led him deeper into the shadows of the building. If they hurried, they should have time for a quickie.

Marcus gave a low, sexy chuckle as he pinned her against a cool marble column. "Seducing me in a national monument, Samara? How irreverent of you."

She gave him a mildly reproving look as she unzipped his pants. "While we're on the topic of seduction, Marcus Wolf, I just want to make one thing crystal clear. From now on, the *only* woman whose ass belongs on your desk is mine. Understood?"

"Yes, ma'am." As Marcus lifted her in his arms, she wrapped her legs around his waist. His eyes glowed hot and intense as he added teasingly, "I'll even carve your name into the wood to mark the territory as yours."

Samara chuckled hoarsely, her skirt hiked up around her thighs as he palmed her buttocks. "Works for me. I'm a woman who believes in keeping what's mine in check."

His husky laugh was muffled against her throat. "Spoken like a true tiger tamer."

"No, darling," Samara breathed, closing her eyes as he impaled her with one long, mind-blowing stroke, "taming *wolves* are much more fun."

Taming the Wolf

Discussion Questions

1. Do you blame Asha for the way she abandoned Samara to pursue her modeling career? Why or why not?

2. Do you think Marcus was wrong for shutting his mother out of his life for twenty-five years? Once you learned the whole story about their marriage, who did you feel the most sympathy for— Celeste Rutherford or Sterling Wolf?

3. Were you surprised by how easily Samara believed Marcus was cheating on her? Under the circumstances, would you have reacted the same way?

4. Although Samara was raised not to trust men, it was important to me that she maintain a healthy attitude toward sex. In other words, I didn't want her emotional scars to carry over into her sex life, because I thought she deserved to be "liberated" in at least one area of her life. How important was this to you? Why?

5. How did you feel about Samara being a recovering alcoholic? Did that make her stronger or weaker as a character?

6. Would you like to see Samara become more involved in her mother's company? Was Asha asking too much of her?

About the Author

Maureen Smith has enjoyed writing for as long as she can remember, and secretly suspects she was born with a pen in her hand. She received a B.A. in English from the University of Maryland, College Park and worked as a freelance writer while she penned her first novel. To her delight, *Ghosts of Fire* was nominated for a Romantic Times Reviewers' Choice Award and an Emma Award for Favorite New Author, and won the Romance in Color Reviewers' Choice Awards for New Author of the Year and Romantic Suspense of the Year. Maureen's second novel, *With Every Breath*, was also nominated for a Romantic Times Reviewers' Choice Award, and garnered four Emma Award nominations in the categories of Favorite Hero, Favorite Romantic Suspense, Author of the Year and Book of the Year.

Maureen lives in San Antonio, TX with her husband, two children, a cat and a miniature schnauzer. She loves to hear from readers and can be reached at author@maureen-smith.com. You may also visit her Web site at www.maureen-smith.com for news and updates on her upcoming releases.

Parker Publishing, LLC

Parker Publishing, LLC

Celebrating Black
Love Life Literature

Mail or fax orders to:
12523 Limonite Avenue
Suite #440-245
Mira Loma, CA 91752
(866) 205-7902
(951) 685-8036 fax

or order from our Web site:
www.parker-publishing.com
orders@parker-publishing.com

Ship to:
Name: _____

Address: _____

_____

City: _____

State: _____ Zip:_____

Phone: _____

Qty	Title	Price	Total

Shipping and handling is $3.50, Priority Mail shipping is $6.00
FREE standard shipping for orders over $30

Alaska, Hawaii, and international orders – call for rates

See Website for special discounts and promotions

Add S&H

CA residents add
7.75% sales tax

Total

Payment methods: We accept Visa, MasterCard, Discovery, or money orders. NO PERSONAL CHECKS.

Payment Method: (circle one): VISA MC DISC Money Order

Name on Card: _____

Card Number: _____ Exp Date: _____

Billing Address: _____

_____

City: _____

State: _____ Zip:_____